PERFECT
HARMONY

• Michele Scott •

PERFECT HARMONY

FAIRMONT RIDING ACADEMY:

A Vivienne Taylor Horse Lover's Mystery

• BOOK 3 •

SKYSCAPE

SKYSCAPE

Text copyright © 2014 Michele Scott
All rights reserved.

Published by Skyscape, New York

www.apub.com

Amazon, the Amazon logo, and Skyscape are trademarks of Amazon.com, Inc., or its affiliates.

ISBN-13: 9781477847794
ISBN-10: 1477847790

Cover design by Krista Vossen
Library of Congress Control Number: 2014907840
Printed in the United States of America

To all the women and girls out there who are totally and completely horse crazy!

CHAPTER *one*

I still can't believe I'm going to Virginia for the entire summer instead of spending it with my mom in Oregon. The truth is, ever since I won the chance to go to Liberty Farms, a world-class training facility on the East Coast, I've been pinching myself, because it seems like a dream.

I sit up straighter as the flight attendant's voice comes over the speaker. "Ladies and gentlemen, the captain has turned on the fasten-seat-belt sign. Please bring your tray tables and seats to their upright and locked positions as we make our final approach into Washington Dulles International Airport."

I stare out the window and send a silent thank-you to my mare, Harmony, whose amazing performance at the scholastic championship event in Kentucky last month made this whole thing possible. I'm excited to see her soon—she'll arrive at Liberty Farms not long after I get there. This summer is going to be a once-in-a-lifetime chance for a kid like me who doesn't come from money, since Fairmont Academy is paying my way. Every step like this I take brings me closer to my dream of one day becoming an Olympic rider in the sport of three-day eventing.

I'm honestly kind of amazed I'm feeling so optimistic, considering that just weeks ago, the death of one my closest friends, Joel Parker, turned my life upside down. If things had gone as planned, Joel would be meeting me at Liberty Farms later today. Instead, he's gone. When I discovered him dead in his room after the competition last month was over, the cops in Kentucky had ruled that it was suicide by overdose. I know in my heart of hearts, though—and I may be the only one who believes this—that Joel did not kill himself. I'm positive that he was murdered. I'm also positive that, this summer, I'm going to find out who killed my friend and why.

Once the plane lands and I grab my two huge duffels at baggage claim, I make my way to the airport shuttle pickup. It seems like it takes forever to drop off the other passengers at various locations around the city, but finally, I'm the only one left and we're traveling on pretty country roads.

I feel a surge of excitement when I notice a wooden sign off to the left that says "Liberty Farms." Outside the window, emerald-green pastures hemmed in by white fences flash past. "Wow," I say, mostly to myself.

The shuttle driver, an older lady with short curly gray hair, looks at me in the rearview mirror and smiles. "It's something, isn't it?"

"Yep," I say as we proceed up the cobblestone drive. I've read up on the place, so I immediately see landmarks I recognize: the two large barns, which can hold a total of forty horses; three large pastures; and a dozen paddocks. What's taking me a little by surprise is that it looks so much like old East Coast money. It's almost intimidating. In the distance, I spot a grand old Southern-style mansion with massive white columns. This place is definitely different than Fairmont, where I go to school in Southern California, which has views of the Pacific Ocean and casual one-story white stucco buildings.

When the van stops in front of one of the barns, the driver looks at me and says, "You need help with your bags?"

I shake my head. "Nope, thanks. I got it."

She gives me a friendly smile. "You're a sweetheart. Now that it's really summer, I'll take any chance to stay inside this air-conditioned van."

I laugh and say good-bye, then go around the back of the van and unload my big duffels. About five seconds later, I understand what the driver was saying—because I'm already drenched in sweat. The humidity is unbelievable. The next minute I start swatting the air around me like a crazy person, because I'm being attacked by a flying black bug that looks almost big enough to be a bird. But despite the heat and the bugs, I feel like pinching myself. It's hard to believe I'm finally here.

CHAPTER *two*

"Welcome to Virginia," I hear someone say. When I look up, I see a blond woman about my mom's age smiling at me. "The land of humidity and giant bugs."

I laugh and put out my hand. "I'm Vivienne," I say.

"I'm Faith Watson, the Liberty Farms coordinator," she says. "I'll take you on a quick tour first, and then show you where you'll be staying. You can leave your bags here for now."

I follow Faith into the barn, and my mouth practically drops open. Each stall is double-size and layered with what looks like at least four feet of shavings. The rehab equipment includes a few water treadmills, a saltwater spa, and a TheraPlate, which kind of looks like a treadmill but is actually a place where horses stand and undergo healing vibration therapy. As I follow Faith around the property, I see two indoor arenas, one with mirrors for dressage lessons and another for jumping, plus two outdoor arenas. I'm totally blown away, especially because I know that the coaches who teach here are as impressive as the facilities. At Fairmont, we work with Kayla and Holden Fairmont, the school's cofounders, as well as the head coach, Christian Albright. All three of them have national reputations. Training with them in California this past year was incredible—and I'm pretty thrilled that Holden will be coaching at Liberty Farms for the summer too. But I'm also excited to meet some of the other legendary coaches who teach here, like the famous Bernard Richardson. Having access to experts like him is going to be amazing.

"Okay," Faith says, when we're done with the tour. "Last stop is your cabin. Maybe you can meet some of your roommates."

I raise my eyebrows. "More than one?"

She laughs. "You'll be bunking with three other girls. This isn't Fairmont Academy."

I'm suddenly horrified that I've given her the impression that I'm some spoiled Fairmont rich kid. "Can't wait to meet them," I say.

She gives me a thumbs-up. "Someone dropped off your bags, so you should be all set."

"Thanks," I say.

When I get inside, I spot a girl with light-brown hair sitting on one of the bunks. She bounds up and comes to my side, holding out her hand to shake.

"Nice to meet you," she says in a Southern accent. "I'm Janna Olsen."

"Vivienne Taylor," I say, holding out my hand. "Your new roommate."

"Well, Vivienne," she drawls, gesturing around the cabin, "it's not exactly the Ritz, but we'll make do, right?"

I nod and look at the setup. The inside of the cabin is clean, but nothing special. There are bunk beds pushed against two of the walls, and four dressers, so we each have a place to store our things. That's it. Nothing fancy. It's definitely not as plush as my suite at Fairmont, which I share with just one girl.

It kind of reminds me of an old-fashioned summer camp. Over the past school year, I've had just one roommate—my friend Martina—so I'm not sure how well I'll deal with this new situation. But since there's no choice, I'm sure that I will find a way to handle it.

Still, I'm nervous. I don't come from the rich kids' club, and even though Janna seems down-to-earth, I'm betting she does. Most of the kids in the equestrian world seem to have bundles of money—at least the ones from Fairmont. Not me, though. I'm a small-town kid with a scholarship, which means that fitting in isn't always easy for me.

"Bathroom is that way," Janna says in her Southern drawl. She pulls her hair up into a ponytail. "One mirror and four girls—should be interesting." She laughs. "Luckily, I don't wear much makeup."

I smile and feel relieved that I might have already met someone I could be friends with. Janna is pretty, but she's no-fuss, and nothing like the tan, blond Barbie types that I've become accustomed to dealing with in California. No . . . Janna is actually paler than me, which is saying a lot. In addition to her fair skin, she has light-blue eyes and an easy smile. She seems a lot nicer than most of the girls at Fairmont, at least on first impression.

"I'm not much for makeup, either," I say. "I'm just here for the riding."

I don't say out loud, of course, that I'm also hoping to solve the mystery of my friend Joel's death. Not exactly icebreaker conversation.

I start putting my clothes away in the empty dresser near my bunk as Janna heads to the bathroom for a quick shower.

A mix of emotions washes over me as I unpack. Mainly, I'm dying to know who else has arrived. One of the first people I'll be looking for is my best friend, Riley Reed, who I got close to at school last year, and who was in Kentucky with me for the championships. He knows all about Liberty Farms, because he used to train here, along with Joel, back before coming to Fairmont. The second person on my list to find is Austen Giles, who I've known since I was about eight years old. Austen and I grew up together as fellow riders and friends—until we kissed for the first time, right before he left for college and I left for Fairmont. My cheeks flush as I remember what he whispered into my ear when we both were home over Christmas break. *Someday, Vivienne Taylor, someday.* It had felt like a promise that we'd be together eventually, like it was inevitable. I'm not exactly sure how I feel about Austen now—all I know is that I love being near him.

Unfortunately, Liberty Farms is also going to be home this summer to some kids I'd rather avoid. For starters, there's Tristan Goode. Up until a couple of weeks ago, he was my boyfriend. But I broke up with him after a mysterious photo was texted to my phone that showed him lying naked in bed—in the bed of his ex, Lydia Gallagher. Finding out he'd betrayed me that way was awful, especially so soon after Joel's death. I was a mess. But the silver lining is that I got away from Tristan before he could hurt me in other ways. I'm guessing by now he's fully back together with Lydia. Seeing the two of them act cuddly is definitely not something I'm looking forward to.

What fills me with the most dread, though, is the idea of getting to the bottom of Joel's death—and finding out that someone I care deeply for might be covering up the truth of what happened that night. Like Riley. As much as I can't wait to see my best friend, I worry that he is hiding something more than his usual secrets. See, the thing is, Joel and Riley are both gay. Well, only Riley is now because Joel is . . . dead. But Riley is, and he's still keeping his big secret from his family. No surprise there, since they're all deeply religious and fiercely conservative. Riley is afraid that if and when they find out, he'll lose everything—especially his horse, Santos, which would totally destroy him.

Sometimes, my thoughts go to a very dark place, and I wonder if Riley might sacrifice just about anything to keep his secret from being exposed. Would he have sacrificed Joel? I find it hard to wrap my brain around the idea that he could have been involved in a murder, but I have to say that I can't 100 percent rule it out. Joel and Riley were on the outs again last semester when Joel's supposed overdose happened. On top of that, there's the fact that this awful rich kid named Chris Haverly, who was with us in Lexington at the championships, seemed to have some kind of sick power over both Riley and Joel. Exactly what he was holding over their heads is one of the mysteries I'm planning to solve. Since Chris rides at Liberty and will be here along with the rest of us this summer, it shouldn't be too hard to learn a little more.

I'm just hoping I won't have to run into Joel's horrible stepmother, Tiffany. She's a well-known East Coast trainer who used to teach at Liberty Farms. *What if Tiffany is a guest coach here?* I quickly try and erase that horrible thought from my mind. I spent an awkward dinner with Joel in Lexington, during which Tiffany threatened to take away Joel's horse, Melody, and give it instead to her daughter, Paisley—Joel's horrible, spoiled stepsister. Fortunately, that didn't happen, since I was able to convince Kayla Fairmont to purchase Melody. I'm not entirely sure that makes Kayla a hero, though.

Janna comes out of the bathroom just as I'm shoving my now-empty duffels under the bunk. "Wonder when we'll meet our other roommates," she says.

"Let's just hope one of them is not Lydia Gallagher," I say. "I don't want to say anything mean about someone from my own school, but let's just say she might not be the easiest person to live with."

Janna smiles. "I've got a few people from my school I don't like either. Okay, so we'll hope for no Lydia."

"Fingers crossed," I say.

"Hey, is your horse here yet? Maybe we could go check out the barns once I'm dressed."

"She's not here, but she should be arriving soon," I say. "I'd love to go down to the barns." I walk over to the door of the cabin and look outside just in time to see a semi pulling around the side of the main barn. The writing on the side of the truck says "Cranston & Co. Haulers."

I know that my girl and the rest of the horses coming from Fairmont are on that truck.

"She's here," I shout with excitement. I'm beyond ready to see Harmony—I hate being separated from her for even a day. Two seconds later, I'm out the door. Janna shouts after me, "Wait up!" but I'm already chasing the truck.

It comes to a stop in front of one of the barns. I spot Faith walking over to the driver, who hands her a clipboard. A couple of grooms arrive to help unload. I eagerly wait for the moment I can bring Harmony off the trailer.

The door on the side of the truck is opened, and the first out is Lydia's horse, Geisha. My stomach sinks. I have nothing against the horse. She's a nice mare, but she is a harsh reminder that my nemesis will be arriving at any moment. As Geisha is led down the ramp, a bolt of anxiety hits me and I feel short of breath. Luckily, the unpleasant feeling lifts quickly. I feel certain it relates to the fact that I'm so not crazy about Lydia. Second out is Tristan's horse, Sebastian. I can't help but grimace as I think of how appropriate it is that their horses traveled together, now that Lydia and Tristan are so cozy. Next, I'm surprised to see Joel's horse, Melody, come off the truck—what in the world is she doing here? I shake my head as I realize I need to start thinking of Melody as Kayla's horse. Now that Joel is dead, the mare belongs to her. I'm burning with curiosity to know why Kayla would send the horse here instead of keeping her in California.

In the next moment, though, I forget my questions as I catch sight of Harmony starting to descend the ramp. Her ears prick forward, and the sunlight hits her shiny gray coat. I walk over to the handler and smile at him. "I can take her. She's mine."

"All yours, kid," he says.

I take the lead rope from him and rub my hand over her face, then give her a kiss on the nose. She's happy to see me, but as she pulls up to her full height, it's clear that she's curious about her new surroundings—all ears and eyes. I sense anxiety in her too, and I can tell she's wondering whether she's here to be sold.

How do I know this?

Yeah, well—that's the funny thing about me. I'm what you would call an "equine communicator." I can read the thoughts of horses, especially if I'm close to them. Nobody knows about this ability except for two other people: my mother, who is very protective of my gift, and Kayla Fairmont. How she found out, I have no clue, but she confronted me about my unusual skills after the championship event in Kentucky where Joel died. I'm still in the dark about exactly how much she knows about my gift. All I know is that when she talked to me about it, she used the most condescending tone imaginable. She lectured me like the world's worst know-it-all.

Here is the thing about communicating with horses, she said. You don't have enough skill and insight yet to really understand how to handle it. Your own thoughts, imaginings, and perceptions can get in the way. You have to be responsible about that. Otherwise, there can be serious problems in interpreting the communication. Sometimes, Vivienne, you need to allow horses to just be horses, because at the end of the day, they aren't human.

Remembering her words makes me roll my eyes. Sure, Kayla Fairmont is a lot older than I am, but just because she's the dean of my school didn't give her the right to read me the riot act. To be honest, the more I've thought about our confrontation, the more I've started questioning whether I can trust Kayla. How did she find out about my abilities? Was she investigating me for some unimaginable—and possibly dark—motive of her own? I wish I had the guts to ask her whether she, too, has some kind of unique ability. Maybe she's some kind of psychic who can read people's inner thoughts, or maybe she can also communicate with horses. My mom has said there are others like me out there—although how she knows, exactly, I'm not sure. So why can't I just ask Kayla a few questions and figure it out once and for all? Something stops me. I suppose it's that authority figure thing. The lady is sort of intimidating.

I feel another wave of anxiety from Harmony as she again tries to understand the unfamiliar surroundings, and I stroke her neck to calm her down. "You're always going to be with me," I say, swallowing hard, because I know that I can't really make such a promise. Harmony isn't my horse, after all. She belongs to Kayla and Holden Fairmont. "You're not up for sale. We're here for some summer camp."

Janna strolls up to me. "She's beautiful, Vivienne."

"Thank you."

She points to one of the paddocks where a horse with a chestnut coat and white stockings on its front legs is grazing. "There's my baby," she says. "His name is Cavalli."

"How long have you been riding him?"

"Just a year. We'd only been together for a short time before I rode him at the qualifying round in Lexington. My other horse had maxed out at prelim, so I got lucky with Cavalli. He's got some serious scope, and his dressage is gorgeous. He was imported from the UK."

I look at her in surprise. "Nice. I'd love to be able to go look at horses abroad someday. You were in Kentucky? I can't believe we didn't get to know each other!"

For the first time since we've met, a dark look crosses her face. "I was kind of glued to my teammates and coach during the competition, so I'm not surprised. I would have been way better off trying to meet new people," she says.

Before I can ask her what she means, I hear a male voice call my name. I swivel my head and see that Tristan is walking toward us. I want to turn my back and walk away, but I also know that I'm going to have to deal with him at some point. I might as well get it over with.

"Guess the next batch has arrived," I say.

Janna's eyes are glued to Tristan as he gets closer.

"He couldn't have been in Lexington too," she says. "I would have noticed someone that gorgeous." Her voice is full of admiration.

"Oh, he was there," I say.

"Vivvie!" he yells, waving to make sure that I see him. How could I not see him? Even from here, those greenish-blue eyes of his stand out against the warm glow of his skin and fair hair. Well, Janna is right about him being gorgeous. There's no denying that Tristan is hot. I can't take that away from him.

He walks up to us with purpose, and my stomach sinks.

"Why haven't you returned my calls? My texts, my e-mails? What the hell is going on?"

"Tristan, this is Janna Olsen."

"Hello." He nods at her and she smiles, returning the hello, then he immediately turns back to me. "What gives, Vivvie?"

"Really? What gives?"

"Very nice to meet you," Janna says in her sweet Southern accent. "Looks like you two have some things to talk about, so I'm just going to see you back at the cabin, Vivienne."

"Thank you," I mutter and start walking toward one of the paddocks to let Harmony graze. Tristan steps in line with me.

"I think you owe me an explanation," he says.

"I owe you an explanation?" I can sense my horse's tension at our conversation, probably because she detects my anger. "Let me see, did you not get the text that I forwarded to you when I went back home? The one with a picture of you lying naked on Lydia's bed? It was sent to me by a blocked number, which I find fascinating."

He tosses up his arms. "And don't you think that may have been taken before you came along, when Lydia and I were going out? Or did you ever wonder if maybe it had been photoshopped? Or did you consider the most likely explanation: that I'd gotten drunk at a party and passed out somewhere random afterward? For your information, I told you the truth when I said that Lydia and I have never had sex. That's true no matter what photo you see."

I roll my eyes, reach an open paddock, and turn Harmony out. I'm positive she isn't too happy with the welcoming she's just received. She tends to like to spend some real time with me when we've been away from each other, and vice versa, but as I already mentioned, this little situation needs to be dealt with quickly, so we can all move on.

"Which is it, Tristan? Is it an old photo? Or was it photo-shopped? Or were you just drunk? Surely you know the answer."

"I don't know. I really don't. But I'm not sleeping with Lydia!"

I cross my arms and look at him coldly, which isn't easy to do, because I don't have proof of anything. Maybe what he's saying is the truth. Maybe. But, facts are, I'm not sure if he's being honest or not. And I have had enough curveballs thrown my way through the years—the one that really stands out is my dad leaving us the day after my tenth birthday—that trusting someone doesn't come easy. And, on top of that, Tristan has lied to me in the past. I sigh and shake my head. "You know what? I wish that I could believe you. I really do." Oh crap, I think, digging my nails into my palms. I feel like I'm about to cry, and I really don't want the waterworks to start. I do everything I can to suppress them. "However, the fact that I have any doubt—and I have plenty of doubt—tells me that it doesn't matter."

"Are you serious?" He raises his voice. "Are you kidding me right now? After everything? After all we've been through this year?"

His cheeks are flushed and his obvious anger is a little upsetting, to say the least. I'm not used to it, and I don't like it at all.

"I don't want to talk about it, Tristan," I say. "Let's just be done." I'm fighting the urge to actually run away from him. Maybe I made a mistake coming to Liberty Farms in the first place. Then I hear my name and it's a voice I recognize and my stomach sinks further.

"Vivienne!"

Tristan turns his head to see who is calling me, and then he turns back to me, now shaking his head. "I get it," he says bitterly. "This isn't about me, or even about Lydia. This is about him." His eyes glow with anger as he jerks his head in the direction of Austen Giles, who is walking our way. "Farm boy. Nice. You could have just broken up with me instead of inventing all the drama, Vivienne."

"Drama? Um . . . the photo I got wasn't invented. And I don't believe that anyone has sent you a naked picture of me in Austen's bed, now have they?"

"No. But nothing surprises me anymore. Who knows, maybe there is one out there."

"You're an ass."

"Right. I am. That I am. And since that is what you think of me, I'll try not to let you down. In fact, I'll live right up to your expectations, starting now."

I'm left speechless as Tristan walks away. Austen, still coming toward me, tries to say hi as they pass each other, but gets no response. Tristan makes a beeline for an airport shuttle that's just pulling up. A second later, I understand why as the driver opens the side door and I see Lydia Gallagher step down onto the cobblestones in a skimpy summer dress, tossing her blond hair like a star arriving on the red carpet. The second she spots Tristan, she runs into his waiting arms.

Yep. It's going to be an interesting summer.

ooks like I interrupted something," Austen says, looking back to see Tristan pulling Lydia close.

The next kid out of the van, who looks like a prep school poster boy with his pink oxford shirt and boat shoes, shouts, "Get a room!" A couple other kids who step out after him start laughing, but Tristan and Lydia stay pasted together. I almost gag as I realize how completely duped I've been.

"My guess is that things didn't go so well between you two after the championships in Lexington," says Austen.

"Not exactly."

"I'm sorry, Vivvie, that I had to tell you what I knew about him."

"It's okay. Otherwise I never would have known that he helped cover up for Lydia. I still can't believe that the whole time we were going out Tristan knew that she'd poisoned my horse. I'm glad you told me. Of course, he claims to be innocent. He has his version of the story."

"This I have to hear," Austen says, running his hand through his thick, dark, wavy hair.

"Let's just say that Tristan has his own ugly secrets," I say. "His dad is a pretty bad guy who's deep into all kinds of illegal stuff. He made the mistake of telling Lydia all about it when they were close. Being the vindictive person she is, she used that information to blackmail him. She said if he reported her for poisoning

Harmony, she would rat out his father—who would in turn destroy Tristan's life completely. So he decided to keep his mouth shut. He said he felt afraid of her."

"Hate to say it," Austen says, "but he doesn't look too terribly afraid of her at the moment."

"No. He doesn't, and that story seems like a stretch. Given how cozy they look now, I'm pretty sure that Tristan has told me a lot of lies."

I don't say this to Austen, but, even though I'm burning up with anger at Tristan right now, I can't lay all the blame on him. There are some truths to Tristan's story—like his dad being a real jerk. Tristan's horse, Sebastian, shared some very dark and ugly things regarding Tristan's father with me during the school year at Fairmont. So the one thing I'm inclined to believe is that Tristan doesn't have a great relationship with his parents. But that's definitely not a good excuse for keeping the truth from me about who poisoned Harmony. The whole thing is just a mess.

"I'm sorry, Viv."

"I know. Thanks."

"I'm also really sorry about your friend Joel. I hope you got my messages. When you didn't return my calls, I thought you were upset with me. I just wanted you to know that if you needed me for anything, I'm always here for you."

I smile. "I know. I wasn't angry or upset with you. I just needed time to deal with what you told me about Tristan. Well, and get over being a little irritated that you hooked up with Lydia in Kentucky when I warned you against it."

He blushes and replies, "You did warn me, and I'm sorry that I didn't listen to you. She is kind of assertive."

"That's one way of putting it. As far as everything else, I really needed some space to figure things out."

"Did you?" he asks.

"Did I what?"

"Figure anything out?"

I sigh because I'm not sure I should share this with him, but then again, I'm not sure whom else I can trust. If there is anyone I can trust this summer, it's Austen, so I decide to divulge. "I think that the answers to what happened to Joel might be found here at Liberty Farms."

He shakes his head. "I don't understand. Didn't he commit suicide?"

"No. I don't think so. I don't believe it."

"Why? I mean, wasn't it an obvious case? When they found him dead in his room, wasn't it clear that he'd overdosed on his prescription meds?" He suddenly seems to notice my expression and reaches out to touch my arm. "Wait, *you* found him, didn't you? Vivvie, I'm so sorry."

"I did find him." I pause for a moment, trying to shove the memory of the night back into the recesses of my mind. Unfortunately, I can't. I remember seeing my friend on the floor, his lips tinged light blue, his hands cold, his face pale, and his eyes—gone. A shiver snakes down my back with the memory and I force myself for the second time today not to cry. "There were medications. But you don't understand."

"Tell me, then," he replies. "Explain."

"You believe me, then? You believe that Joel didn't kill himself?"

He shrugs. "Vivienne, I don't know. I didn't know the guy other than just meeting him in Kentucky, but I've known you since we were little kids, and you've never lied to me or made things up. You've never been that girl who buys into drama. You're Vivienne Taylor for God's sake. You're the most honest, sweet, and trustworthy person I know."

It's my turn to blush. "Thank you."

"So, tell me why you think Joel didn't take his life."

"For starters," I say, pausing as Harmony lifts her head up to look at me. I know she's wondering when she's going to get some time with me. I send her a quick image of myself hugging her around the neck. She takes a few steps and decides to roll. After that she gets up and tears around the pasture, bucking and tossing her head. I laugh. "Looks like someone needed to let off some steam."

"Cooped up in that trailer for that long, they usually do. Now, continue telling me what you were telling me."

"What you don't know about when we were out at the championships is that Joel was on the verge of losing his horse, Melody, to his new stepmother and stepsister. His dad had told him that if he didn't win the event that the horse would go home with them and become his stepsister, Paisley's, new horse. Joel would have been crushed if that had happened. If they'd taken Melody away from him, I could maybe wrap my brain around him wanting to take his own life. Maybe."

"His family sounds awful. How could they be so cold?"

"Right, I know."

"But they didn't take Melody away from Joel."

"Because I interfered."

"Of course you did." He nods his head and smiles. "How'd you pull it off?"

"Long story short, I persuaded Kayla Fairmont to make an offer on Melody. The kind of offer that Joel's dad couldn't refuse."

"I probably shouldn't ask you how you persuaded her to spend that much on a horse she didn't need, should I?"

I shook my head. "Probably not. It might discredit the sweetness you think I have going for me."

"Doubtful. Seriously doubtful."

I try not to blush again, but I can feel the heat rise to my cheeks. It's a little weird for me to feel this way—but the fact is, I like that he's flirting with me.

"Anyway, Kayla bought the horse and told Joel he never had to worry about her being taken from him again. He was ecstatic. I mean, he was so thrilled. He loved that horse as much as I love Harmony, or as much as you love Axel," I say, referring to Austen's horse.

"Right. I'd probably throw down if someone threatened to take him from me."

"You see."

"But there's more to your story than boy-loves-horse."

I nod. "True. Did you meet that Chris Haverly kid who was at the champs? He was just hanging around because he could."

"Briefly. His family has zillions and he struts around like that makes him special."

"That's the guy."

"What about him?"

"He's creepy weird, obnoxious, and pompous, and he totally has this jerk factor about him, and not just in terms of girls. He scared Joel. It was like Chris was holding something over his head."

"Did Joel tell you that?"

"No, but it was obvious to me that Chris made him nervous. I saw them talking a few times, and each time it seemed tense. One time especially, Joel seemed really distressed afterward. I had to wonder what was going on."

I don't divulge that I also received some information from Joel's horse that there was some bad blood between Joel and Chris from when they'd worked together at a horse farm.

"What are you getting at?" he asks.

"I wish I knew. I'm just sure Chris and Joel had some kind of dark secret and it's possible that Chris was blackmailing or threatening Joel."

"Wow."

"There's more. I think my friend Riley knows what the secret is. I think he's involved."

"Have you asked him?"

"I did before Joel died and they both told me to leave it all alone."

"Well, that's a pretty clear message. Did you try talking to Riley again, after Joel died?"

"No. I was a mess. I wasn't in the headspace to talk to anyone. Like I told you, I needed some space and time to recover after everything that happened."

He nods. I look over again and see Harmony coming toward us. "I think she wants my attention."

"If you want, I can show you her stall."

I smile. "That's right. You're a working student here this summer."

"I am."

"Does that mean you have to groom my horse?"

"Don't push your luck, Miss Taylor."

I smile, happy for Austen that he has this chance to be one of the summer's working students. Yes, there's hard labor involved. They have to deal with tacking and untacking horses, cleaning tack, mucking stalls, and feeding. But in exchange, working students get the chance to be taught by the coach they work for; sometimes, they get board and training for their horse, and even room and board for themselves. I know that Austen is receiving all of the above from Bernard Richardson, who he's working for here. Bernard is one of the top event riders in the country—in the world, really. He won the Rolex three times, and almost won the

Grand Slam once. At the Pan Am, he won an individual gold and a team bronze, and he was on the Olympic team twice. Impressive, to say the least, and definitely someone Austen and his horse can learn a lot from.

"Did you get to bring Axel with you?" I ask.

"I did." He smiles. "And it happens that he's in the stall across from Harmony."

"Really, now?"

"Really."

"How did that happen?"

He shakes his head and shrugs. "No idea. Pure luck."

"Sounds like an inside job," I say, laughing. I walk over to the side of the paddock and get Harmony's attention. "Hey, big girl. Want to go see your new home?" I hook the lead rope back onto her halter and unlatch the gate. We start toward the main barn.

"You planning to ask Riley a few things? I know he's coming; I saw his name on the list. Maybe he can share what he knows about Joel and this Haverly kid?"

"He's supposed to be here, but I didn't see his horse, Santos, come off the horse trailer with Harmony. That worries me, because Santos didn't pass the jog out at the championships. Riley was worried there might be something really wrong. I haven't heard."

"Well, I might have some answers for you about who Riley *is* riding this summer. Because the roster I saw showed that Riley would be riding a horse named Melody."

As I raise my eyebrows in surprise, I see awareness dawn on Austen's face. "Melody—the horse you were just talking about."

"That explains why Kayla Fairmont sent Melody here on the trailer," I say.

"So Riley can ride her."

"I still think of her as Joel's horse," I say. "It's definitely a little strange."

"There's more to this story about Joel, isn't there?"

"There is."

He glances at his watch. "I want to hear it, but the rest of the staff is due here any moment, and we have a mandatory meeting in about fifteen minutes. Since everyone is still arriving and orientation isn't until tomorrow, want to go grab some dinner with me tonight? I found a good burger place just down the road."

"Already learning your way around here?"

"You know me, Vivvie. I had to find the good places to eat first thing. I've been here for a week now, so I have a few down."

"Nice. Yeah, let's get burgers," I say. "It's a plan."

Austen pats Harmony's neck and leads her toward her new stall while I think about how much I like the idea of going out with him tonight. First, it'll give me a chance to talk more about my suspicions regarding Joel's death. I trust Austen, and I know he'll tell me if my theories sound completely ludicrous. Second, I don't really want to eat here tonight with all the new arrivals—particularly Lydia and Tristan. An extra bonus is that I'll have time to clear my head before I see Riley. I'm nervous now that I know he'll be riding Melody, because things will be doubly awful if my suspicions are confirmed that Riley was involved in hurting Joel. To know something like that and see him riding Joel's horse would kill me.

Austen opens the wooden door to Harmony's stall and she cruises on in. "Here's your new home, beautiful."

"Hi, big boy," I say, when I see Austen's handsome gray gelding, Axel, peering at us from his stall. He lets out a low nicker to say hello to the newcomer. "A pair of gorgeous gray horses."

"We do have a lot in common, don't we?" he says.

"Yeah. I guess that we do."

"Should we meet back here around six thirty?" Austen grins. "I'll have finished feeding about then."

"Works for me." I watch him walk over and pet his horse on the neck before he heads out, and I can't help but smile. This summer is going to have its challenges, but there are definitely some pros to being here.

CHAPTER *four*

I decide to stay with Harmony for a while, because the last thing I want right now is to run into anyone else I know. I finally give her that huge hug she's been waiting for and that's when she starts communicating; I understand her thoughts most clearly when we're touching or very close.

Unfortunately, I don't like what she's saying. It's about the obstruction in her eye—again. The problem started in Kentucky, and once I'd investigated with the onsite vet there, and my mom, who is also a vet, we realized that Harmony has a uveal cyst. Although these sorts of cysts don't hurt a horse, they can distract them and, for some horses, cause them to spook more easily. A lot of horses get them and do just fine. However, for other horses, it's really bothersome and they don't adjust well, because they can't see shadows clearly.

My direct communication with horses usually happens in pictures. Visual images just seem to be the easiest and best way to "talk." So now, I show Harmony an image of her eye, and she shows me an image of me, but it's only half of me. Clearly, her vision is being blocked and she's unhappy about it. I sigh and pull out my cell phone and call my mom.

"Schnoopy!" my mom exclaims when she answers the phone. "How are you?" Schnoopy has pretty much been my lifelong nickname, thanks to my mother. Not exactly sure where it came from, but it's what she calls me.

"I'm okay."

"Uh-oh. What's wrong?"

Knowing I can't go into all the details about Tristan and Lydia, or bring up my issues about trusting Riley, or even address my concerns about what really happened to Joel, I focus on my horse. I blurt out, "It's Harmony, Mom. Her eye is worse. She's been telling me about it and I'm worried."

"Sounds to me like the cyst needs to be removed."

"No. I don't want to do that to her."

"Honey, it could impede her jumping. The cyst could cause you, well . . . it could cause both of you to get hurt. Fixing it involves a basic surgery and I'm positive there are capable vets out there who can handle it. She won't even have to be laid down. They can do it with what's called a diode laser."

I shake my head. "I want you to do it."

"Ah, Schnoop, I don't have a license to practice in Virginia. And remember, I'm leaving tomorrow with some friends on a hiking trip through Europe."

I swallow hard. I wish she could come be with me and do this surgery, but she's right. My mom has earned this vacation big time. She does so much for my brother and me. Now, she's finally saved enough money to make this trip while I'm at Liberty Farms, and my brother is away at summer camp. "I know, Mom. You go and have fun."

"I'm sorry, babe. E-mail me. I think there might be hot spots occasionally on the hiking trails where I can get e-mail. I'm not sure about the cell coverage. I'll call you as soon as I can. You have to trust me, though, that her eye can easily be taken care of."

"I know." She's right, of course, but Harmony means the world to me. I'm probably biased, but my mother is an amazing vet, and I want only the best for my horse. "I just wish there was a way you could take a look at her."

"Listen to me," she says. "Get her settled and go find Holden. He's out there, isn't he?"

"Yes. I think he's arriving sometime this evening." All the kids from our school had been relieved when we'd heard that Holden Fairmont was going to coach us at Liberty Farms this summer. There were going to be a lot of unknowns, but one thing for sure was that Holden knew how to look out for his students.

"Good. Get with him. He and I have spoken a couple of times about the issue and he's very aware of it."

"You have?"

"Yes."

"Oh." I'm surprised that I'm just learning this from my mom, but whatever.

"It'll be fine. I promise you it will. Now, how is everything else going?"

I lie and tell her that everything is great. I don't want to worry her. I want her to relax and have a good time on her trip. She tells me that she needs to get going, because she has to get my brother packed for camp. "Love you, Schnoopy, and I'll call as soon as I can."

"Love you too, Mom. Have a good time."

I hang up the phone and spend the next hour with Harmony before I decide it's time to go back to the cabin and get ready for the evening. When I open the cabin door, I'm accosted by the overwhelming scent of strong perfume mixed with hair spray. I know before I even look around that this is *not* a good sign.

My worry is confirmed when in the next second I see Lydia Gallagher putting her clothes away in one of the dressers, wearing a set of expensive-looking headphones over her ears.

Janna is on her bed reading but sets her Kindle aside when she sees me, and gives me a knowing look.

"Hey," Janna says. "Your horse good?"

"She is. Thanks."

"What? Did you say something?" Lydia turns around to look at Janna as she takes off her headphones. Then she spots me. Her jaw drops. "Oh no. No. You and I can't sleep in the same cabin."

I smile. "Feeling is mutual."

"What are you going to do about it?" she asks.

"Ignore you," I reply.

"I need to get this changed. This isn't going to work at all." She tosses the headphones onto the bed and leaves, slamming the door behind her.

I look at Janna and we both start cracking up. "I see you met the wicked witch."

"I'll say. I think your plan is perfect," Janna replies. "Ignore her. I'll join you."

"Thanks," I reply.

"Hey, they dropped off orientation packets. I put yours on your bed."

"Oh good. Thank you." I pull the paperwork out of the packet and start looking it over. "Early start," I say, noticing that we'll be meeting at seven in the morning.

"Yeah. We probably will be riding pretty early out here. Even with the fans in the indoor arena, the days we school cross-country will likely be miserable. Gets pretty hot and humid."

I nod. "I don't mind early. But did you see this? There's a switch in the teachers. Kim Skinner isn't going to be here after all," I say, kind of bummed. Kim is one of the best dressage coaches and riders in the country, and I was really looking forward to working with her. Dressage is definitely a weak point for Harmony and me.

"I saw that. Not sure why she isn't coming, but it's a bummer. It doesn't say who's replacing her, though."

"No. Just reads 'TBD.' It looks like they'll be lining up a few other things at the last minute too. I noticed some of the lessons aren't assigned to a specific coach yet. Oh well, I'm sure whoever we get will be great." I notice Janna check her watch. "Want to get something to eat with me? I'm kind of hungry. I have my car, so I thought I'd drive into town and check things out."

I know I should invite her to go with Austen and me, but I really want to finish talking to him about my suspicions around Joel's death; and truth be told, I was kind of looking forward to our time together with nobody else around. "I've actually got plans already with an old friend from home. He's one of the working students here this summer."

"Oh. Okay." She forces a smile, but I can hear the disappointment in her voice. "Well, I've got other options. There's a guy here for the summer who I met at champs in Kentucky. He was pretty nice to me down there when I was feeling rotten because of some problems with my team. He's kind of cute too. When I ran into him earlier, he mentioned he'd like to hang out."

"Oh yeah?" I watch as she quickly types out a text.

"Yeah. His name is Chris Haverly. His family owns Haverly watches."

I'm not sure how to react to this. I mean, Janna is entitled to have anyone she wants for a friend, and I don't know for a fact that Chris is a bad guy. I just know his creep factor is way up there. And if the guy is a killer, or had any part in Joel's death, I should at least warn my new friend. "You know what, you can come with us tonight," I blurt out.

Just then her phone dings with an incoming text, and she looks up and shakes her head. "No. You go. He just texted me back and said that he'd love to hang out." Janna is all smiles. I bite my tongue so I won't say anything bad about Chris. Why couldn't I just have invited her to come with us for burgers? I guess even I have to admit I'm feeling a little possessive about my time with Austen.

She jumps up. "Oh no. I forgot to lock my tack trunk. See you tonight. Have fun!"

Before I can warn her . . . before I can get another word out, Janna is out the door, and I'm left wondering what kind of person I am. Am I just paranoid? I mean, if I told her what I really think—that Chris Haverly might have known a thing or two about my friend Joel's death—would she think I was insane?

Probably. After the door slams shut behind her, I take a few minutes to think over the situation. What should I tell Janna about Chris Haverly the next time I see her? I brainstorm ideas as I go through my drawers and try to decide what to wear for my meet-up with Austen. I remember that he once told me that he thought I looked nice when I wore a green sweater. I find a green sleeveless blouse and a pair of jean shorts that I'll admit are a little bit shorter than some of my other pairs. I chastise myself for being so girly. Guess I have to admit that my infatuation with my old friend has grown into something a little bit bigger, and that—yes, I want him to really notice me.

CHAPTER five

Y ou couldn't have said anything," Austen says, picking up his monstrous cheeseburger. "Not without seeming weird."

I poke a French fry into some ketchup, thinking about how often Austen and I like the same things—like this diner. I don't know if he was actually trying to pick a place I'd like, but if so, he did a good job. The walls are painted in bright primary colors and even though it's packed with people, it has a friendly, cozy feel. And Austen was right about the burgers. They're delicious. "You're right, I couldn't have warned her," I say. "But if she gets in tight with that guy, I'll have to say something. She's a really sweet girl and guys like that can't be trusted."

Austen sets his soda down. "Vivvie, you can't always come to everyone's rescue, you know. Sometimes you have to let people figure things out on their own. As much as you want to help, it can actually cause problems. For you."

"What do you mean?"

"Let's just say that this Haverly kid *is* a bad guy. What happens when he finds out you're warning people off of him? He might even come after you. Then I'd have to kill him, and then I'd go to jail." He smiles. "And I don't want to go to jail, because then how would I ever get to spend time with you again? And, by the way, I like that blouse on you."

I smile back. Ha! "Thank you. But what if . . ."

Austen lays his hand on mine. "I know what you're going to say, and that's all that there is right now—what-ifs. Hold off before you start making assumptions."

"Maybe you're right." I sigh. "What do you think I should do?"

"Finish telling me what you know, and then I'm going to help you find the answers." He smiles and those dimples of his that I've always thought were cute, even when we were, like, twelve, make an appearance. I can't help but notice they're more adorable than ever. "Really? You're really going to help me find the answers?"

"Yeah. Really. That's what friends do for each other."

I try not to look surprised. *Friends?* Okay. So, that's what we are. We're friends. We've always been friends and we will always be friends. But now I'm wondering, does he remember our kiss last fall? What about the time in the barn when he said that one day it would be him and me? Maybe he thinks that's all ancient history. Thing is, that doesn't explain the flirting he's been subtly dropping in. Guess all I can do is try to ignore those cute dimples and get down to business.

"Okay, let me catch you up on some of the stuff that happened in Lexington," I say. "To start with, like I said, Riley and Joel both admitted they shared some dark secret with Chris Haverly that I was better off not knowing about. Now Joel is dead and Riley isn't talking."

"You have no idea what the unspoken secret was about?"

I tap my fingers on the table. "Well, Joel's stepmother, Tiffany, was suspected in a scandal of over-drugging ponies. It happened at a place where all three of the guys worked together—maybe they knew some incriminating details? Who knows. Apparently, at the same barn, Joel's horse, Melody, was drugged and went down during a show—and the little girl who was riding her got badly hurt. Maybe Tiffany was involved in that too?" I hope that Austen doesn't start questioning exactly where I've gotten my info. I can't tell him that I gathered some of it from Melody herself.

"So, Joel never told you any hard facts," Austen says.

"Not really," I say.

"But I see where you're going. Are you thinking this dark secret between Joel, Riley, and the Chris kid has something to do with the stepmom supposedly drugging ponies?"

I shrug. "Maybe. I don't know. She was never convicted, so nobody knows what part she actually played. All I know for sure is that Joel hated his stepmom and her daughter, Paisley. That girl definitely seemed like an awful stepsister to get stuck with—mean and vindictive, and not just because she wanted Joel's horse. She put off a bad vibe in general. And she had the weirdest boyfriend too. He got all aggro on Joel during a dinner we all had together. Granted, Joel was pretty angry after they threatened to take away Melody, but there was something more going on. I think Paisley's boyfriend was shady. I have to wonder if they'll show up this summer. Their family has strong ties to Liberty Farms, because Tiffany worked here as a successful trainer for years."

"I've been here for a week and haven't seen any of these people you're talking about, except for that Chris kid."

My stomach sinks because, although I should be elated at the possibility of not seeing Paisley, her weird boyfriend, and Joel's stepmother, I also *do* want to see them. If anyone will have the answers I'm seeking about Joel's death, it's them. "Maybe they'll show up."

"I don't know. Are you sure you're not on a wild goose chase?"

"I'm sure."

"Okay, then. Tomorrow, I start making friends with Chris Haverly."

"What?" I almost choke on a French fry.

"Yeah. If you think this guy is up to something and that he might know what happened to Joel, then I need to work on getting him to trust me."

My stomach sinks, but what he's saying makes sense. I once told Riley that keeping your enemies closer than your friends was the best way to get answers; apparently, Austen has the same philosophy.

And, speaking of Riley, I'm going to have to do with him exactly what Austen plans to do with Chris: I need to go back to making him my BFF. The icky part is, I'll be trying to build fake trust between us—to get him to confide in me. Does that make me a liar? I'm not sure I want to know.

CHAPTER *six*

On the drive back, Austen is quiet, which is unusual for him, since he usually banters nonstop. I shift uncomfortably in my seat, because I'm not used to this more thoughtful side of my friend. Maybe he's regretting his offer to help me figure out what happened to Joel.

He's had the stereo turned up on a Radiohead song. I turn it down and he glances at me. "Everything okay?" he asks.

"I don't know. Is it? You've been really quiet since we left the restaurant."

He doesn't answer right away, and it increases my doubts. He pulls the car to the side of the road and parks. "I could lie and tell you that everything is okay, and that I was just deep in thought. I mean . . ." He pauses and glances at me. "I mean, I was deep in thought, but only because I've been trying to figure out how to tell you something all evening. I couldn't get a word in edgewise with all our talk about the Joel situation. And here's the thing—I do want to help you with that. I think you're right that something bad might have happened. But there's also something else on my mind."

"You're confusing me, Austen," I say.

"I'm sorry, Viv. It's just that, well, there are a couple things that I have to say out loud, but I'm not sure how to get started."

I take his hand and squeeze. "We're friends. You can say anything to me. You know that, right?"

He nods. "Friends. Yeah. I know. Okay, here goes. I think that you know how I feel about you. I haven't exactly made that a secret in the past six months. When you wound up with Tristan, I was pretty crushed, but I kept reminding myself that we were friends and that we'd always be friends."

"You're right. We will."

"I don't know any other way to say this so that you get it, but I love you, Vivienne. When we were eight and you pushed me into the pond on that trail ride that we were all on, and you laughed like a lunatic because I was wet and muddy, I loved you then. Ever since I was a little kid, I've felt this way. All the years of me teasing you, joking with you, and acting like a total goofball was just my way of covering up how much I think about you. You've been the only girl who has mattered in my world for a really long time."

I stare at him for a few seconds as my brain processes what he's said. Then, instead of saying a word, I wrap my arms around him and kiss him hard. I've kissed Austen before, but, right away, this feels different. It has more behind it. I don't feel embarrassed or like I'm holding back, and I'm not scared. When our lips meet I feel like I'm melting from the inside out, not that it's possible, but the sensation is like something solid turning to liquid. He starts to explore my mouth with his tongue, and my entire body tingles. As the kiss goes on and time seems to stop, I feel like I'm floating in a place where I can't think but can only feel. His hand moves to my lower back and I press against him, making the kiss deeper with a kind of intensity that's totally new to me.

Slowly, the two of us pull apart. He sits back and so do I, neither of us saying anything for a minute. I'm still trying to catch my breath. Being with Tristan never, ever felt like this, even though I thought it was incredible at the time.

He breaks the silence with, "What does this mean?"

I smile at him. "It means that, I guess, I feel about you a lot the way you feel about me." As the words come out, I know they're weak, because I love him too. But I just broke up with someone who I thought I loved and I'm not sure how to make this type of transition so quickly.

He nods and laughs. "You are so you."

"What does that mean?"

"It means just that. Don't worry about it. I think I know you well enough to know what kind of a kiss that was. But the thing is, if we're really going to take this next step, and try to step out of the friend zone, we might have some challenges. Big ones, that go beyond the fact that we might not know how to act around each other once we're more than friends."

"Challenges?"

"Yeah. Challenges. The first one is that you just got out of a relationship. You're my friend first, so I respect that, and I don't want you to feel a ton of pressure to make some big decision about us."

I nod. "I appreciate that. I really do. But, honestly, the further away I get from Tristan emotionally, the more I realize that we weren't really meant to be together. We're too different. He's far better suited for Lydia, which maybe he knew all along. Because, according to a revealing photo I received via text, they were back together before Tristan and I ever officially broke up."

"Ouch."

"Yep."

"But that's what I mean," he says. "I don't want be your rebound after a bad thing like that. I don't want you to be with me just because you know me well and it's easy."

I frown. "Austen, you just said it . . . we were friends first. We've known each other for over ten years. We've grown up together.

Being with you could never be about a rebound. It would be about us exploring new feelings together and seeing where they lead us."

He reaches over and pulls me in close to his chest, where I can hear his heart beating loud and fast. "I like that."

I notice something that I'm not sure I ever noticed before about him—he smells really, really good, like spice and soap, and something almost citrus-like, I think. I don't know why, but the way he smells and feels sends my own heartbeat into overdrive. I wonder if he can tell. I'm pretty sure I could stay like this for a very long time—in this kind of surreal state where I'm just beginning to realize that the boy I've known my whole life has just declared his love for me. And that, for the first time, I might be sure that I love him too.

Then I remember the word he just used after his declaration—*challenges*. I speak up. "We dealt with challenge number one. You're worried about me using you as a rebound, and now that you know that can't be the case, what else is on your list?"

"This one might be a bit tough."

"Okay."

"You're here on scholarship and you're seventeen."

"A month and a half to go until I'm eighteen," I chime in.

"Yes, but those six weeks matter. I'm here as a working student and will be nineteen in a week. One of the first rules we were given when we arrived is that as working students we aren't allowed to 'fraternize' with the students who are here to train. Most of us are older than all of you and I think that's the main reason. There are some legalities there."

"Oh."

"Yeah. Oh. I don't want to lose my job and I don't want you to lose your scholarship. But I also don't want to lose you. This is our chance to see if the 'new us' works. We're both going back to separate schools in the fall, so now is the time. We might not have another chance to find out where this thing might be headed."

I sigh, feeling truly sorry for the first time that Austen ended up at UC Davis in Northern California instead of, say, UCLA, where he'd be closer to me and the Fairmont campus. Then again, Davis is a great school for equestrians, and I wouldn't want anything to stand in the way of Austen getting to spend time with horses at college.

"Then there is only one thing to do."

"What's that?" he asks.

"We'll have to sneak around."

His eyes widen and one of his silly grins spreads across his face. "We could get into a lot of trouble if we get caught."

"Well, really, what could we get caught at?"

He laughs. "Technically, I'm not even supposed to take you off the farm without one other person with us, so I've already broken the rules tonight."

"We've broken a lot of rules in our day. Remember when we were little kids and Gail told us we weren't supposed to ride without an adult?" I smile as I think of our former coach. "Broke that one a few times."

"And we got busted when we jumped without her there and I wound up falling off and breaking my arm."

"I still can't believe that happened," I say. "It was a little cross rail."

"My horse wasn't exactly coordinated."

"You're right. You had that funky chestnut pony, Harry, who just wanted to be a trail horse." As the words come out, I realize that they shouldn't have.

"He did only want to be a trail horse, you're right," says Austen. "The only time he was ever sure-footed was on the trails."

I swallow hard. Being able to read horses' feelings and thoughts means you have to be a little bit paranoid about what you say; you never want to give away a detail that could only have come directly from the horse's mouth, so to speak. I remember the day quite well when Austen's pony tripped on the cross rail and Austen flew off, landing on his right arm and screeching in pain as it broke. Gail had arrived about ten minutes after his accident, and I knew on top of everything else that we were going to get a real earful, because we had broken the rules. Our other friend, Mia, had called Austen's mom. I'd brought Austen some ice, and then put Harry back in Gail's barn. I'd whispered to Harry as I stroked his face, "Why did you get caught up in the cross rail?"

In his way, through images, Harry had shown me that he didn't feel safe picking up his legs and knees. He'd also showed me an image of a shady path through the woods, and I'd realized that he felt safer and happier on a trail ride. Had I just given myself away by making it clear I knew the horse's feelings? I watch Austen's face, then feel relieved as his normal expression proves without a doubt that he still has no inkling about my weird gift. It was a stroke of luck that my little mistake could be so easily passed off.

"We've definitely broken a few rules in our day. That's true." Austen laughs and I feel my paranoia completely subside. "But this time, the consequences could be a bit more severe if we're found out. It's kind of like we're at camp—you're the kid and I'm the counselor."

I sock him gently on the shoulder. He feigns as if he's been hurt.

"I am not a kid," I say. "And you are not my counselor."

"Ah, you're good with being a rule breaker, then?"

"I'm good with it," I reply. "Besides, if we're going to find out what really happened to Joel, I think we'll be doing plenty of sneaking around in that area too."

"I think you're right."

I wait for him to turn the engine back on, but I can tell he has something else he wants to say. "What is it?" I ask. "Maybe another challenge for us will be that we know each other well enough to know when there's something more to say, or something wrong, or . . ."

"It's your dad, Vivvie."

"What?" I shake my head. "What're you talking about? My dad?"

He faces me and takes both of my hands. "I didn't know how to tell you. I just found out myself before I picked you up. I wanted to tell you first thing."

"Tell me what?" I can hear and feel the emotion catching in the back of my throat.

"Your dad trains just down the road. He lives only a mile away. And he teaches at Liberty Farms."

CHAPTER *seven*

I feel completely shell-shocked as Austen starts the car and drives us back to Liberty Farms. Instead of parking in an obvious place, he kills the headlights and we pull into a dark spot by the barns so I can get out of the car unnoticed.

He reaches over and puts a hand on my leg. "I would've told you at dinner, but I didn't know how to," he says. "It's kind of a big thing . . . it's a huge thing, actually. And we were already talking about a big thing with Joel. And then I had to explain how I felt about you, and I don't know—maybe there was some part of me that wanted to completely ignore it, and hope it would go away. To be honest, all of me wanted that, because I know how badly your father hurt you and what you went through after he left. Let's face it . . . you kind of have trust issues, and who wouldn't after all that you've been through? I blame him for hurting you."

I look at him with tears in my eyes and lay my hand over his. "You're right. You are. I don't know how you could've told me in any other way than you did. I know this had to be hard for you."

"You're not mad at me?"

"No." I shake my head and Austen wipes away my tears with his free hand, then pulls me in close.

"What are you going to do?" he asks.

I slump back in the leather seat of the car. "I don't know. I kind of want to run home."

"You can't do that."

"I know. I didn't say that I was going to. Just that I kind of want to. Maybe it's time that I deal with it. Maybe it's time that I confront my dad and hash this out. I mean, it can't all be coincidence that I'm here for the summer and my father lives up the road."

"Life works like that sometimes, I think. It's all kind of mysterious."

I nod and turn to get out of the car, then think better of it and turn back to Austen for a quick kiss. But what I expect to be a peck turns into something more when I can't pull my lips away from his and he cups the back of my head. As we fit ourselves together perfectly, my insides feel like they're turning to liquid again. Knowing I should go, and worried we'll be seen, I pull away and stare at him.

"Where did you learn to kiss like that? Or maybe I don't want to know," I say. "I just can't believe I never guessed things could be like this."

He smiles. "Believe me, Vivvie. I never *learned* anything. Let's just say you inspire me. And don't worry. Nothing I've ever been through can compare to these kisses. They're different. *We're* different."

I nod. "Okay, well that's good news. I'm glad to hear you're not some secret celebrity kisser or something."

He laughs. "You should go. I'll stay here in the car. We really don't want to be seen."

"I'd kiss you again, but then I'll never go," I say. With that, I hop out of the car and head back to the cabin.

Luckily, nobody else is around when I arrive, which is a relief. I'm glad neither Lydia nor Janna are back yet. I can't help but wonder who our new roommate is. There's a backpack and suitcase on the floor near Lydia's bunk that I don't recognize. Obviously

Lydia's dream of being moved to another cabin isn't becoming a reality since her crap is still here.

I brush my teeth and climb into my bunk, but once there, I realize there's no way I'm going right to sleep. Inevitably I find myself thinking about my father, and remembering the day I woke up and found out he was gone. I also can't stop thinking about Austen. Diverse feelings all around, from anger and sadness over my dad to pure elation over what's happening between Austen and me.

Finally, I hear Janna's footsteps, but I pretend to be asleep.

More thoughts race through my mind as Janna starts to snore, then I hear the giggling that I know belongs to Lydia and Tristan's deep voice outside. I pull a pillow over my head and keep it there for a long time, so I won't have to see that wicked little bitch come inside. It's around then that I fall asleep.

When I wake up, it's still dark outside, so I know it's early. I stretch and yawn. Then I blink several times as I notice who is in the top bunk across from mine. "Emily?" I'm too surprised to remember to whisper.

Her eyes open and she sits up. "Hey, Vivienne."

"Why are you two *talking*?" Lydia yells. "It's the middle of the night. Shut up."

"What's going on?" Janna asks sleepily.

"Nothing," Emily Davenport and I answer simultaneously. We decide to ignore Lydia, who buries her head under her pillow.

"So you're our fourth roommate?" I ask.

She nods. "Here I am."

I know Emily pretty well, because she also attends Fairmont. She barely qualified to come and train for the summer at Liberty Farms. And I hadn't expected to see her, since a week before we were all supposed to arrive, I received an e-mail from her saying that she wasn't coming. She'd just left it at that—no explanation.

Not that she owes me one. I have a kind of weird friendship with Emily, probably because right after we first met at Fairmont, she helped me catch a killer. It's a strange way to get acquainted. We'd never been typical BFFs, but we'd gotten to know each other pretty well during the school year. Like, I know she has a crazy ambitious horse-show mom who puts a ton of pressure on her to perform, even though she has clearly said she hates competitive riding and just wants to be a vet. I also know she has some confidence problems. There's no other way to explain why she used to hang out with Lydia and her crew—who I call the DZ, which means "drama zone"—even though they weren't that nice to her. Anyway, the girl has some issues, and she takes meds for depression too. In short, Emily can be unpredictable. I never know what she's going to do next.

"I thought you'd decided not to come," I say.

She crawls out of bed and takes the rubber band she has on her wrist off, pulling her wavy hair back into a bushy ponytail. "Where's the coffee?" she asks.

"I said shut up," Lydia repeats.

We both ignore her. Again.

"There's one of those Keurig machines at the main house. Want to head down?" I put on a pair of shorts and a T-shirt, knowing that the summer heat will already be apparent outside, even at six in the morning.

"Yeah. Let me change."

A few minutes later we walk into the main house, which is called the Commons House. It's the spot where all the students get breakfast and coffee.

"How did you manage to get Lydia as a roommate?" Emily asks. "Bet you didn't see that coming."

I shrug. "Luck of the draw. you still haven't answered me. I didn't think you were coming."

"I wasn't. I told my mom that I didn't want to come out here, that I wanted to do normal teenage things for one summer—like go to the beach, shop . . . you know, what most girls our age do. Or do an internship at a vet's office. Both those ideas went over like buckets of shiznick."

"Got it. At least you told her. You're starting to voice yourself. That's good."

"I don't need a counseling session, Vivienne." She looks around. "What I do need is a hot cup of coffee."

"Got it." I know better than to get defensive or try to argue with her. I really wasn't trying to counsel her, but Emily is the kind of person who sees things exactly how she wants to see them.

"My horse is being flown in today, since we missed the transport, so I need to get with it so I'll be awake when she gets here."

With coffee and croissants in hand, I show Emily around the Commons House, since Faith gave me the tour upon arrival. It's a two-story house that serves as the main gathering place for all the students; it's where we're supposed to meet each morning to receive our daily schedules. It's equipped with a kitchen, bathroom, large family room, and a game room with a pool table and large-screen TV connected to an Xbox. There are also a couple of bedrooms upstairs, in case guests come to visit. It's cozy and kind of reminds me of home.

The grand Southern-style mansion I saw from the airport shuttle when I first arrived sits a little farther back on the property than the Commons House and the barns, and there is nothing about it that reminds me of home. I've been wondering who lives there. I'm guessing that it's whoever owns this place. I just wish I knew who that was. Before I came out here, I looked all over the Internet to see who owns Liberty Farms, but there was no real information. It had been for sale recently and all I could find out was that it had been sold. I don't know. Maybe Faith lives there, or maybe it's where the top trainers get to stay.

There are a few other structures around the property too, including a ramshackle farmhouse that Faith told me about. Apparently it once housed a family of slaves on the property, and there are rumors that it is now haunted. Nobody has been enthusiastic about renovating it in recent years, so it is basically awaiting demolition.

As Emily and I finish our tour of the place and head back to the kitchen, I see Chris Haverly walk through the double doors. Austen is behind him and he slyly winks at me. Hmm. He certainly isn't wasting time in getting to be Chris's friend.

As I grab an orange juice, I sense someone watching me and I turn to see Tristan in the corner of the room. I feel heat rise to my cheeks as he shoots me a disgusted glance and then goes back to looking at his phone.

"Do I detect a chill?" Emily nods her head toward Tristan.

"We, uh, we aren't together any longer."

"Oh. Interesting. Anything to do with your friend from back home?" Now she nods her head toward Austen.

"No." Another thing about Emily is that she can change her loyalties pretty quickly, so the last thing I want is for her to find out about Austen and me. I'm super aware that we need to be very careful about the new status of our relationship. "It has to do with a photo someone texted to my phone. You might want to ask Lydia."

"Ah. Okay. Where's your pal Riley?" she says.

"I thought he'd be here by now," I say, realizing that it *is* strange he hasn't turned up yet. "I'm a little worried about him."

"Poor you," she says snidely, and jets off back to the breakfast table and starts piling a plate high with eggs.

I can't say that I'm all that unhappy that Emily has left my side, taking her sour attitude with her, but I definitely want to question her about her last hours with Joel.

Emily had been Joel's "girlfriend" in Lexington before he'd died—sadly, she'd been clueless that she was just playing a part, and that Joel was actually gay. For a long time, no one knew about that part of his life except for Riley, Tristan, and me. When Joel had finally come clean with Emily after the championships, she hadn't exactly been happy about the reveal.

I know I'm paranoid, but the thought had crossed my mind more than once: What if Emily got so upset when Joel told her he was gay that she decided to take revenge? What if she'd been drunk—the girl definitely consumes more alcohol than your average high school kid—and not thinking clearly? If so, could she have done something spiteful, never thinking it could cause a tragedy? Joel supposedly overdosed on sleeping pills. I don't have access to an autopsy report, of course, but I can't help wondering what kind of sleeping pills were in his system. I know Emily takes all sorts of meds for her depression and whatever else she has going on.

Beyond these suspicions, I don't like the fact that she has been so tight-lipped about her last interactions with Joel. Not that I asked her directly, but there's part of me that imagines she might want to find comfort in talking it out. But she's never really tried to bring it up with me.

Almost like she has something to hide.

CHAPTER *eight*

A minute after Faith signals the students to gather for the morning meeting, Lydia makes her entrance. I try not to roll my eyes at her polished look. I mean, seriously, how does the girl wake up in a bunk bed and walk in here ten minutes later dressed in her polo and breeches with hair and makeup that look like she just walked out of a Victoria's Secret catalog? It just isn't right.

She sits down on the small couch next to Tristan and leans her head on his shoulder. I try to keep my expression neutral, even though the display sort of disgusts me. Why does seeing them together get a rise out of me? Maybe because only a few short weeks ago I was ready to declare my love for Tristan. I mean, I was ready to lose my virginity to the guy. Thank God that didn't happen. Especially now that I see how easily he moved on! I glance at Austen and he smiles at me, his eyes warm and mischievous, and my pulse speeds up. I remember our kiss last night and try not to blush.

Janna walks in and makes her way over to me. "Hey, sorry I didn't roll out of bed when you got up. I would've loved to have gotten some breakfast with you and the new roomie, but I was so tired. I kind of was out late with Chris." She smiles.

"Oh." What I want to say is, "Oh no."

"Who is that talking to him, by the way?" she asks.

I glance around and see that Emily is chatting with Chris. "That's our new roomie. She goes to Fairmont too. She's nice, but I can also say she's a little bit weird."

"I can handle nice and weird," she says. "Anything over Lydia; you're so right about her. She isn't nice at all. She yelled at me to hurry up in the bathroom."

"I'm sure she did. Like I suggested, ignoring her is best."

"Deal. I have to tell you about Chris. He's super sweet and interesting. He knows a ton about this place too."

"Really?"

"Yeah. Oh, wait, but there was something else I found out from him I wanted to tell you."

"Okay, shoot."

"You know the TBD instructor on the schedule? I found out who it's going to be. Some lady named Tiffany something-or-other. Supposedly she has a great reputation. I guess she also lives in the big mansion here. Supposedly she and her husband just bought the place."

I stare at her. Seriously? Joel's stepmother owns Liberty Farms?

"Everything okay? You look pale."

I nod. "Fine. Just still bummed out I won't get to train with Kim Skinner."

"Well, I totally want to hear your take on Chris; I really kind of like him. But it looks like we're about to start. I'll fill you in later."

"Okay." I'd love to know what else she learned from Chris. I also want to tell Janna to stay away from him, but then I remember Austen's words from last night: *You can't always come to everyone's rescue . . .*

I can tell the meeting is about to start, because Austen and the three other working students are gathering at the front of the room—then I do a double take. One of the working students by

Austen's side is none other than Joel's stepsister, Paisley. Now, that is odd. Beyond odd. It is downright strange.

I'd only shared one meal with Paisley, back when Joel was alive, and she'd seemed spoiled and arrogant. The type who wanted to seem like a rich blue blood with East Coast money—even though she wasn't, of course. Her mom, Tiffany, had married into Joel's father's wealth. So, why was she here? Were they *making* her work? Because the girl I'd met with Joel didn't strike me as the type willing to be a working student. She seemed more interested in stealing Joel's horse for herself and cozying up to her weird boyfriend—I think his name was James—than doing something productive. Austen will work his butt off as a working student, but Paisley? I can't see it.

The other mystery at hand is why Austen didn't know last night that Paisley and Tiffany would be involved at Liberty Farms this summer. When we'd talked at the diner, he'd said that he wasn't aware of any of Joel's former friends or family being on the grounds—just Chris Haverly, whose connection to Joel was still uncertain. I try to catch Austen's eye so he'll realize that the girl next to him is the same "Paisley" we talked about over cheeseburgers.

Faith stands up next to the working students and asks for our attention. "Riders, we're happy to have you here at Liberty Farms. You are a group of eighteen talented individuals from around the country. You're the best young riders we have, and you will all be receiving quality instruction and care. You'll be learning from the best. It won't be easy. You'll be challenged. It'll be fun too. We ride five days a week and take Sundays and Mondays off. We encourage you to use that time to go into town, see some sites, and get some culture. Riding lessons begin at seven thirty a.m. due to the summer heat and humidity and typically finish by noon. Then it's lunch, and afterward you'll be expected to clean tack, and do whatever else you need to for and with your horses. The pool will open at one p.m. each day, and as long as you are finished with your horses, you are free to use it. The gym is open from five thirty a.m. to nine p.m., and you can check the schedule for special classes such as yoga, strength training, and cardio dance."

I can hear a few of the guys chuckle at the mention of cardio dance.

Faith smiles. "Don't knock it until you try it, guys. It's a lot harder than it might sound. And our philosophy here is that if you're asking your equine athlete for his or her all, then you should expect yourselves to also be on your game one hundred percent. You are in a unique sport with a unique partner, and you are both expected to be in optimum shape. You've all been given the book of rules, so I don't need to go over them unless anyone has questions. Anyone?"

"I have a question," says a guy with reddish-blond hair. I notice his wrinkle-free oxford shirt and recognize him as the preppy kid who'd heckled Lydia and Tristan when they were having their oh-so-sweet reunion next to the airport shuttle.

I can tell by the way he's raising his hand that he's probably about to make another joke.

"Sure, Wills, what is it?" Faith says.

Wills? I didn't know anyone gave kids names like that anymore.

"Is there a rule against bringing our horse with us to cardio dance?" This gets chuckles from everyone.

Faith smiles slightly but shakes her head. "Against the rules," she says. "Other questions?"

A few giggles.

"I know Wills was joking, but this is as good a time as any to remind you how seriously we take discipline at Liberty Farms. The rules are the rules. That includes things like getting caught in the opposite sex's room after ten o'clock curfew. Break these rules, and you could face being expelled from the program."

"Ouch," Wills says. "Okay, so I'll go to cardio dance alone."

More laughter. Faith can't help but smile broadly.

"All right then, if there aren't any more questions regarding the rules, I say we introduce our coaches for the summer."

I feel anxiety in the pit of my stomach knowing that my father will probably be among those introduced. I twist my hands together but try to keep my eyes trained on Faith, rather than search the room to see if he's walked in.

"I know there were bios in the binders you received," Faith says, "but we've made a few changes, so I'll talk about those first. To start, I'd like to introduce Tiffany Parker, who will be with us this summer in place of Kim Skinner, who had to withdraw for family reasons."

I don't wait for Faith to say the obvious—that Tiffany actually got this job because she and Joel's dad recently bought Liberty Farms. It would seem tacky, so that little fact is clearly going to be swept under the rug.

Faith continues, "I know many of you were looking forward to working with Kim, but we are very lucky that Tiffany could step in. She has taught at Liberty before, but most recently was on hiatus. Her family has recently purchased the facility. Tiffany comes to us with a successful background in the hunter and jumper world, so she'll be working with you in your stadium jump lessons . . ."

I didn't hear much more of what Faith went on to say about Tiffany—about her awards and accolades and accomplishments—because all I could think about was the accusations against her. Of course, she'd never been convicted of drugging ponies. But I knew she'd done something awful to the pony that Melody had shown me last semester; and I'd seen with my own eyes how coldly she'd threatened to separate Joel from his horse. I can feel my ears growing red, which is something they tend to do when I start to get angry. This isn't good at all. The last thing I want is Joel's wicked stepmonster coaching me in any situation. And it is awful that she owns the place—or, at least, Joel's dad does. Now I know the truth: the fancy Southern-style mansion on the hill belongs to the Parker family.

I think I might be sick! The last thing any of them deserve is to own this historic place and live in a beautiful house while my friend is six feet under. I take in a deep breath and work on keeping my cool.

The sight of Tiffany standing up there all blond, tan, and perky makes me want to gag. "It's so wonderful to be home. My family and I have just returned from a few weeks in Hawaii."

That explains why Austen hadn't seen or heard of any of them. This revelation makes me even sicker. A few weeks in Hawaii! Who does that? And who does that shortly after their son has died? I can't imagine what Joel's father is like.

Tiffany continues, "I'm so looking forward to working with each and every one of you. It's going to be a fabulous summer."

Oh brother. As I witness the spectacle of Tiffany Parker greeting us, a horrible thought occurs to me. Did Kayla send Melody here because she'd sold the horse back to Joel's father and Tiffany? I pray that isn't the case. I love Melody too much to see her put into the hands of such horrible people.

The next intro at least makes me happy when Faith says, "Among our other very capable and excellent coaches is one man who some of you work with on a regular basis already, but we are happy to have him here. Holden Fairmont."

A second later, Holden jogs up to join the group at the front of the room, waving and smiling at us. "Thanks, guys. We're all going to work hard and have a great summer." He steps back and

Faith continues detailing Holden's accomplishments, which I'm already aware of.

She then introduces Bernard Richardson. Just his presence alone is kind of intimidating. He's tall and lithe, with graying hair and dark eyes. I glance at Austen, who I know is in awe of the guy.

He also tells us how hard we're going to work, and what a great summer it's going to be. I can't believe I'll get to train with him. I definitely don't like the fact that I'll have to work with Tiffany, but Holden and Bernard will be great. As I wait for the final introduction, I feel myself holding my breath—thank God Austen broke the news to me last night or the shock of finding out my father will be teaching here might have killed me.

"And our final new addition for the summer lives and works here in Virginia. He's been touted as one of the top event trainers in this part of the world . . ." Suddenly, my heartbeat is pounding in my ears and I realize there's no way I'm going to be able to just sit here and politely applaud for the father who left me and my brother. So, as my father comes from around the corner to say his niceties to the crowd, I back away and turn around, going out the side door.

I know I was noticed. How could I not be in such a small group?

But I'm sorry. I had to get out of that room. I start walking quickly, not wanting anyone to come after me, and then I start running, hoping that I don't barf. As I run, the tears begin—and the only place I know to go to for solace is my mare's stall.

I make it to the barn and open up the stall door. Harmony is in her run and she turns, walking toward me. She knows I'm upset as she reaches me and nuzzles me, and I bury my head into her neck, crying and saying over and over again, "I hate him . . . I hate my father."

CHAPTER *nine*

I'm not sure how long I'm in Harmony's stall, because the first thing I do is curl up against the wall and drift to sleep with her standing over me.

It's Riley's voice that brings me fully back to the moment and the harsh realities. "Thought I might find you here," he says. He comes into the stall, closes the door, and sits down beside me.

I sit up, rubbing the sleep from my eyes. "Where have you been?"

"Had to go to church camp for the two weeks I was home before I was allowed to come here. It's been solidified that I'm going to hell."

"No, you're not," I reply.

"If my parents knew the truth about their little choirboy, then yes, I'm sure hell would be the next stop for me." I shake my head, wishing he didn't have to go through such difficulty. He puts an arm around me. "What gives, Viv? I was walking into the meeting room when I saw you bound out of there like you were a rabbit being chased by a coyote."

This makes me a laugh a little. "You do have a way with words, Ri."

"I do, don't I? Come on, what gives, my little warrior? It takes a lot to make you go running. I know how tough you are. Seen it firsthand. But it is good to see you, even if you were bolting away."

I lean my head on his shoulder. "It's good to see you too."
Harmony nudges me. She wants more attention. I run my hand
over her nose and proceed to tell Riley about my father's presence. Having him next to me, being the friend I've grown to
love, makes me question how I could ever suspect him of being
involved in Joel's death. It's hard to keep my guard up, because I
believe that Riley is a good guy. But what if the facts turn out to
prove otherwise?

"All summer long your dad will be teaching here?" he asks,
raising his eyebrows. "Wow, Vivvie. That does suck. That sucks
big time."

"I know," I reply.

"All right, we can do this one of two ways."

"We can?"

"Yes," he says. "One, you can totally act like you don't know
who he is and just be a student and take the lessons . . ."

"You think that's realistic?"

He shakes his head. "Probably not. I am really good at ignoring things, but I'm not you. You probably need to face this one
head on, Viv. It's time to confront your dad. It's been how long?"

"Almost eight years. My birthday is coming up in August."

"Right. It's time. You're going to turn eighteen and technically
you'll be an adult. I say that you need to be an adult in this situation and handle it."

"I don't know if I can. I don't know if I want to. What I want
to do is run and hide—bury myself behind a rock."

"No can do. I won't allow it. I think you can deal with this better than you realize. I think you have to. You never give yourself
enough credit. The only option you have if you can't ignore him is
to go home. That's not a good option. That would be like running
and hiding. You don't really think that's a good idea, do you?"

I shake my head slowly. "No. I know what being here can do for my riding career. I've got to focus on those goals, and you're right, the only way to really deal with this is to face it."

"Right. Deal with it then."

I sigh. "There's more. Joel's stepmonster is one of our coaches. And did you know that his dad bought this place for her? They own Liberty Farms!"

"Tiffany?"

"Yep."

"Shit. That's pure insanity. She's a nut job, Viv. You'll see. I can't believe it."

"I know, and her daughter, Paisley, is a working student. Isn't that weird? And to top it all off, Chris Haverly is here too."

Riley is quiet for a long time. He finally says, "I can't stand that guy. And Paisley is a working student? What is going on? That girl has always had grooms. I can't imagine her lifting a finger to do any of the dirty work around here."

"I know. None of it makes much sense. Riley . . ." I lift my head and look at him.

"Yeah?"

"What happened between you and Joel and Chris Haverly? Both of you guys told me to leave it alone last semester and now Joel is dead, and I really can't . . . I don't believe he killed himself. Do you know something? Does Chris?"

Riley again grows quiet. He finally responds in a whisper. "I'm not sure what I know, Viv."

"Do you think Joel killed himself?"

He shrugs.

"You're still afraid, aren't you? I can tell."

He stands up and reaches for my hand. "What I don't want is for you to get hurt. Joel and I told you last semester to stay out of things, and that was good advice. If we started digging, we'd probably find something, but we are better off leaving it alone. I've lost one friend, and I'm not going to lose you too."

I start to say something when another voice interrupts us. "I thought I heard someone talking." Chris Haverly stands outside Harmony's stall. "Hey, Reed. You made it. Going to be like old times, my man. Good deal. Too bad Joel isn't here for it. RIP. That's all I can say."

"We were having private conversation," I say.

"Oh, lookie here—isn't that Miss Vivienne Taylor? We met at the championships. Delighted to see you again."

"Right. Feeling isn't mutual." I give him my best "you disgust me" look.

"She's a feisty one." He looks at Riley.

"Leave her alone, Chris."

"Ah, it's okay. She'll learn to like me soon enough. They all do. You'll see, sweetheart. I'm a really nice guy. Your roomie Janna has already discovered just how nice I can be."

"Don't hold your breath when it comes to me." I cross my arms and feel as if I've been violated by him. I've got to warn Janna away from him. This guy is bad news no matter what.

He grins. "It's been a real pleasure, Vivienne. Now I'll let you two get back to your private conversation."

Haverly leaves us and I look at Riley, who has gone pale. "Don't mess with him, Viv. Promise me. Please don't mess with him. He's from a powerful family, and no matter what he does, he'll always get away with it. You've got to trust me."

I shake my head. "I can't promise you anything when it comes to that guy. I'm sorry . . . no one is above the law, not even someone as rich as he is. Here's the thing: I think Chris Haverly knows what happened to Joel. And I plan to prove it, whether you want to help me or not."

CHAPTER *ten*

After my discussion with Riley, I walk back to the Commons House to get my schedule, feeling a little dejected. I wasn't expecting to give Riley an ultimatum about helping me, but my emotions ran away with me. And if he knows something about Joel and Chris, I refuse to let him pretend that he doesn't. He has to make a choice, and either get on board to help find justice for Joel or admit that he's too cowardly to try.

When I walk inside, Faith is the only one still around. She comes over and pats my arm. "Are you okay?"

"Yep. Just felt a little bit sick to my stomach and needed some air," I say.

"Just remember, Vivvie," she says, her face kind. "You're here to improve yourself as an equestrian. That should be your main goal. Keeping your focus is even more important when you encounter unexpected challenges."

I shoot her a grateful look. "Thanks," I say. "Maybe I just need a pep talk."

"I think tomorrow will be an easier day," she says, handing me my daily schedule for the week. My eyes scan the paper. At least I won't be riding with my father today. Then, for the first time, I wonder: *Does anyone, other than Austen and Riley know that he is my dad?* I hope it's not common knowledge, because one thing for sure is that I don't want to chitchat with someone horrible like Lydia about my childhood issues.

I stash my schedule in my bag and say good-bye to Faith. Then I head back to the barn to tack Harmony for my jump lesson—with none other than Tiffany. Going into the jump arena, I spot her with Paisley, setting the jumps.

I'm happy to see that Riley is also in this lesson. Wills, who looks perfectly ironed and totally Ivy League as usual, is also with our group.

"Hello, Vivienne," says Tiffany, walking toward me. "Nice to see you again." I feel Harmony tense up as she reaches my side. That tension could be pure feedback of the feelings my horse is getting from me, but if I had to guess, I'm thinking that Harmony is one amazing judge of character. She knows that this woman is not a good person—at all. "I know that our initial introduction at dinner with Joel was not ideal, and I want to apologize." She looks down. "It may not have seemed like it at the time—because, like every family, we have conflicts—but I really did love Joel and am sorry he's gone."

A chill runs through me as she says these words. Fact is—I do not believe her. She can't even look me in the eyes. Nobody who loved Joel would treat him the way she'd treated him that night, coldly telling him she was going to take away his horse and give it to Paisley. I don't buy her act. Not one little bit.

However, for the sake of achieving justice for my friend, I muster my best fake smile and say, "I understand. Those were tough times. No hard feelings. I'm just here to learn, and I'm so excited to be learning from someone like you." Yeah—I kind of taste the puke in my mouth, but I'm going to get those answers that I'm seeking, and if that means I have to make friends with my worst enemies, then so be it.

"Good. Good to hear." Now she looks up at me, and mimics my fake smile with her own. "Fresh start and bygones. Good, good." She claps her hands. "Let's get started, shall we? Why don't you go ahead and begin your hack while Paisley and I finish setting the jumps."

I nod and glance over at Paisley, who is glaring at me.

Riley already has Melody up into a trot, but I notice right away that the horse isn't showing her usual calm. She hops up and down, so Ri halts her, backs her, then coaxes her forward again. They do several transitions together that don't look quite right, and as Harmony and I trot past, I say, "Everything okay?"

"Yeah. She's a little wound up. Probably from the long haul out and not being exercised for a few days."

"Probably. Be careful," I reply. It's totally possible that Melody's mood is due to her not getting enough exercise over the past few days. Horses who are used to working almost daily can get a little pent up and act kind of nutty when they're first let out again. But, if I'm going to trust my gut here, I'd be willing to bet that what's making Melody nervous is Tiffany. If I can get some time alone with Melody later, I'll be able to find out—hopefully, anyway. I also need to ask Riley about how he convinced Kayla to send Melody here for him to ride—or did Kayla offer? I'm curious as to how that all transpired. I didn't ask earlier, because our conversation had seemed intense enough.

"Okay, guys," says Tiffany. "Let's go up into a canter and into your two point."

We do our hack around for a few minutes and then Tiffany calls us over. "Okay, gang. Today we're going to work on a six-stride line and the goal is to do it in seven and not six. The purpose for this is to get your horse rounder. I want nice and round and for you to compress the stride. Sometimes these event horses can get a little flat after being out on cross-country, and I want you to work on collecting them. What I especially want you to work on is putting your leg on the horse, without increasing speed. Vivienne, want to give it a shot?"

"Sure," I reply with some trepidation. Not because I'm intimidated, but because it's Tiffany and she kind of freaks me out.

I put Harmony into a nice collected canter and come around the turn heading to the oxer.

"Good. Count the stride. Sit up; leg on. Compress," Tiffany says.

Over the oxer and the vertical . . . we finish the exercise.

"Nice job. But she really bulged that shoulder on the outside around the bend to the oxer, didn't she? Let's do it again and I want you to counter bend her in that turn."

I nod in agreement and go back out onto the rail and start over. This time our approach is better.

"Still popping that outside shoulder some, but better. Very nice on the collection, though, and getting her round. I liked your leg. I liked the cadence. Pretty. We'll keep working on getting her straighter on the approach to the oxer. Riley? You ready?"

"Yep."

Riley heads out with Melody to work the exercise, but Mel is really wound tight and rushes the jump. Instead of doing a seven or six stride, the horse does it in five.

"Let's do it again," Tiffany says. "Think compress. Stretch up and ride each stride. Ride the line."

Riley nods and goes back out to try again. Melody is too quick and rushed on their next two tries, though, and leaves a stride out, so Tiffany directs Riley to do some halt transitions and really work on getting the mare to slow it down. It takes some time for Tiffany to talk Riley through it, but after working the exercise repeatedly, Melody finally seems to relax and does the line correctly.

Forty minutes later, as we are cooling our horses down, I privately admit to myself that Tiffany's lesson wasn't half bad. I hate to say it, because I don't like the woman, but I try to always be honest with myself and others when possible. And the truth is that Tiffany did a good job in coaching Riley and Melody through the hard stuff. She even helped Harmony and me on our approach. But she isn't winning me over yet. Not by a long shot. I'm aware that she was just a little too nice during our lesson—a little too approving. I've been riding most of my life, and compliments don't easily fly off a coach's tongue. You have to really earn it, so the flattery she was doling out seemed a little fake. Still. I won't ignore the fact that maybe I did learn something, and that Harmony and I improved our performance.

"Thanks, guys," Tiffany says, interrupting my train of thought. "I'll see you in a few days. Good job today. And if you need anything before that, feel free to visit me up at the house." She turns and points to the imposing mansion on a knoll in the distance.

I raise my eyebrows. "Nice place," I say.

"It is. You should come by and visit. Take a dip in the pool with Paisley and some of her friends. In fact, I've invited some of the working students to come over this weekend for a swim party on the Fourth of July. I'm sure it's fine if I also invite some of the students."

"Thank you," Riley says.

"Yeah. Thanks," I answer back.

Wills pipes in, "I'll so be there!"

He is someone, like Lydia, who I may have to learn to ignore. My impression of Wills is that he's the kind of kid who's a little insecure and likes to hide behind his preppy clothes—and act like a joker to fit in. The type who puts a whoopee cushion on someone's seat and thinks it's hysterical even while he's wearing a perfectly ironed oxford and acting like he's completely innocent. The thing about Wills is, I'm not sure he'd know an actual serious life problem if it smacked him in the face.

Riley and I leave the arena together and I can't hold my tongue for much longer. I finally say, "Why the hell was she so nicey nice to me?"

He shrugs. "Who knows? Maybe she's changed. I haven't ridden with her since right before I moved to Fairmont at the start of freshman year. Maybe the allegations about drugging ponies, not to mention what happened to Joel, caused her to actually become a better person."

"Call me a cynic, but tigers don't change their stripes."

"Cynic."

"I'll own that," I reply. "Change just doesn't come all that easily, Ri."

CHAPTER *eleven*

I've got Harmony in the wash rack, and she's happy. My horse loves being rinsed off. She doesn't like her face being squirted, but she does love when I hold the hose up to her mouth so she can take a sip of water and play with the running stream. I can't help but laugh at her when I do this.

Riley is just putting Melody into the wash rack next to us when his phone rings. "Hello. This is he. Yeah. Hi, Dr. Moore. Okay. Okay." He pauses. I'm trying not to eavesdrop. "What? No. That's . . . Oh my God." He smacks his forehead with the palm of his hand and looks down at the ground, shaking his head. "I'll talk to my parents. I'll see what I can do. Yeah. Okay. Thank you. I understand." He hangs up the phone and I look over to see him shake his head, looking pretty forlorn.

"Everything okay?"

"Not really. Santos has a suspensory tear at the sesamoid. He's done. There's no way my dad will do what it takes to rehab him, especially knowing that it's a risk. My dad is going to freak out at the cost. I need to call home and talk to him. I mean, maybe . . . maybe if I beg him."

"I'm sorry, Ri. He's such a great horse." I see Riley start to tear up at the possibility of Santos's career ending and my heart breaks for him.

"Yeah. This sucks. I want him to be here so badly with me. I have so many plans. You know I've been saving money so we can leave the States when I graduate." He wipes his face and glances around.

"I know," I reply. Riley has been biding his time. He has a decent amount of money coming to him at graduation, and he's planning to keep his secret regarding his sexuality until after the money is in his bank account. He believes that as soon as his parents learn that he's gay, they'll cut him out of their lives forever.

"What's worse is that I like Melody. She's a nice mare. But she's not Santos. Plus, she was Joel's, so it feels kind of wrong for me to be riding her."

"I can understand that, but I think Joel would have wanted this. I think he'd be happy about it. How did you get to ride on her, anyway?"

"Kayla suggested it. She's been taking care of Santos for me." His phone rings again and he looks at it. "Great. It's my dad. I bet the vet or Kayla already called him."

"Want me to rinse her and you can take care of that?" I ask. "I'm finished here."

"You sure?"

"Of course. Go ahead. I know what it means for you to have Santos get better. I'm sure you miss him."

"You have no idea."

"Go. I've got her. Find me later."

Riley nods, and takes off while answering his phone call. I hope everything will be okay. I know his parents are really tough on him—especially his dad. Thinking of his parents reminds me that my own father is somewhere on the grounds at this moment. It's strange to know that the parent who abandoned me is nearby. The issues I have with him aren't exactly the same as what Riley's dealing with, but in some weird way, it relates.

Why can't the people who are supposed to love you the most simply accept you for who you are? How can a parent feel okay leaving a child? Do they stop loving you? I don't have the answers to these questions, and I'm not sure I will ever find them. But then again, I know there's going to come a moment, probably in the very near future, when I'll have the opportunity to ask my dad those kinds of questions. And I can't help but be curious as to how he might answer them.

As I put Harmony away and go over to rinse Melody, I sense she is still somewhat anxious. I speak softly to her and touch her heart center. This is my chance to communicate with her. She was definitely edgy out in the arena. "It's okay, baby girl. It's okay. I know it's confusing to be here, especially without Joel." I show her an image of Joel's face.

She tenses up further and her nostrils flair wide as her breath becomes rapid. I stroke her neck. "Hey, hey, I promise that it's okay. I'm here, and I'm going to help. I'll help you and I'll find out about Joel."

She then shows me a flash of a face. It's a girl's face, I think. I also get a flash of dark hair. Next, she shows me the pony— the same one she's been showing me for months—the dead pony. After that she pulls back on the cross ties and starts to scramble as she slips some on the wet, slippery surface.

"Whoa, whoa! Easy, sweet girl. It's okay." She busts one side of the cross ties and rears up. She comes down on all fours and just as I think she's going to break the other cross tie and run like hell, I do something instinctively. I show her an image of Fairmont in which she's grazing with other horses she knows—like Santos and Harmony. She begins to settle as she understands that she'll be going back to Fairmont. "I promise you, sweet girl, you'll go back to school with us. We won't leave you here. Something bad happened here. I know it, and I'm going to find out what it is."

I clip a lead rope onto her halter, and unhook the cross tie on the other side. She jigs out of the cross tie, but I'm not worried.

She's definitely settling down. As I lead her back into the barn, I catch Chris Haverly watching us from the side of the barn. I look right at him. He wiggles his fingers at me. "Hello, Vivienne Taylor," he says. "You sure have a way with horses. Nice job in handling that crazy one there."

I once again sense that tension from her, but I keep sending her the image of Fairmont and the pastures. "She's not crazy. She's just a little wound up today. Makes me wonder."

"Oh yeah? What makes you wonder?"

"Horses have good instincts. Better than people. I had no idea you were watching us, but I think she did. And she didn't like it."

"You're cute."

"You're an ass, and the horse here agrees. Go crawl back under your rock."

"Ooh, sassy. I like it. I like sass. Just wait, girlfriend, you and I are going to be very close before the summer is over."

I keep on walking along with Melody without responding to what Chris Haverly said to me. I can't help feeling like his words are a threat.

CHAPTER *twelve*

After I put the horses away, I head up to the Commons House to grab a sandwich. I'd like to eat with Austen, but I don't see him, which I realize is maybe a good thing. I know we have to be careful. Tristan and Lydia are at a table eating with some of the kids from other schools. He looks kind of lost. I turn away when he spots me.

Chris Haverly is eating with Paisley and that Wills kid. I don't see Janna anywhere, but I avoid eye contact as much as possible. I'm on a bit of a mission.

Turkey and cheese in hand, along with a bottle of water, I go to the cabin where I climb on my bunk and turn on my laptop. First, I go into the documents I keep protected by a password. A few months ago I started keeping notes on the horses who communicate with me and what they've said. My idea is to, hopefully, begin to better understand what I'm capable of doing with my gift.

One of the horses who I've had ongoing conversations with over the past few months is Melody. Ever since I started communicating with her back at Fairmont, I've been suspicious that she was the victim of a crime, because she has repeatedly shown me images of herself being drugged by someone—a male someone, who happens to be wearing a very nice watch. And who around here is a terrible guy who also happens to come from a family that makes some of the world's premier watches? Yep, I'm feeling pretty sure that the perp is Chris Haverly. The question is, why would Chris be giving Melody an unwanted injection? And does it connect to the fact that Tiffany was suspected of drugging ponies? Joel certainly never told me that Melody suffered through a situation like this. Maybe he wasn't aware of it? All I know is that I tend to trust horses more than I do people—and that Melody definitely lived through this bad experience.

Horses don't lie. And Melody has shared enough details with me that I know it's for real: I've seen where the needle went in and sensed the drugged dizziness she felt entering the jump arena. The next image she always shows me is her getting caught up on the jump and going down along with the little girl riding her. Then, every time, I get the image of the dead pony—which, unfortunately, makes no sense at all to me. But her communications have been consistent. I just wish I could understand them better.

Joel told me out on a trail ride last semester that a little girl had owned Melody before he had and that she'd been horribly hurt while jumping her. What did it all mean?

I scan the notes on my laptop again, hoping I'll find some new answers, but come up with nada. I set my laptop aside and lie back on my pillow, staring up at the ceiling—and will myself to figure this out.

I sort through the puzzle pieces I have. First, there's the fact that Joel's stepmom lost her job here at Liberty for drugging ponies. There was a bit of a scandal and she lost some clients. However, the equestrian community does have a tendency to be quick to forgive. There are also those in the horse world who honestly don't care all that much—people who see the animals as easy to replace. These types tend to have deep pockets and can buy new horses on a whim. I realize that it's pretty disgusting, but it happens to be the truth.

I keep returning to my idea that Riley must know more than he's telling me. He's definitely got some inside dirt on Chris

Haverly, and he also trained with Tiffany. Maybe he remembers the pony that died?

Looks like Riley and I have some more talking to do.

CHAPTER *thirteen*

I shoot Riley a text and jump down off the bunk. As I do, the door opens and Janna pops in, all excited and peppy. She'd make a good cheerleader. "Hey," she says. "How was your lesson?"

"Good." I'm not willing to add more to it than that. "And you?"

"It was great. I worked with Holden. He's wonderful." She flashes her bright-white smile.

"I can't disagree with you there."

"He's gorgeous too. I mean, I know I shouldn't say that because he's old enough to be our dad, but I am telling you, he's like a Brad Pitt or a George Clooney, or maybe both of them rolled into one."

I laugh. "I guess. I never really think of him like that. He's my coach, and a mentor."

"Oh, come on, you must think he's hot."

I shrug. "Like I said, it's hard for me to think of Holden as anything besides one of the best coaches I've ever had."

"Right. Besides, you have your hands full."

"What's that supposed to mean?" I ask.

"Oh, I don't know. I got the feeling that Tristan is pretty into you."

"Yeah, Tristan and I used to be a thing. But we're so over. He's back together with his ex, the ever-charming Lydia, and the two of them are perfect for one another."

"I don't want to brag, but if there is one thing I know, it's guys. And that guy is still way into you. You're wrong about him and Lydia."

"I don't think so," I reply.

"Oh yes, he is. I can tell by the way he looks at you and watches you. Whatever he did to screw things up, he's feeling pretty damn sorry about it now."

"You know what, Janna, I don't really want to talk about it. It's over. He's with Lydia and I'm good with that."

"I'm sure you are. You've got that other one drooling over you too."

There is an edge to my new friend's voice. Something I haven't heard in the past few days since meeting her. And it's bugging me big time. "What are you talking about?"

"Oh, come on. The working student—all brooding blue eyes, and dark wavy hair, and dimples, and muscles. Oh man, do I hope to see him at the pool. Speaking of, get your suit on. I heard everyone is going to the pool for the afternoon."

My stomach tightens. "First off, no one is drooling over me. Especially not a working student. Against the rules."

"Rules schmules—so meant to be broken."

"You're wrong. I've known Austen since we were kids. He's a friend and that's all." I hope she didn't see us together. Paranoia is creeping over me and I feel a surge of worry. I hate that we have to hide being together, but we both have a lot to lose if anyone busts us.

"Whatever you say." She winks at me, then heads into the bathroom to change for swimming.

Yeah, this other side of Janna—I'm not liking it so much. I hope I didn't misjudge her. All I want to do is get out of here and talk with Riley.

When she comes back out dressed for the pool, she says, "Get your suit."

"Thanks, but I don't really feel like going to the pool." As the words come out of my mouth, Lydia walks in.

"Not going to the pool, Viv? Gee, why not? You afraid you might see someone you don't want to see?"

I roll my eyes at her. I do that a lot when it comes to Lydia Gallagher. "And who wouldn't I want to see?" I ask. I look down at my phone as Riley returns my text. Of course, he's going to the pool. Guess that I'm going for a swim after all. I look back at Lydia.

She shrugs. "Don't know. I just know you're full of all sorts of little secrets and lies."

I pull my suit from the drawer and head to the bathroom. I hear Lydia laugh her evil cackle.

"Why are you so mean to her?" Janna says as I close the bathroom door.

"Mind your own business, mousy," Lydia shoots back. "We have history. Your new BFF knows exactly why I love to get under her skin. Ask her about it."

Oh great. First off, she's right—Lydia does get to me. Badly. I wish I could hide my annoyance better. Secondly, now Janna is going to want to give me the third degree. "Mousy?" I hear Janna say through the bathroom door.

"It fits."

I sigh, slip into my suit, and put on a sundress, then walk out of the bathroom. It looks like Janna is going to start pulling hair or throwing punches, so I grab her arm. "Leave Queen B to herself."

We walk out and I notice that Janna's hands are visibly shaking with anger. "You okay?"

"Is she always such a bitch?"

"Yes," I reply. "She is."

"Want to tell me your story with her?"

I shake my head. "Not right now."

"Okay. Let's go swim, then."

I breathe a sigh of relief. Looks like Janna is going to mind her own business for a bit.

As we walk, I broach the subject of Chris Haverly. "Have you seen more of Chris? Seems like you really like him."

"We haven't gone out again, but I think I do like him. I mean, he's really nice."

"He is?"

"Yeah. He took me to a very expensive restaurant, and said I could order anything that I wanted, then we went out to an under-twenty-one club where we danced for a while. After that, we came back here. We took a walk and he even picked a rose for me. It was really sweet."

"That was it?" I ask.

She glances at me. "What do you mean? Are you asking me if he tried something?"

"Did he?"

"No. He was perfectly respectful. He just loves bringing girls to the club with him."

There's an edge to her voice that makes me wonder what she isn't telling me.

"We had a really good time. We did."

"That's great. I'm happy you guys had fun."

I'm lying through my teeth, of course. I'm worried about Janna hanging out with the devil, but then again, I can't police everything. And, selfishly, I realize that maybe her proximity to Chris might help feed me clues. I do find it rather interesting that he wined and dined her. It's not that Janna isn't a cute girl, but I pegged Chris Haverly as a guy who goes for the Lydia types— glossy. And that he's so into the club? There's something weird about that too.

At the pool, I lay my towel on a lounge chair. "Let's sit here."
Then I look around and spot Austen. He's on the other side
of the pool seated by Chris, which makes me cringe. But at least
I know what he's doing and I'm grateful for the help. I don't see
Riley yet.

Janna immediately says, "Let's go over there." She points to
Chris and Austen.

I shake my head. "You know, I like it here."

"Don't be a party pooper. You can be my wing woman. And
there's your friend. Don't you want to catch up on old times?"

If she only knew. I realize there's no point in arguing with her,
so I tag along and find myself awkwardly in a lounge chair next
to Austen.

"Hi, guys. We thought we'd join you," Janna says.

"I was just getting to know my new friend here," says Chris.

Austen smiles in a friendly way that impresses me. He can
really fake it.

"So, Austen," Chris says. "What do you *do* out there in
Oregon?"

Chris looks at me and raises his eyebrows in a way that insin-
uates nothing good.

My heart stops for a second as I worry that maybe Chris suspects we're together. But then I calm down as I realize there's no
way that can be the case. He's just being a jerk and trying to rub
everyone the wrong way.

"It's nothing compared to here," Austen says, clearly wanting
to pull Chris's eyes away from me.

Chris turns back to him. "Do you go for trail rides in the
mountains? Go hunting? What?"

Austen laughs. "Not so much on the hunting."

"You should come out with us sometime," says Chris. "*Us* meaning me and James. Do you know him? Blond guy, Paisley's boyfriend?"

"Haven't met him," says Austen.

I hope you don't have to, I think. I still remember how awful the guy was when I joined Joel for dinner that night with Tiffany and Paisley in Lexington.

"Anyway," Chris continues, "James and I go shooting pretty often. My family has an amazing collection of rifles. Sometimes we even break out the antiques."

"Sounds fun," says Austen. He actually manages to sound truly genuine.

Before long, our strange little group grows; first Emily joins us, and then Wills shows up. Next comes Paisley, wearing a skimpy bikini with her light-brown hair looking windblown and teased, who sits down on the opposite side of Austen and flutters her freaking eyelashes at him. What the hell?

And as if it can't get any more surreal and bizarre, what I should've expected happens—Lydia comes walking through the gate wearing what I'm not sure could be quantified as a bathing suit, or even a bikini. It's even tinier than Paisley's. It's kind of hard not to notice the guys' jaws dropping. I can't say that I blame them as boobs galore sashays across the pool deck toward us.

"Oh man, would you look at that," Wills says. "What's her name again?"

"Viper," I reply. It escapes my mouth before I can stop myself.

"Do I detect some jealousy?" Wills asks.

"Not an ounce," I say.

We all watch as Lydia turns, clearly waiting for Tristan, who's now walking toward the pool, and I can't help but feel like she's purposefully giving us the perfect view of her tiny little hiney. I hate her. Oh yes, that's been established.

Janna leans in and whispers something to Wills.

"No worries there. Tell you what, Vivienne, you'll have your golden boy back in no time. That girl—the viper—she's going to be mine. Promise you that. I'll just use the Wills swag on her."

"Wills swag? Give me a break." Chris laughs. "You wish, man. You have no game. We all know that. Or, did you learn a little something out at juvie?"

Whoa! What? Juvie?

Wills doesn't reply. His freckled face turns bright red. Why is it that Chris can say so much crap to people and they don't ever come back at him? I mean, I don't know the story as far as Wills going to juvie, but, if some ass were giving me grief like that, I'd have a comeback.

"Game. Whatever," Chris continues.

I can't bite my tongue any longer. "Oh, 'cause you have such good game, Haverly?" I say.

"Mhmm, talk about viper. Vivienne Taylor bites," Chris replies.

Austen gives me a look. He's warning me.

"I just think you're a bully, and I call it like I see it," I say.

"Kids, kids, let's all get along. Okay?" Wills chimes in. "Chris didn't mean anything by what he said to me."

Chris shakes his head. "Just like Vivienne, I call it like I see it."

Gag. Oh God. Am I seriously at a first-rate equestrian program, or did someone just check me into a loony bin? I'm pretty much done with the day's drama. Where is Riley?

I don't see my friend, but I do notice that as Tristan comes through the gate, Lydia reaches her arms around him and gives him a kiss.

"Ah, there's golden boy now," Chris comments. He glances at me. "Sure you don't want him back?"

I ignore him.

"Lighten up," Emily says. "You don't know all the crap Vivienne has been through."

Now, that's kind of a shocker to have Emily defend me, especially since she seems like she's hardly paying attention to anything half the time. I know Austen wants to come to my rescue, but if he opens his mouth and starts talking, we might be outed.

Lydia and Tristan join our group, and she immediately hands him a bottle of suntan lotion. All the guys stare as she rolls onto her stomach and unties her top so he can rub the lotion on her. I swallow hard as I watch him, because it really wasn't that long ago that he snuck up on me—before we were ever together—and did the exact same thing to me by the pool at Fairmont. I glance away.

As this little show is happening, with all eyes on it, I feel my fingers being tickled. I look down and see that it's Austen and he's handing me a napkin. I give him an odd look.

"Open it," he whispers.

I do as he says. He's written, *9:00 behind barn two tonight.*

I nod, smile, and close my eyes, leaning against the lounge chair. Lydia and Tristan can go ahead with their little spectacle. It's the last thing I'm worried about. One thing is bothering me, though. What is the deal with Wills? Why did he spend time at juvie? Clearly, he's known Chris for some time—and I'm guessing Chris knows the whole story of whatever got Wills into hot water. All the more reason for me to find Riley and see if he understands Wills's connection to all of this. Did Wills know Joel? If he did, he might have some answers for me.

I send Riley a text asking where he is. I don't get a response. Aggravating! He said he was going to be here! That was the real reason that I came, so that we could talk. But, looking at the crowd around me, I'm not sure if we'd have any privacy to really talk, anyway. Heck, Austen and I have to exchange notes to have any kind of conversation with one another, so we don't blow our cover. Clearly, Riley and I will have to find somewhere much more private than the pool to have our talk.

I steal another glance at Austen, and somehow the dysfunctional bunch around me stops bothering me for a moment—all because of the napkin in my hand and what's written on it. I guess that nothing else really matters in this moment. I smile slyly at Austen, and he smiles back. I can't wait for nine tonight.

CHAPTER *fourteen*

ydia is still out, presumably with Tristan. It's eight thirty. Emily isn't around, either, and God only knows where she might be. But Janna won't shut the hell up! All I want to do is be inconspicuous as I try to put on a little lip gloss and look somewhat cute for Austen. Fat chance of that happening while I'm getting the third degree. I'm also really irritated that I haven't heard back from Riley. I've called and texted. I need to find out what cabin number he's in and track him down.

"What did happen between you and Lydia?" Janna asks after she's already asked me how I got accepted to Fairmont, what life is like at home, what it's like in Southern California, how I met Tristan, and on and on.

"Oh no," I say, suddenly struck with brilliance.

"What?" Her eyes widen.

"I forgot to call my mom at eight. I promised her that I would tonight. It's the one night this week she's not on call for work. She's going to be mad at me. She loves to gab."

"Oh."

This is obviously a lie. My mom is somewhere in France right about now. Of course, I *would* actually like to call her. I'm more than ready to tell her that my dad is teaching here for the summer, and ask her how to handle it. But I can't e-mail a question like that; it'll only stress her out. Knowing my mom, she'd be on the first plane back here. She can be slightly protective of me, and

I refuse to ruin her vacation. She deserves it and had really been looking forward to it. All I can hope is that my lie fools Janna. "I'm just going to take a walk and call her. I'll be back."

"Oh. Okay. Be careful. Kind of dark out there."

"I'll be fine. I'm not too worried. Not going far."

I grab my phone and flee the cabin. I'm sans lip gloss and I never even got to pull a brush through my hair, but it is what it is, I suppose.

I walk as quickly as I can to the barns, not wanting to be seen. I'm early because I had to escape Janna as soon as I possibly could. I couldn't take her jabbering any longer.

When I'm almost there, I hear two voices, clearly a girl and a boy, coming down the path toward me. I quickly pull behind one of the smaller sheds near the barns, hoping they'll pass without noticing me.

They do exactly that, but my jaw drops when I see who it is: Tristan and Emily. What in the world are those two doing together at this time of night? It can't possibly be that he's cheating on Lydia. Emily has pretty dark hair and a kind of cool style, but I'm surprised that Tristan can handle her complicated personality. I thought he was all about hanging out with superficial blondes these days. The first thing that crosses my mind is that they are down here getting drunk. I know Emily likes to sneak alcohol when she can. That's not really Tristan's scene, though. I shake my head to clear it. I'd like to get to the bottom of what those two are up to, that much is for sure. I check the clock on my phone and see I still have some time to kill before Austen shows up. I decide to visit Harmony for a few minutes. I turn the corner into the barn and I have another one of those *stop and look* moments.

Wills is standing in front of Melody's stall, petting her. And he looks to be talking to her. He spots me. "Oh, hey. Nice horse," he says.

"She is. You know her?"

"Uh, well, kind of, but not that well." He looks at his watch. "Oops, I gotta head back. I'm actually meeting with Faith. She wants to talk to me, I guess. Probably in trouble. I kind of put out a couple plates of horse cookies in the Commons House as if they were regular cookies." He smiles sheepishly.

"Ah, well, I think most of us would know the difference."

"You'd be surprised," he says. "All right, well, I'm out. Gotta go take my punishment."

I watch him leave the barn and I'm mystified. I would've liked to ask him how he knows Melody—and whether he knew Joel. Although these two questions are just the tip of the iceberg, because there are other mysteries about Wills that I'd like solved. For example, I want to know why he's buds with a jerk like Chris Haverly, not to mention the story of how he ended up in juvie.

I head to Harmony's stall, my mind still racing. When I walk up, her head is buried in her feeder. I go to pet her and she shies away. "It's me, silly girl." She walks forward again and puts her head back in. I stare at her in surprise. I mean, yes, my horse likes to eat, but it's strange for her not to respond to my voice—she must not have heard me with her head buried in the feeder. Then it hits me. She didn't respond, because she didn't hear me, yes, but the bigger problem is that she couldn't see me, either. I swallow hard as I realize that I neglected to speak with Holden about the problem with her eye. Instead of watching the peep show by the pool and socializing, I should have been taking care of my horse.

Stupid, stupid, stupid.

The list of what I need to deal with is getting longer by the minute. Solving Harmony's eye problems, dealing with my father being a coach, explaining the situation to my mom, figuring out how to handle my feelings for Austen, solving the mystery of what really happened to Joel . . . Oh brother. *Can I just please tell my brain to shut up?*

I walk into Harmony's stall and as she continues eating, I stroke her neck and say, "I'll get your eye taken care of. You don't have to worry about it." I feel so guilty that I haven't done this for her sooner. What the hell is wrong with me that I forgot to take care of this? All of a sudden, I'm crying. Jeez! Tears too? I'm at least two weeks from my period. I'm seriously having some issues.

Your dad is what's wrong.

I take a step back and look at Harmony. Oh my . . . this takes me by total surprise. "Are you talking to me, girl?"

Yes.

Okay now, I've had this special, secret gift since before I can really remember. My first experience that stands out in terms of a horse communicating happened when I was five and our neighbor's pony bucked me off his back. I landed hard and was crying on the ground when the pony came over to me with his head down. I suddenly had a clear image of a knife in his back. I looked up at my mom who was hovering over me, making sure that I was okay, and I said, "His back hurts him." From then on, things like that happened a lot, and eventually my mom became completely convinced that I could communicate with horses. And she was right. Over the years, I've learned to expect communication from horses through pictures of events, snippets of memories, or waves of emotions—never words. If a horse shows me something they witnessed with their own eyes, I might hear dialogue between two people. But hearing a horse's voice in my head? No. Not ever.

"My dad, huh?" I say, out loud.

Yes. That's why you keep getting upset, and forgetful.

Oh wow, wow, wow—mind-blowing wow.

"Viv?"

Austen's voice pulls me out of the incredible moment I'm sharing with Harmony, and I look up, surprised, as he peers around the corner.

"Hi," I say, sounding as stunned as I feel.

"Come on. Let's go out the back. It's dark and we won't be seen."

"Night, sweet girl," I say to Harmony. I want to say so much more, but the timing isn't going to allow for it.

Instead, I walk out of the stall and take Austen's hand. We walk around to the back side of the barns. "You okay?" he asks.

"Yeah. Sure. Why?"

"I don't know. You just seemed a little off when I walked up."

"Oh. I was lost in thought. Kind of a strange day, you know."

"I would agree with you." He puts his hands on my waist. A silken warmth begins to travel through me. God, it's strange that I'm feeling this way about Austen, but I can't deny that it's nice. I lean my head against his chest and he leans in. I can hear him breathe me in.

"You smell so good, Vivvie. You know what the weirdest part of the day was for me?"

"What?" I ask, pulling away and looking into those big blue eyes of his, which I can see in the moonlight shining down on us.

"It's that I was so close to you at the pool, but there was nothing I could do to defend you when Chris was being such a jerk. Not without everyone knowing how I really feel. I knew that if I opened my mouth it would be all over."

I nod. "I knew it too. It didn't matter, though, because I knew exactly what you were thinking."

He takes my hand and we start walking. "That's the best part about this thing between us. We both know each other so well we can basically read each others' minds."

I laugh. "Yeah. I suppose we can."

"At least I seem to be charming Chris Haverly," he says.

"I noticed. And?"

"He's an ass. You pegged him."

"Not only an ass but a creeper, right?"

"I won't argue that. He's a big partier. Invited me to some rave next weekend."

"A rave?" I didn't like the sound of that.

"I know what you're thinking. But I told him that we had to invite you too."

"I'll think about it," I say. "But if I go, it might just start World War Three," I add, giving him a slight smack on his shoulder. "Then again, I don't really want you going alone."

"You don't have to worry about me getting into any kind of trouble. You should know by now that I'm a pretty straight and narrow kind of guy."

"I do know that," I reply.

"Haverly, though, not so much. Hopefully if I go out and party with him, I'll be able to find out exactly what he's involved in. For me to get what his deal is, I'm going to have to play along."

"I know. I don't like it, though." We stop walking when we reach an old pine tree. Austen sets down his backpack and unzips it, pulling out a blanket. We sit down and I smile. "You think of everything, don't you?"

"I try."

Feeling a little awkward, like this is the first time I've ever been alone with him, I return to the topic that's both easy to talk about and still making me burn with curiosity: whether Austen learned anything else about Chris Haverly. "Anything else on the creeper besides he's a partier and an ass?"

"Not yet. But, it's there. I know it. That guy is bad news. He just is. My gut says so. And I don't like the way he is with that girl from your cabin."

"Janna?"

"Yeah, that's her. He was kind of a jerk to her at the pool after you left. When she got up, he yanked her back down into her lounge chair so hard that I bet he bruised her arm. Then I overheard him saying something about how 'close' she was going to feel to him before the summer was over."

My heartbeat picks up as I feel a wave of concern for her, and I remember that Chris said something similarly threatening to me. "God, I have to warn her to stay away from him before it's too late. What does she see in him?"

"I hate to say this, but you're probably going to have to let her fend for herself," he says. "She looked pretty into him at the pool."

From the backpack, Austen pulls out a Twix, my favorite candy bar since I was about eight years old, and hands it to me.

"Yum," I say. "You're too much."

Next he pulls a Breyer model horse out of the backpack. My eyes mist with tears as I recognize the figurine. "Thought you might like this," he says, pressing it into my hands.

I can't speak for a moment. Then I manage to say, "You kept this?"

"Of course. My tenth birthday. Not that I was into Breyers like you and the girls, but I thought it was pretty sweet when you gave me this and told me that it was your horse, Dean." He laughs. "Do you remember what happened after you gave it to me? What you said?"

I blush remembering the silliness of my younger self. "I told you that my horse would be watching over you at night, because he was good at keeping bad dreams away. I can't believe I was so dumb."

He reaches out and touches the ends of my hair and then traces my face with his fingers. "It wasn't dumb. Not at all."

I blurt out, "Do you believe in soul mates?"

He wraps his arms around me and pulls me into him. "Of course I do. I'm with mine right now."

That's when he kisses me, and that crazy silken warmth that's becoming so familiar washes over me. I feel his hand, calloused from riding, slip under my shirt and I feel a burning sensation almost like fire where he touches my bare skin. The warmth inside me turns into a heat that I'm certain I've never felt before. Our kiss grows deeper and longer and my body wants more, surprising me, because I want more than kissing now. I feel like I'll do anything to get closer to him. Then, suddenly, he stops kissing me and pulls away. "Austen?"

"I love you. You know that. So, the last thing I'm going to do is rush this. You're special. You always have been. And if things work out the way I hope, then we have our entire future ahead of us—together. Let's slow it down. Okay?"

"Okay." I nod. "Can I ask you something? If you want to, you can tell me that it's none of my business."

"You can ask me, but I already know what the question is, and the answer is yes. Yeah, Viv, I'm still a virgin."

"I am too," I reply quickly.

He kisses me gently on the lips. "I was hoping you'd say that. I didn't know, because of you and Tristan."

"No. We didn't."

"Then we have something to look forward to, but first, I really think we need to get used to what's happening between us right now. We've been friends. Now we're something more, and after, we'll be even more. I say we enjoy the ride."

"I totally agree."

We sit in silence for several moments, looking up at the stars and just being together. I want to pinch myself to be sure this is for real. But it is. It is perfect and as it was always meant to be.

CHAPTER *fifteen*

I t's getting late, and I don't want any of your roomies reporting you. Seems like you have a nosy one in the crowd," Austen says as we start to make our way back.

"There's nosy, moody, and bitchy. Add a few more and I'd feel like I'm among the seven dwarves on steroids."

He laughs. "Good one, Viv. Good one."

"I'm occasionally good for a joke or two."

It's still humid and the scent of earth, pasture, and horse mingles in the night air. "You know, with all our relationship kind of talk back there, I failed to ask you if you'd learned anything about Paisley, Tiffany's daughter."

He lets out a low whistle. "She's a weird one. Haverly is an ass, but that chick is crazy."

"Why do you say that?"

"For starters, I asked her to clean out the feed buckets, and I thought she was going to cry. I'm head working student, so I can make that call." He puffed out his chest.

"You are, are you?"

"I am."

"Such prestige."

"Stop. You're teasing me now," he says. "Anyway, she was cleaning buckets and I was washing out the tack area while soaking bits, and I saw her mom come in—"

"Tiffany."

"The one and only. I overheard bits and pieces of their conversation. Paisley was complaining about being a working student. Her mom was all over her that she had to do this, that her stepdad was making them all learn responsibility. Paisley started crying, and I heard her say that he'd never been like that before Joel died."

"Interesting."

"There's more. Tiffany seemed really pissed off, and even told Paisley that her marriage could be over if Paisley didn't start acting more responsibly. I had to walk away then, because one of the horses was banging on his stall. I don't know what happened between them after that, but when Tiffany left, Paisley was in tears and talking under her breath. When I asked her if she was okay, she told me to 'f' off."

"She did?"

"Yep, and she said the entire thing."

"Hmm."

"Yep. I agree. Hmm. What do you make of it?" he asks.

"Dysfunction junction. I'm thinking their family is sort of falling apart. It sounds like Joel's dad has gotten tired of being the money tree and like he insisted that Paisley do something on her own for a change."

"I think you're right."

"Anything else?"

"Hey, I think I did pretty good on the first day of the job, don't you? I'm like a regular private investigator."

"I suppose you are. And yes, you did a great job today."

"What do I get for it?" he asks.

We stop just outside the barns, both of us knowing that in moments we have to go our separate ways for the night and all day tomorrow we have to act like there is nothing at all between us. I take hold of the collar of his shirt on either side and pull him toward me. I kiss him hard, pushing my body into his, and then slide my mouth around to his ear, nipping at it with my teeth ever so slightly. I even surprise myself by this move.

His arms wrap around my waist tightly and he picks me up and whispers, "Jesus, Viv, where did you learn that?"

I laugh. "Guess I've watched my share of *Pretty Little Liars.*"

"Watch some more, will you?"

"Deal."

"There is one more thing before you go, and I've been trying to figure out how to tell you all evening."

"It's about my dad. Isn't it?"

"Yes."

"Lay it on me."

He sighs. "You're scheduled to ride with him tomorrow. I saw the roster before I came to meet you."

I cluck my tongue. "Okay."

He takes both of my hands in his. "It's going to be okay. You're not in this alone."

"I know. Thank you."

I put my arms around his neck and he holds me tight. If I could stay here forever, I'm pretty sure that I would. I would remain in Austen's arms without a care and let all this other stuff fall by the wayside—this complicated stuff that I'm beginning to hate.

Something tells me that being an adult can sometimes really suck.

CHAPTER *sixteen*

I'll never forget the morning my life changed drastically within a matter of minutes. It was the day after my tenth birthday.

The day before had been so much fun.

My friends and I had been out at Gail's place, where we rode, then my mom had picked us up and taken us all out for pizza. My dad wasn't there for pizza that evening, and maybe that should have been a tip-off for me. But he'd shown up with my birthday cake.

And now as I look back and remember that night and the next day with a little more clarity, I understand that there were clues that I would wake up on the morning of August 10 to find my father gone—not just for the day, week, or month . . . but for all the years afterward.

Like, when he'd hugged me that night before bed, his grip had been a little tighter. And he'd said, "I love you," which wasn't something he said all that often. He'd told me that he was proud of me and that I was a great kid. Even remembering this part is hard. Why did he have to be like that? He should've just left.

Before that day, though, my father had been a decent dad. He worked for an equestrian magazine and he trained event horses. Once he left us, his career took off. He remarried. We weren't in touch, and I never talked about him. I convinced myself that our paths would never cross. I had so much anger and hurt, but ignored it so long it just turned into numbness. Which somehow I thought meant I was okay.

But I've been lying to myself for a long time it seems. Even my horse knows it. I still can't get over the fact that she was directly speaking to me last night. Crazy!

As far as my father goes, I have to face the facts. My dad is still in my world—the world of horses, the world of eventing. And believing that I would never see him again just because I lived on the West Coast and he lived on the East Coast? That was pure wishful thinking. Given his prominent role in the horse world, and my ambitions to make the Olympic team, it was inevitable that this day would eventually come. The world of three-day eventing is not all that big when it comes down to it.

I pull on my britches, slip on my riding boots, and tie back my hair. I don't want to admit that I'm probably feeling more fragile than I've ever felt before, as if I could fall apart if someone said the wrong word to me. Thank God everyone has already left the cabin, because I don't want anyone guessing how awful I feel inside. Now, as I open it, Austen is standing there. He remembered. He's waiting for me.

"Hey. Good morning. How you doing?" He reaches for my hand and I give it to him. He pulls me in, holding me there on the front steps of the cabin. He doesn't need me to answer. He knows exactly how I'm doing. So much for keeping it a secret that I feel awful and depressed. Who am I kidding? This is my best friend, and now so much more. He whispers in my ear. "It's going to be okay. I'll be right there with you."

I nod and fight back the tears. I pull away and say, "We better not let anyone see us. I couldn't take it if you were kicked out of here for 'fraternizing.'" I hold up my fingers and make little quote mark impressions in the air and try to laugh it all off.

"A friendly hug won't get me fired." He winks at me, then puts his arm around me. "Come on, you can do this. And when you start to freak out inside, which I know you will because I know you . . ."

"Yes, you do." I laugh nervously again.

"You look at me, and I'll give you our sign. Okay?"

"Our sign?"

"Yeah. Come on. You know the sign."

"I do?" I ask, confused.

He crosses his arms and shakes his head. "Really? You don't remember our sign? When we were little kids and I'd do this . . ." He takes one pointed finger in between the other on the other hand and his thumb and he tugs on it."

"Oh my God!" I laugh for real this time. "How could I forget?"

"I know. How could you forget?"

"The fart sign."

He nods. "The fart sign."

When we were kids at the barn, Austen had a thing about fart noises, like most of the other boys I knew. He loved to get under all the girls' skin by making farting and burping noises nonstop. I have to admit that I found it rather amusing. When Gail would be giving us a lesson and call us into the middle of the ring to go over something, every time I'd look over at Austen, he'd give me the fart sign to try to make me laugh. It worked a lot of the time, and when it didn't, I had to look away so that I wouldn't start cracking up and get into trouble. "I'm not sure that's a good idea. I might bust up."

"That's exactly why it's a great idea. Come on, you know I make you laugh."

"Yes, you do. This just isn't a funny situation."

We start walking to the barn. "I know it isn't. Trust me. I can't even imagine how difficult this is for you. I'm not trying to make light of it. I was there after your dad left. We may have been kids, Viv, but I was there and I know what it did to you. I saw how hard it was for you. But you have to face this. You have to deal with your father. He's here and you're in this program and I don't think you want to leave."

I shake my head. "No. I've worked too hard to leave here. And now . . . there's you. I wouldn't want to leave you." I want to ask him if he, too, has been consulting with my horse, not to mention Riley—who told me practically the same thing. They are all apparently on the same wavelength.

"Good. Because I wouldn't want you to leave me, either! So, face him. I think that maybe you'll find once you do that, you'll finally be able to heal—and move on."

I don't respond for a minute as what he said sinks in. Then I stop walking a few yards from the barn. He looks at me. "What?"

"I love you."

He smiles. "I love you too. We've established that."

"No. I really love you. Like, I honestly have never felt like this before." I laugh. "I know my timing is weird. I should have said it to you the other night when you told me you loved me, but I was caught off guard."

His blue eyes gaze into mine. "You're telling me now."

"Yes," I say. "And . . ." I take a step closer to him, but he pulls away a bit and lightly gives me the type of punch on my arm that says, *we're just friends.*

"I really want to kiss you right now, but we have company," he says under his breath. Together, we turn to see Tristan and Lydia inside the barn, studying us through the open doors. He smiles. "Just know that later on, I'm going to kiss you. And I might not stop."

"Is that a promise?"

"Oh yes, it is." He makes the fart sign. "Ready?"

"As I'll ever be." I make the fart sign back and we walk into the barn.

CHAPTER seventeen

I take Harmony out of the stall and start tacking her, doing my best to ignore Tristan and Lydia. I spot Riley taking Melody out of her stall. I walk up to him after putting my horse in the cross ties. "We still haven't really had the chance to talk," I say. Ever since he didn't respond to my texts at the pool, I have had the feeling that Riley has been avoiding me. "I'm getting worried. Are you okay?"

He turns to me and I can tell he's been crying. His eyes are puffy and red. "Riley," I gasp. "What happened?"

"It's Santos. He's done. His career is over. I talked with the vet. There's no hope. It's my fault."

"What do you mean?" I shake my head, confused by this.

"Well, after he pulled up lame in Lexington, and we took him home, he seemed somewhat better. My parents wouldn't even spend the money to have him ultrasounded. Then, all the stuff with Joel . . . I had Santos on stall rest and iced him. What I didn't think about was that he could have torn the suspensory, since I let him just stand in the stall. Because the injury happened at the sesamoid, we didn't see any heat or swelling. It's been too much time standing on it without treatment. He'll never compete again. My horse is now a lawn ornament."

I put my arms around him and give him a hug. "I'm so sorry, Ri."

"I know. I can't cry anymore. It's just that I had so many plans. Germany! I planned to go to Germany with him and get the best dressage training possible, Vivvie. Not now." He tears up.

"Hey, hey. I know. I know. I do. We've talked. But keep it together. Go out there and ride Mel for now. Focus, Ri. And let's talk later." I'm trying to walk a fine line. I want to be empathetic and supportive, but I also want to give him the pep talk I know he needs. Losing your horse is the worst experience ever. The plus side is that Santos is still alive. But his injury is career ending. That much I do know. I so feel for Riley, but I also know that if he dwells on this before he goes out for his lesson, then he's only defeating his goals. Santos won't be able to take Riley to the next level of his career, but I refuse to believe that Riley won't find another way. As his friend, my instinct right now says to keep him focused.

"You're right," he replies. "Let's definitely talk later. Dinner? You and me?"

"Of course." I'd made plans with Austen, but considering what Riley is going through, I'm sure Austen will understand. But boy do I want that kiss he promised me.

"Good. Finish tacking up. You're right. We need to stay the course."

I hug him again, quickly, so that no one sees. I don't want anyone to get wind that he's upset, because I'm sure the questions will start flying then. And Lydia would probably be the first person inquiring. Riley feels the same way that I do about her. I smile and give him one last piece of advice. "Ride, Ri. Go ride your heart out."

"Okay."

I'm doing my best to go back to my business with Harmony, but my stomach is churning. I'm worried about Riley and now I also have to deal with the fact that in moments I'm going to come face-to-face with my father. When he'd been introduced by Faith at the meeting, I hadn't taken the time to focus on him. This sounds awful, but I can't even remember right now what he looked like.

Austen walks past me a few times, and I can tell he's trying to get a read on my emotional state without being obvious. The next time he walks past, I look at him and smile. I make the fart sign and he smiles back.

Lydia starts to walk past me with her brush box in hand. She stops and smiles that wicked smile of hers. "Is it true that Frank Taylor is your dad?"

I keep brushing Harmony and decide ignoring her might be the best tactic. That's been my motto all along with her.

"Vivienne, I asked you a question."

I turn and face her. "It's none of your business."

Tristan walks up then and grabs the brush box from her. "Come on, Lydia, leave her alone. It isn't your business."

"Why not? I want to know. I mean, he's one of our new coaches and one of the top trainers in the country. They do have the same last name, and rumors travel quickly in small groups. I sort of heard it through the grapevine. Plus, who could've missed her storming out of the meeting yesterday? That was quite dramatic, Viv. Could've won an Academy Award for that, I think." She crosses her arms and looks at Tristan, and then back at me. "Don't you find it fascinating that she's never mentioned it before? That her dad is none other than *the* Frank Taylor? I do. Makes me wonder if that's how she got her scholarship to Fairmont—you know, did good old dad pull some strings?"

Although I should know better than to get closer to a viper like Lydia, I move away from Harmony and take a couple steps toward my nemesis. She tosses her blond hair over one shoulder like she's ready to fight.

"Lydia, stop it," Tristan says.

I sigh again. "You know, you're such a bitch. The truth is that, yes, he's my father, but he left our family when I was ten and I haven't seen him since. So, no, he didn't help, and I earned my scholarship all on my own. Not something you can relate to. Are you happy now? Happy that I told you my deep, dark secret, so you can run off and tell everyone some twisted version of my life story? Because that is what you do. Change the truth to fit your needs. Tell lies if you have to. I really don't get it. You must be really bored to spend so much time making things up."

"Oh, I'm hardly bored." She bats those stupid eyelashes of hers at Tristan, who turns red. "Ouch. That must of hurt; poor Vivvie, Daddy leaving you and Mommy."

I have patience, and I'm not easily angered, but, yes, I'm going to hit this bitch. I pull my right arm back and go to swing, when I suddenly feel a hand grab my elbow and stop my punch in midair. It's Austen. "She's not worth it. She really isn't. Don't listen to her crap."

"Oh, how cute, Prince Charming to the rescue."

"Lydia . . ." Tristan pleads.

"I'm going. I can't wait for this lesson to begin. I'm sure it's going to be fascinating." She struts away.

Tristan turns to me. "I'm sorry."

"You didn't do anything," I reply.

"I know, but I'm, I'm sorry for—"

Austen cuts in. "She gets it, bro. You're sorry. You guys better finish tacking. Your lesson starts in five."

I see dejection in Tristan's eyes and I can't help but feel bad for him. I know it's stupid. I know he lied to me, and he's back with Lydia, and, trust me, I have no interest in getting back together with him. But I still feel bad when I realize that he is truly sorry.

The next few minutes move too quickly for me as I lead Harmony to the mounting block and get on. Austen walks up next to us. "You'll be fine. Treat this like any other lesson. Okay?"

I nod. "Yeah." It's all I can muster. I'm so not okay.

"I'll be on the rail of the arena. I'm water boy today." He holds up four bottles of water—two in each hand.

"Okay." My insides are fluttering, but in a bad way, and Harmony is sensing my tension as she hops up and down. I take a deep breath and place my hand on her neck, leaning in close. "It's okay," I whisper. "We're okay." I do my best to muster some kind of calming energy, and create a picture that shows her that I'm still in control.

I spot Holden walking toward us from the top arena. "Hey, Vivienne, listen, there's been a change to the schedule."

"There has?" I ask.

He nods. "Yes. You'll be having a private lesson with me today, instead of working with . . . Mr. Taylor."

At first I'm not sure what to say to this. I'm not sure what to feel. A familiar sense of abandonment surfaces, but it's mixed with relief and some anger too. I shake my head. "You know who he is, don't you? You know who he is to me?"

Holden slowly nods. "I do. We spoke last night. He felt that it would be a lot of pressure for you to be taught by him and I agreed."

"Pressure for him, or for me?" Tears sting my eyes. "Is he just too afraid to face me? Because he's a coward, is that it? It's fine! He's nobody to me."

"Hey, hey, listen, maybe today isn't the best day for you to ride. Maybe you just need to think."

I shake my head. "Nope. No. I'm good. I need to ride. That's why I'm here. I need to get in the ring and focus." I'm now giving myself the necessary pep talk. It's true, though. What good would it do me to go back to the cabin and mull this all over? No good at all. I'd just start to feel sorry for myself, and that would be plain stupid.

"Okay then, let's get it done."

We head to the smaller dressage court. I glance over to the larger one, which is on the opposite side of the jump arena. I can see my father in there beginning to teach Lydia, Tristan, and Riley. Austen is over there as well. He spots me and I can feel him sending me some good vibes.

I decide to ignore all of that and just go to work with Harmony. Our lesson starts out with working on extended trot. Once I have her working forward with a nice extension, Holden has me do some leg yields with her and sit the trot. "Leg on. Good, good. I like this, Vivienne. Now, I want you to go back to a collected trot doing a shoulder-in to the right."

We do what he asks, and Harmony feels like she's dancing in midair. She's light and fluid. We typically don't do so well in dressage, but today we both seem to be in sync. Maybe it's Holden. I think there's something about him that gives us both a great deal of confidence.

"This is very pretty. Now, let's work on collecting and extending the canter. Do that a few times."

We do exactly what he's asking.

"Okay, let's do some walk to canter and canter to walk transitions," he says.

Everything is going smoothly. I take in a deep breath and relax as we move into the downward. I feel her come over her back and the connection is so sweet and as perfect as it could be. I look at Holden and say, "Who knew that I would love dressage—ever?"

"When ridden correctly, it is the best feeling in the world, isn't it?" He smiles.

"Truly!"

By the time Harmony and I are finished with the lesson, I've nearly forgotten everything else—nearly.

I walk Harmony over to Holden. "I know I mentioned the thing with her eye to you, but I'd really like to have it looked at. She's not entirely herself and I just want to be sure we're good to go before we start schooling cross-country."

He shoves his hands into his breeches. "I understand. Why don't I give the vet a call today and schedule something. He's supposed to be great. Faith and all of the other trainers and coaches here have given him kudos."

"Okay. Let me know." It takes all I have not to blurt out the fact that Harmony keeps telling me herself that her eye is bothering her. Wouldn't that be great? I can see it now: "Hey, Holden . . . I'm like a teenage female Dr. Dolittle, only with horses, but yeah . . . and Harmony is saying that she isn't seeing so well out of her right eye and it bugs her." No, no, no. There's no way I'm going to do that—unless I want to be committed to a mental hospital. Although, given how crazy I'm feeling these days, maybe that's where I belong.

I can't help but take another glance over to the large dressage court before walking Harmony back to the barn. Looks like Riley is running through a test on Melody, and the other two are watching. I hear my dad say, "Good job, Riley!"

He sounds sincere. He sounds like my dad. I want to put Harmony away quickly. Maybe we can just keep avoiding each other all summer. Maybe I can just have private lessons with Holden on the days that I'm supposed to be coached by . . . by . . . my father. That would work for me. Avoidance. Riley didn't think I'd be good at it, but it turns out I can be. In fact, avoidance might be what I prefer.

I have Harmony in the wash rack for her rinse when everyone else comes into the barn. I don't look up. I just keep rinsing. I go to turn the water off and start scraping her down. And there he is. Right off to the side of the cross ties. Frank—my father.

"Hi, Vivienne."

I can't speak. I just stare up at him for several long seconds, until I finally hear myself say, "Hello." He looks a little bit older. But even with a few more wrinkles around his warm brown eyes and his blond hair looking thinner, he's definitely my dad. I've never thought we looked alike. I definitely take after my mom with auburn hair and hazel eyes. I have to tilt my head up to look into his face. He's tall, over six feet. Not like me. I'm more like my mom in that department too, since I'm not quite five three. He takes a step forward and I hold up my hand. "I don't want you to hug me."

He nods. "I think we need to talk."

Part of me wants to respond with, "What's the point?" and walk away. There's definitely something nice about the avoidance strategy. But instead, I think of all the advice I've gotten from Riley, Austen—and heck, even Harmony—and instead, I say, "I guess we should."

"How about dinner this weekend?" he asks. "You can come to the farm."

I don't know about that. Dinner? That sounds like a long time to sit and visit. Before I can respond, he adds, "You can bring Austen. I haven't had a chance to visit with him and I'd like to see him too."

I start to shake my head, when Austen walks right up to us and says, "That sounds great, Mr. Taylor. We'll be there. What time?"

I give Austen one of my "are you kidding me?" looks.

"Friday night. Seven?" Frank says.

"Seven it is," Austen replies.

He walks away and I turn to Austen, "Really? What did you just do?"

"Trust me. Okay? Trust me."

I shake my head, untie Harmony, and say, "Fine. But I don't like you very much right now."

"I'm good with that," he replies. "You'll like me again. I know you will." He makes the fart sign and, yes, I can't help but laugh. If there's one thing I know is true, it's that Austen is good for me.

"By the way, we are going to have to wait on seeing each other tonight," I say. "I'm having dinner with Riley. He's had some bad news about his horse." I tell him about Santos.

He frowns. "That's rotten."

"I know. He's pretty bummed. I'm also hoping that I can ask him some things about Joel and their old crew. I don't want to push it, though. I'll see how it all goes tonight."

"Am I going to see you at all later?" He smiles.

"I'd like that."

"Even though you're mad at me?" he asks.

"That's right; I am mad at you. Telling my dad we would come to dinner at his house!"

"Tackle this thing head on, sweetie. It's the only way to do it. You're strong and you can handle it. You can't just go all summer without dealing with it."

"I know. I know. I wish he wasn't here. I wish I could've just kept on going the way I have been for so long."

"Maybe you'll finally get the answers you need from him."

"Maybe," I reply, realizing that this summer certainly has a theme to it—truth seeking. It appears I'm on several truth-seeking adventures. Where this is all going to lead me, I really don't know.

CHAPTER *eighteen*

R iley has his Jeep with him, so we decide to go into town and find a place to eat. The lush green land-scape looks really pretty in the dusky light. But I'm glad the Jeep has AC, since it's still really hot and humid even as dusk is descending.

We find a place that looks promising and head in. We both order the specialty—fish n' chips. As we wait for our food, I finally say, "How are you?" I know the answer already, but I need to ask.

"I can't believe it, Vivvie. I had everything planned out perfectly. I've even been in touch with Klaus Schwitzer about going to Germany to train with him. He was totally open to it, but now . . ." He gazes down.

"I didn't know the plan had gotten that far," I say. I don't bother talking about how amazing Klaus Schwitzer is, because it might bum him out. But the truth is, it sounds like quite an opportunity, since Schwitzer is one of the world's most respected dressage riders, not to mention an Olympian and a world-class coach and trainer. I know how much Riley loves dressage and wants to excel in the sport. Being able to go work for someone like Klaus would be incredible for him. "You can't give up on this chance," I say.

He looks up at me. "Really? How do you suppose I make it happen? I don't even have a horse. I'm sure my parents won't be willing to buy me a new one. I'll have enough to buy one with the money I get when I graduate, but then there won't be enough left over to go to Germany."

"I know there's a way. There are all sorts of grants and ways to get it done. We'll find you a way."

He smiles. "You're always an optimist."

"Is there another way to be?"

"I guess not. I don't know how you do it. I guess I should take note. How are you dealing with this stuff with your dad?"

The waitress sets our order down. It smells and looks delicious. I take a bite before answering his question. Perfectly greasy, flaky, and tasty. "I'm not handling it all that well. But let me tell you, I think I could be better at avoidance than you give me credit for. My first instinct is definitely to run away and ignore the problem. But both you and Austen have convinced me that's not the way to go." I can't tell him that my horse has given me the same advice. "In fact, Austen and I are going to dinner at my dad's house in a few days. He wants to talk."

"Big step."

"Yeah, but I don't want him back in my life, Ri. I've done pretty well without him. I'm sorry, but there are just certain things a parent can't take back or do over. Frank acting like my dad now, when I'm almost eighteen, doesn't really seem like a good plan for me."

"I can understand that. How will you deal with him this summer, then?"

"I haven't thought too much about it. I guess I'll hear him out and go from there. Any ideas?"

"You'll know more after the dinner. If you're still opposed to any kind of relationship at that point, you do what you need to. If it were me, I'd be as professional as possible. Take the lessons. The man is good at what he does."

"Yeah? Was it a good lesson with him today?"

"It was. I haven't been that confident on Mel yet, and Frank helped me. He helped me get into sync with her."

"That's good." It is good, but to know that my dad is good at something kind of bothers me. Some part of me kind of wishes he wouldn't be good at anything—I guess an angry part. But it's nice to hear he helped Riley.

"Oh my gosh, Riley. I know this might sound crazy, but what if you found a way to buy Melody back from Kayla? That way we know for sure Tiffany would never get her. Plus, you two seem to be clicking now. She does really well with guys. She adored Joel."

Riley slowly nods. "Maybe. Maybe that would work. You don't think Kayla would sell her back to Tiffany?"

"That I don't know. I'd like to say no, but you know how the horse business is. And, with Kayla, maybe you could work out a payment plan, or maybe even work off some of the money by doing things around Fairmont."

He smiles. "Have I told you lately that you're full of crazy ideas?"

"What other way is there to be?"

"Right." He dunks a couple of French fries into some ketchup and eats them. "This food is good."

"It is. Hey, so is it weird to have Tiffany coaching? I know you worked with her before you came to Fairmont." I don't want to bombard him with questions, but I really do want him to open up.

"Yeah, I rode with her for a couple of years. But I wanted to event, so after doing her jump lessons, I eventually moved on. Joel stayed and did the jumpers. His real three-day eventing experience only started when he came to Fairmont."

"What do you think of her?"

He takes a sip from his drink. "I think she's dirty. She only has the job here now because she and Joel's dad bought the place. I don't like her, but she's a decent instructor, so I'll take what I can get out of it. I suggest you do the same."

"Who owned Liberty Farms before, when you were here?"

"Irene Yates. She was an old horsewoman with good sense. She was kind of grumpy, but you couldn't help but love her. She loved running this place. She adored the horses and she liked me, so we never had any issues."

"What happened?"

"She got Alzheimer's, and her kids put her in a home. I heard she died a few months ago."

"Makes sense. The Parker family then comes in and buys the estate, and now they're the new owners. Was Mrs. Yates the one who fired Tiffany?"

"I wasn't here then. I was already at Fairmont, but my guess would be yes. Irene was by the book and if there was any whiff of a scandal like what surrounded Tiffany after the accident with the pony, then I'm sure she was unhappy."

"Why do you think they're so secretive about owning Liberty Farms?" I ask.

He shoves another fry into his mouth and studies me. "I didn't know that it was a secret."

"I spent months trying to find out who owned the place before we came out here, with no luck."

He leans back in the booth and studies me. "I think they want to keep a low profile. Maybe their plan is to keep Tiffany's name out of the headlines, and they hope that once people come out and see the farm, they'll forget about the scandal. That would be my thinking. But, you're not all that concerned about who, how, and why they own Liberty Farms. This is about Joel. Isn't it?"

"Yes."

"Vivvie, I told you not to mess with that."

"Why?" I lower my voice. "Riley, what's the deal? What do you know? Why was Joel afraid of Chris? For that matter, why is everyone afraid of that guy? Even that kid Wills acted subservient to him at the pool, even though he normally jokes with everyone. Talk to me."

"Oh, Wills is unpredictable. I met him a few times around here before leaving for Fairmont. He and his little sister, Anna."

"He spent some time in juvie apparently. Chris was giving him hell about it in front of everyone, and, like I said, the kid didn't do a damn thing to defend himself. What is Chris Haverly's story, Ri?"

"Not here, okay? I'll tell you what I do know," he whispers, "but not here."

"Then finish your dinner, because I need to know."

CHAPTER nineteen

Once we're back in the Jeep and heading to the farm, I say, "Start talking."

"Look, Vivvie, I've told you that I don't know much, but everyone is afraid of Chris because he's untouchable."

"What do you mean he's untouchable?"

"His family is extremely wealthy."

"That doesn't mean anything to me. So what?"

"It's not just that. His uncle is Senator Haverly. Did you know that?"

"The senator who the news keeps saying is going to run for the presidency?"

"Yeah."

"Not only does Chris Haverly come from old money, but his family is tied into Washington politics," Riley says.

"Okay. I'm confused, why does that make everyone afraid of him? More to the point, what is there to be afraid of?"

"What I know is secondhand. Okay?"

"It's better than anything I have."

"I met Chris at Liberty Farms through Tiffany and Paisley. He started riding there about six months before I moved to Fairmont. I didn't like him from the get-go. He digs up dirt on people. It's creepy."

"What do you mean?"

"I mean, the guy is a lunatic, like serial-killer kind of crazy, okay? Within a month of meeting him, he pulls me aside one day—and keep in mind that I'd *never* talked to him—and seems to know everything about me. He tells me he knows my parents are religious fanatics and that he's positive I'm gay, but haven't told my family. I denied that, of course. He tells me what kind of home we live in, how many siblings I have, where I go to school, and on and on."

"What was the point?"

"I never found out exactly what he wanted. I asked him, of course, but he just said that, in time, he'd tell me. That sounded ominous. But luckily for me, I'd already gotten into Fairmont and was moving on. Joel obviously was stuck there, however."

"Right. He didn't escape until last year. But you said that there was a secret and it was dangerous."

He nods. "I don't know how true it is, though. It was Joel who told me, once he and I became friends again at Fairmont. Remember how I was so afraid that Joel was coming to Fairmont to get back at me for breaking up with him?"

"Yes. I remember," I reply.

"That wasn't it at all. Joel was running away from Liberty Farms. He said that Haverly and James, Paisley's boyfriend, were into making some kind of designer drug and they were selling it at raves and boarding schools and stuff."

"What?"

"Yeah. Crazy. I guess Haverly is some kind of genius chemist and James helps him every step of the way. His plan was to black-mail Joel into selling his drugs all over the East Coast equestrian circuit. That's when Joel decided to get as far away as he could from Liberty Farms and came to Fairmont. But California wasn't far enough away to escape Chris, and pretty soon Chris got in touch with Joel at Fairmont and threatened to ruin his life if he didn't deal like Chris wanted."

"Oh my God," I reply. "No wonder he was afraid of him."

"So am I. Look at the family he comes from. You cross people like that and you wind up dead," Riley says.

I notice the tight grip he has on the steering wheel. "Like Joel," I reply.

Riley doesn't answer right away. "Maybe. I don't know. I really don't. Maybe he was threatened. Maybe they did kill him, Vivvie. But it looked like an overdose, so how do we prove that it wasn't? And we don't know that it wasn't just what it looked like."

"Come on, Riley! You don't really believe that, do you? Joel had just had an amazing week at championships, he'd learned Melody was going to be his to keep, and then he goes and kills himself. Do you really believe that?" I yell.

"No. I guess I don't."

"Me neither. You've got a choice to make. Either you can keep your head buried in the sand and let Chris and whoever else is involved get away with all of this, or you can help me prove that they killed him."

Riley pulls the Jeep to the side of the road and puts it into park. "There's no choice, I guess. I'll help."

I heave a sigh of relief. "You have no idea how long I've been wanting to hear you say that."

CHAPTER *twenty*

As Austen and I drive out to Frank's farm, I press my forehead against the cool window.

"You okay?" Austen says.

I nod. "I kind of wish you, me, and Riley were at the burger place tonight talking about how to handle Chris Haverly instead of going to see my long-lost dad," I say.

"I get it," he says.

But as much as I'm filled with dread, it's nice to have Austen with me—and the week that just finished was actually a pretty good one. Harmony and I are making progress with the coaches. I still dislike Tiffany more than ever, but her lessons are decent, if also full of horrible fake niceness. I like Bernard's coaching much better, even though he's quiet and kind of stern. He's a good teacher and even helped me through an episode where Harmony was spooking easily and stopping repeatedly on the cross-country course. Of course, my lessons with Holden are always amazing—in terms of coaches, he is my comfort zone for sure. I thought I'd be doing lessons with my dad by now, but so far, Holden has always stepped in, so I haven't had to.

As for Harmony's eye, things are in a holding pattern. Holden told me that the vet had been out of town and is due back any day. He said that we could use another vet, but that he'd prefer to wait for Dr. Vermisio, who came highly recommended. I agreed to wait.

Austen pulls the car into Frank's driveway and my stomach clenches into a knot. The first thing I notice is that his farm is really nice. It's a large, pretty two-story redbrick, and the barn matches. There's a big pasture out back. As we slow to a stop in the circular drive, I realize that clearly Frank has done all right for himself. Off to the side of the house, I notice a swing set.

"I don't think I can do this," I say.

Austen squeezes my hand. "You need to. Don't do this for him. As far as I'm concerned, he doesn't deserve it. Do it for you and do it for your mom. Get your answers and then tell him how this summer is going to go down. If you don't want to be his daughter, you don't have to. He hasn't been a dad to you. If I were you, I wouldn't feel any obligation."

"I don't."

"You shouldn't. But the deal is that he's coaching at Liberty, and from what I've seen, I can say that he looks to be a good coach. See him in that light, because that's all he needs to be to you."

"Then why do we even need to have this conversation here? Over dinner? Seems simpler to just do it at Liberty and get it over with."

"He invited us and I think even though he didn't do the right thing by you and your mom and brother, that doesn't mean you can't choose to do the right thing. Coming here is probably the right thing."

"I hope so."

"Me too."

I see a young girl run out of the house, and a petite redheaded woman walk out behind her. They get into a BMW sedan and drive past us. "I'm guessing that's my stepmother and her daughter. Wonder why they aren't staying for dinner?"

Austen shrugs.

"Probably for the best," I say.

We get out of the car and head up the porch steps. Before we even get a chance to knock, Frank opens the door. He's holding a glass of red wine in his hand and swings the door wide. "Hey, kids, come on in." He smiles the smile that I remember.

The house smells of cinnamon and apple pie—my guess is potpourri. I can also smell garlic. My dad—*think of him as Frank, I chastise myself*—was always a good cook. My stomach rumbles.

"I've got a pot of spaghetti cooking. That was always one of Vivvie's favorite dishes."

I can't even respond to that. Does he really expect that I'm going to walk in here and back into his life and be his daughter again?

He shows us into the family room, which is light and airy, painted in a soft green and white. The kitchen opens up into the family room and there is a big-screen TV with bookshelves on either side. From where I'm standing on the hardwood floor, I can see photos of Frank and his other family—his new family. I'm a little dizzy, so I sit down on the dark-brown leather sofa. Austen sits next to me.

"Would you like something to drink, guys?" Frank asks, taking a sip of his wine.

"I'll have some water," I reply, feeling parched.

"Me too," Austen adds.

Frank walks into the kitchen and quickly brings us back glasses of water. "Well, dinner is ready. You hungry?"

I tell him that I am, but it's not really the truth. I want to bolt out of here. We sit down to eat and I can't help myself. I ask, "Where's the rest of your family?"

Frank looks down at his plate and then up at me. "We thought it was best for this first dinner if Kimberly and Jade went out for a while."

I want to ask which one was Kimberly, and which one was Jade. I'm sort of figuring that my half sister's name is Jade, if I were to be logical about recently popular baby names. I want to ask how old she is, but I bite my tongue. I also want to add that there probably won't be any more dinners. This one is to set things straight and clear the air. After this, we can be coach and student for the rest of the summer, just like everyone else. But fortunately, I manage to keep my mouth shut. I don't say anything. I take a bite of the spaghetti and it tastes just like I remember—delicious.

"You're in college now, huh, Austen?"

"I am, sir. I'm at UC Davis."

"Vet school, you thinking?"

"Maybe. Not sure yet. I know I want to do something with horses. Not sure if being a vet is my thing, though. Maybe just want my own place to run."

Frank nods. "Tough business—the horse business. But, if you run it wisely and you're a good trainer, you can make a living at it."

"Looks like you've done well," I say.

"I've done all right."

We eat for a few minutes in what is now nothing less than an awkward silence.

"And how about you, Vivvie, where do you see yourself going to college and what do you plan to do?"

I set my fork down. I can't take this any longer. I look straight at the man who fathered me, who left us without an explanation, and who didn't even care enough to check on how we picked up the pieces.

"Can we cut the crap, please?" The silence in the room is intense. "I came here for answers. I came here to find out why you left my mother, your ten-year-old daughter, and a one-year-old baby? I mean, who does that? What kind of man are you? Who are you? All I know is that one day you were my dad bringing me a birthday cake, teaching me how to ride, and driving me to lessons when you could. The next thing I know, you're gone. Just gone, and now I'm here and you expect me to tell you all about my future as if I've just come in from school for the day and we're having this nice little conversation about what my plans are. Really?"

Austen is staring at me. Frank is too.

"Okay. Okay. You're right, Vivienne. I owe you a lot, but there is so much more to all of this than just me walking out, and, to be honest, this should be a conversation that involves your mother," Frank says.

"Please," I say in disgust. "How is my mom even necessary here? Are you going to try to put blame on her? You left us. We didn't hear from you. She cried at night for a long time after you left. I know because I was there. You weren't."

"I was hoping this could go down some other way, but it's apparent that your mom hasn't spoken with you."

"I'm confused."

"Austen, maybe you should take a walk, so I can speak with Vivienne alone."

Austen stands up and I grab his arm. "No! No. He stays with me." I look up at him. "Please."

Austen sits back down.

I face Frank again and say, "Okay. Whatever it is, it's time that I know."

He sighs heavily, takes a sip from his wine, and, after what feels like eternity, stares into my eyes and says, "I'm not your biological father. I'm not even your brother's father."

CHAPTER *twenty-one*

I'm stunned to the point of speechlessness. Austen isn't saying anything, either. He's probably stunned too. I finally say, "What are you talking about? That's not true."

He sets down his empty wineglass and pours another one from the bottle on the table. "This was why I'd hoped your mom had talked to you. I'm going to tell you what I know and what happened, from my perspective, seven years ago. You can choose to believe me or not, but it's true. First off, I want you to know that I've always loved you and I have always thought of you as my daughter."

I'm so sick to my stomach.

"When I met your mom, we fell for each other quickly. It was short and sweet. I met her at a horse show and we clicked. She'd just ended a relationship with someone else." He takes another sip of his wine.

"She found out she was pregnant soon after we started dating. She didn't know whom the baby belonged to. I was crazy about her and I told her that I didn't care whose baby it was. That baby was you. At the time, I was telling the truth. I didn't care who the father was. But as the years wore on, and I started to travel for work, she would get angry with me and throw it in my face that you weren't mine. I guess I didn't live up to her expectations. Things got worse after we found out that I wasn't able to . . . to contribute—to procreate," he says, looking away from me.

A wave of nausea passes over me.

"Your brother is from a sperm donor."

"You're lying. You have to be lying! And if you loved me so much, if all this is true, how could you just leave?"

As I stare him down, I realize that in my gut, I believe him when he says he's not my biological father. But my baby brother? It seems impossible that my life could be based on so many lies.

"I'm not perfect, and I built up some resentment toward your mother over the years. I had an affair—with Kimberly. We fell in love. When your mother found out about our affair, and told me that I had no rights to either one of you, I hired an attorney. I fought, but she fought harder, and I guess my fault is that I gave up. I started to feel as if you'd be better off without me, so I left. Then Kimberly and I got married, and we adopted Jade."

"I need to go," I say, standing up. "I've got to get out of here."

Frank stands and comes around to my side of the table. He places his large hands on my shoulders. "I love you, Vivienne. You've always been my daughter. I want to make things right between us. Can you give me a chance?"

"I think all I can do right now is be your student and have you be my coach. That's about it. As far as being my parent, if what you say is the truth, I'm not sure I want either you or my mom in my life." I head to the door with Austen behind me. I'm fighting back tears. I can't believe this. I can't believe that my mom, who is my confidante, my favorite person in the world, the one I've always looked up to, has been keeping all of this from me my entire life! Why would she do this?

We get into the car and drive back to Liberty Farms in silence. Once Austen parks the car, I fall into him and he holds me as I cry. Not only did the man I once thought was really my dad abandon me, but, in so many ways, my mother did something even worse.

CHAPTER *twenty-two*

Viv, you okay, baby?" Austen asks after I think I've cried my brains out and been quiet for a while.

"No."

"Do you believe him?"

"I don't know. Some of it makes sense, and some of it is so crazy nuts that it makes no sense at all. If he isn't my dad, then who is? And why did they keep this from me?"

"I don't know. I know your mom, though, and you mean the world to her. I'm guessing that she never expected to divorce your dad—"

"Frank."

"Frank. I'm sure that she always figured he'd play the role of being your dad."

"Then why kick him out like that? I mean, okay, I get that he had an affair and that can cause some issues. But then she could have just divorced him and at least tried to keep things as normal as possible. I had no idea he wasn't my biological father, so why not just let me have that relationship with him? And, God . . . my brother."

"I have two theories, if you want to hear them."

"Of course I do. If you can bring any sort of reason to this, I'll listen."

"The first one is that anger makes people do crazy things they don't feel they can go back on. Maybe your mom reacted strongly at first and now has regrets."

"Maybe. I don't know. I just have no clue what to think. What's your other theory?"

"That Frank is lying. I believe, I think, that he's not your biological dad. But I'm not sure I buy that he still wanted to be your dad after he met Kimberly and moved on by starting a family with her."

"What?"

"I'm not saying that to hurt you. But, I've heard a lot of kids' stories at college and the thing is, lots of us have screwed up families. If there's one thing I've learned at this point, it's that, ultimately, a lot of us have selfish parents."

"What makes you think that applies to Frank?" I ask.

"I'm just saying, maybe your mom knew best when she kicked him out and wouldn't let him have contact with you. Maybe she sensed he was ready to move on. You were just a little kid, so you wouldn't have understood. When we're young we see grown-ups through rose-colored glasses. Like I did with my dad."

"What do you mean?" I ask.

"Because he was my dad, I always brushed off the fact that he had serious issues with depression. As a little kid, I always listened to my mom's explanations. She was always telling us that he was exhausted from work. But now I know that isn't true. Funny thing is, my mom could have probably helped my dad if she'd forced him to face his problems. She just enabled the behavior instead. Last time I was home over break, I let both of them have it. I'm over it. I see my parents for who they really are. It isn't as if they aren't good people. But they do have faults. The good thing about me saying things directly is that it forced my dad to actually get some help."

"I had no idea."

"Of course you wouldn't, because I never talked about it. I'd been taught to ignore it like my mom did for so long. But I wasn't really ignoring it. I'd been shoving down the knowledge that he had a problem, and now that I'm an adult, I'm done with that kind of thing. I'm not going to fool myself, or anyone else for that matter, about anything. Maybe you didn't realize as a kid that Frank was ready to move on from your family. Maybe your mom saw it, though, and did what she could to prevent you from getting hurt."

I slowly nod. "Well, she couldn't protect me forever."

"I think you need to talk with your mom. But go easy on her. Something tells me that she was more in the right than the wrong on this one."

"I really hope so. What do I do now?"

"You ride. You do what you told him you would. He's the coach. You're the student. Keep it on the surface for now."

"Okay. I'll ride. But that won't help me forget all my problems. No matter how things end up with my dad, I still plan to find out what happened to Joel. I talked with Riley. He wants to help us too."

I fill him in on my most recent conversation with Riley.

"I'm happy he finally copped to what he knows, and that he wants to help. You know that I'm all in. I told you that. But for tonight, let all of that go, get some rest, and remember that tomorrow is a new day. I'm never going to let you down. I won't."

"I know. You and Harmony are the only ones I can count on."

"I'll be here for you. You have my word." He kisses me gently and draws me close with his strong arms, sealing the promise.

hey say that lack of sleep is never a good thing. It isn't. I can attest to the fact that I'm running on sheer adrenaline this morning after maybe an hour's worth of sleep. The good news is that Holden sent a text as I rolled out of bed to say that the vet would be arriving within the hour to look at Harmony's eye. Not only is this good news, but it also distracts me from having to think about everything Frank said at dinner.

I dress quickly, wash my face, and pull back my hair. I can feel Lydia watching me and I do everything in my power to ignore her. I'm glad Emily is still asleep, because she's been especially moody and inconsistent the last few days. Of course, now I'm wondering if that has anything to do with her nighttime outing to the barn with Tristan. As for Janna, she's lying on her bunk, rubbing the sleep out of her eyes, probably because she was out late again with Chris Haverly. We are quite a dysfunctional group. Maybe that's why we all ride. Seems that horse people need horses. They tend to ground us and keep us from going out of our minds. At least that's what they do for me.

"Bye, Janna, see you at the barn later."

"Oh, no kisses for me?" Lydia spouts.

I walk out, shutting the door behind me. That one better seriously watch out, because I'm in no mood for her games. If I could call my mom right now, I would. I'm kind of over her being away on vacation, but I know I won't be able to reach her. She's probably traversing the Swiss Alps about now.

The question I keep circling back to is pretty simple: If Frank is not my father, then who is? I have a right to know. I'll have to wait until my mom returns before I get that answer.

As I head into the deserted Commons House to grab some coffee, I realize there's something a little weird about the vet coming so early, before seven a.m. My guess is that he's busy and making a concession to fit Harmony into his schedule, especially since he just got back from a trip.

Once I'm out on the path to the barns, I see Holden just ahead and call out to him. He turns and smiles. "Good morning," he says.

I jog up to him. "Good morning."

"You doing okay?"

I shrug. I know he can't be aware of what happened last night. At the same time, he does know that Frank and I aren't exactly close as father and daughter.

"I'm okay. I'll be fine. Don't worry about keeping me off of Mr. Taylor's schedule. I can handle it."

I think about telling him what I've learned, but decide against it. I need answers from my mom before I seek advice. Plus, I have to wonder what he'll think of my family after he hears all of this, and it's important to me what Holden thinks. He's my mentor and coach and I respect him. Half the teenage girls around here are gaga over him, but not me. I just think he's an extraordinary teacher who I've been privileged to work with.

"Maybe we should discuss it."

"No. We don't need to. I came here to improve my skills, and whatever personal situation I have with him will be left outside the rings and cross-country course. Don't worry."

Holden frowns. "I do worry. I worry about you. It's part of the job."

"Thanks, but I'll be fine."

"If you need me to listen, I'm a good listener, and on occasion I've been known to give good advice."

I smile up at him. "I'll keep that in mind."

"You do that. Sorry the vet is coming so early. I guess he's booked all week, and I know this is important to you, so we convinced him to fit us in. We've waited for weeks now, so we probably need to get on it."

"Yep."

"Good. There's his truck now."

I see the vet truck pull up to the side of the barn and I quicken my pace to get Harmony out of the stall. She's not going to like being taken away from her breakfast. "I'll meet you guys in the cross ties," I say to Holden.

"Deal."

I'm right about Harmony and breakfast. As I open the stall door, she gives me a look that says "Go away."

"Need to check that eye, big girl. You've been telling me that it hurts. What do you say? I'll give you extra treats today. Maybe a carrot or two or three." I show her my offer in the form of a picture, and she responds, giving no more pushback as I put her halter on. "You do love your food, don't you?"

Yes.

I laugh. "Thank God for this horse," I say out loud.

I walk her out and hook the sides of her halter to the cross ties.

"You must be Vivienne."

I turn around to see a man of about thirty. He's tall and lanky with light thinning hair and deep-blue eyes. I go to shake his hand as he says, "I'm Dr. Vermisio." As I reach my hand out to return the intro, I see a younger man walking up behind him and I suck in a deep breath. The vet finishes with, "And this is James. He does ride-alongs with me and helps me out. He's my nephew."

"Well, hello, Vivienne. Nice to see you."

I'm basically speechless; it's none other than Paisley's boyfriend—the weird one who came to that dinner Joel brought me to in Lexington. He's the one who Riley heard was in cahoots with Chris Haverly and his drug deals! I try to force a smile and speak, but I can't. I don't want him near my horse.

"Cat got your tongue, Vivienne? You do remember me, don't you?" James says.

I nod.

"You two know each other?" Dr. Vermisio asks.

"We've met," I reply.

Holden walks up about that time and, thankfully, the next few minutes are taken up by his explanation of Harmony's eye problem. James takes a step forward as if he's going to unhook Harmony from the cross ties. I step in front of him. "What are you doing?" I ask.

"I was just going to take a look."

I frown and look over at Holden. He says, "I think Vivienne can probably hold her while Dr. Vermisio takes a look."

"Okay," James replies, and shrugs as if he's baffled.

What baffles me is that he thought I'd let him handle my horse. After seeing him be such a jerk to Joel in Lexington? No way. Plus, if what I've learned is true, he's also involved in this scary-sounding drug scene with Chris Haverly.

I stay close to Harmony as Dr. Vermisio steps forward and does a cursory exam and then takes a deep look at her eye. He nods a few times, then hems and haws—not a reassuring bedside manner, I must say. I'm keeping one eye on James, because I really don't trust the guy. And I'm trying to communicate with

Harmony to let her know that the vet is just doing his job, and won't harm her.

Dr. Vermisio finally steps back. He crosses his arms and rocks back onto his heels. "Holden mentioned that your mom is a vet in Oregon and that you've already guessed that your horse has a uveal cyst. Well, you're right, so the only question is what to do next. You probably know that some horses do fine with these cysts and don't need to have them removed. Others don't adjust well. From what Holden says, your horse is in the second category. So, considering your sport and all of the jumping you do, I'd say we go ahead and treat it. We can easily take care of it with a laser."

I'm quiet because I knew this was probably going to be the prognosis. At the same time, I was hoping there was another solution besides laser treatment. "What does the procedure consist of?"

"I'll sedate her. And then I'll use the laser on the eye. She doesn't need to be laid down. She just needs to be a little bit drunk. Horses don't like the sound of the laser, and I need her to stay still. James can help with that."

"No. I will," I chime in.

James crosses his arms.

"Very good, then. I can't do her until after the weekend. I'm completely booked."

"What about downtime?"

"A day because of the sedation. She'll be ready to work for you the next day. Should we say Monday morning? You guys don't ride on Mondays, anyway, right?"

"That's right," Holden says. "Monday morning should work just fine."

"Great."

Dr. Vermisio's cell rings. "I have to take this," he says, and walks back toward his truck.

"I'll go over and deal with the bill," Holden says and also walks to the vet truck.

I feel James staring at me. I finally decide to stare back. I'm not going to let either him or Chris Haverly intimidate me. "What?" I ask.

"Nothing," he replies. "Nice horse. Dr. Vermisio will get her all fixed up for you." He winks at me and I feel nauseous.

"You know why I don't like you, don't you?"

He shakes his head. "I didn't know that you didn't like me. You don't even know me."

"That dinner in Lexington was enough for me. The way you treated Joel . . ."

"Joel brought that upon himself. He had issues. I mean, look at what he did."

I feel my ears beginning to burn as the anger wells up inside me and, before I can control it, I spit out, "Joel didn't kill himself, and I'm going to prove it."

For a few seconds, James says nothing. In fact, his eyes widen, and I'm positive he's gone a little pale. He begins to laugh. "You're an odd one."

"Speak for yourself."

Before I can come up with anything else to say, Dr. Vermisio returns and so does Holden. We coordinate our schedules and confirm the time for Harmony's surgery on Monday.

As the vet and the jerk leave, Holden smiles at me. "She'll be good as new in no time."

"I know, but I don't want that James guy near my horse."

Holden makes a face. "Yeah. I sensed a little tension there. What gives?"

"Let's just say that I don't get a good feeling from him."

"That's your prerogative," Holden replies.

What I want to add is that I saw an expression cross James's face that has me convinced he knows exactly what happened the night Joel died.

CHAPTER *twenty-four*

The day passes in a blur of lessons and busywork, so it's not until I'm done with dinner that I have time to think about e-mailing my mom. Not sure what to write, though. *Um . . . hi, Mom. It's me. Your Schnoopy. I just need to ask you, what's the deal? My dad says that he isn't my dad. So then, who is? Is this all true? Why have you been lying to me my entire life?*

Yeah, that probably wouldn't go over so well. But, trust me . . . it's kind of what I want to write. I'm really confused. My mom is my mom. I love her with every fiber of my being, so all of this has sent me into a spiral. And I can't even get in touch with her.

Instead of bothering to even attempt writing something to her, I send Austen a text to please call me. I've decided there's absolutely no way I should join him for that rave with Chris Haverly and company. On the other hand, I want to remind him to be careful.

My cell rings about five minutes later. I pop off the bunk, because Emily is in the cabin and I want privacy. I start walking toward the barn. "Hey," I say.

"Hey, yourself," he replies in a low tone.

"Where are you?"

"On my way to meet up with Chris."

"I don't think that's a good idea," I say. "Not after what we've learned."

"Sweetie, I'm a big boy. I'll be fine."

"I know, but everyone is afraid of Chris, and for good reason."

"Viv, we know the guy is probably selling drugs, not to mention manufacturing them. If I can start with getting that proof, then we can find out how he's connected to Joel's death and why."

I notice that my teeth are grinding together in anxiety and I tell myself to take a deep breath. For the first time, I'm having second thoughts about pursuing this whole thing. I love Austen and if something happened to him I wouldn't know what to do. "Maybe we should forget about it."

"No. If this guy and his buddies are who we think they are, Joel isn't their only victim. There are others. I guarantee it. These guys have to go down. The one and only way is to get proof of what they've done."

"What if we go to the police with what we know?" It's a reach, but I have to say it.

"If Chris Haverly is as wealthy and connected as we think he is, I'm pretty sure the cops around here would laugh in our faces."

"You have a point," I say. "I wish I could argue, but I can't."

"Tell you what, I've got good radar. You know that. If I feel at any moment I'm in some kind of bad situation, I will get a hold of you. Okay?"

I fight back tears, which I seem to have had to do a lot lately, and I hate that. "I'm scared," I say.

"I know. That's how Chris has gotten away with what he has. He intimidates people and they keep their mouths shut. We can't let him do that to us. Let's just keep doing what we're doing. If I can get in tight with him, I think we can figure this out."

"Okay, but please be careful."

"I will. I love you," he says.

"I love you too. Let me know the minute you're away from that guy."

"I will."

We hang up, and as I get down close to the barn I spot Chris getting into Riley's Jeep. How come nobody told me this part of the plan? Since when is Riley so involved? I feel sick with worry. Then I see Austen get into his own car. I want to bolt down to him, but I know that would be a bad idea, so I call him instead. "Did you see Riley? He's driving Chris."

"I did."

"What do you think that's all about?"

"If I had to guess, I'd say that Riley is probably doing what I'm doing. Getting close to the enemy. You said that he'd agreed to help."

"Great. Now I have the both of you to worry about."

"Don't think like that. If Riley is planning to help, think of it as two of us working on the same team. I have to go now, Viv. I've gotta drive."

"Okay." I hang up, but I don't like it. Not at all. I should be with them. I should be helping, but I haven't exactly buddied up to either Chris or James. I've done just the opposite and made sure they know that I'm clearly their enemy.

I've sent my BFF and my boyfriend into the devil's den. What have I gotten us all into?

CHAPTER *twenty-five*

After hanging up the phone, I feel knots of tension in my shoulders and realize how badly the whole situation is putting me on edge. The one place I can think of to calm down is with the horses.

Harmony hears me walking down the barn aisle and pops her nose out of the stall window. "Hey, pretty girl," I call out.

She lets out a low nicker. Austen's gelding, Axel, steps forward as I come closer, and then Melody, who resides a few doors down from Axel, also frisks toward the front of her stall. I sense that she's calling out to me, and I realize I'm definitely going to need to go say hello.

First, I stop at Harmony's stall and pat and plant a kiss on her nose. "I'll be back in a few. Looks like someone else wants to talk to me."

Whatever.

I stop and laugh. "Did you just say 'whatever' to me?"

Yes. It's fine.

This new way of communicating with her is amazing and crazy. I really do feel like a Dr. Dolittle. Harmony actually talks to me now! "I promise you. I'll be back."

I know. She needs you. Then Harmony nods her head as if she's gesturing toward Mel. I walk a little bit farther into the barn to check on Melody, hoping she can help me get to the bottom of something: why in the world Wills was in front of her stall earlier.

Yes, it looked like he was just innocently petting her—but it put my senses on high alert. I don't think his intentions were necessarily sinister, but I'd still like to know more. I'm hoping maybe Melody will give me some answers.

I approach Mel and pet her nose. I run my hand down her neck. I feel that nervous energy that she sometimes puts off, and I say, "It's okay, sweetie girl. I'm here. What do you want to tell me?"

She flashes a picture of Joel.

"I know you miss him. I'm sorry." I continue stroking her neck. Next, she shows me an image of darkness so thick and complete that it's almost like my head is full of smoke. That's really the only way that I can describe it.

"What is it?" A sharp pain jabs at my stomach and a bitter taste fills my mouth. "Ouch," I say. "Girl, what are you trying to tell me?"

The darkness lifts for a moment and I see a flash of Emily's face, her expression angry. Then Melody shows me Joel again, and my stomach begins to twist like I need to vomit. Is Melody feeling sick? What's the bitter taste in my mouth about?

"You have to be more clear, Mel," I say.

It takes a few seconds but I get something a little bit more clear. Unfortunately, it's also baffling. She shows me that picture of Emily's face again, then she shows me Emily smiling. She shows me Joel and Emily talking but I can't tell what they're saying. The images are blurry. What I see next is Emily handing Joel a large cup and then she takes something from her purse and hands it to him. What it is, I can't tell, but it makes me wonder a few things: When was this? And what did she give Joel? Was it the night that he died? Was there something in that drink? Is that why I have such a bitter taste in my mouth, and such nausea in my stomach?

I don't have the answers, but I will get them. One thing I do know right now is that my suspicions about Emily and the possibility that she was in some way involved with Joel's death are now at the next level. From what I've just seen, I don't think she's the innocent she's been claiming to be. Then there's the issue of what in the world she's doing in secret with Tristan.

I finish up with Mel and then visit with Harmony, who gives me an earful about her eye, and repeatedly shows me pictures of carrots in her bucket. "I know you want more carrots, girl," I say. "Tomorrow." After a few more kisses, I walk back to the cabin feeling exhausted. I crawl into bed and turn my phone on vibrate to avoid having it ring later and wake any of my cabinmates—I have a feeling Austen will call me late, when he's back from the night out with Chris. And if there's any news flash, I want to get it right away.

CHAPTER *twenty-six*

I wake up the next morning before dawn and pull my pillow over my head as I realize it's Sunday—and the Fourth of July. That means the pool party at Tiffany's place. This is going to prove to be an interesting day, I'm sure of that.

Then, with a jolt, I realize it's getting light outside, and that I slept through the entire night. If Austen or Riley texted me, the phone set to vibrate certainly didn't wake me up! I feel for my phone and start to panic as I realize it's gone. I know it was next to me on the bed when I fell asleep. It must've fallen off.

I hear someone snoring, and look around to see that my cabinmates are all still asleep. I climb down off the bunk and, sure enough, find my phone on the ground. Good thing I have a case on it so it didn't break. Kind of stupid of me to keep it on the bunk all night while I toss and turn.

I pick up my phone and am relieved to see that Austen did text me—after two in the morning. *Home. Much to tell. You better be asleep! I love you.*

My body relaxes as a sense of relief washes over me. I wonder what he has to tell me! I'm hoping that we'll have some time alone to talk at Tiffany's.

There's another text. This one is from Riley. It came in around the same time that Austen's did. *Need a powwow. I'll drive to Tiffany's today. Meet Austen and me at Jeep at ten.*

I feel elated but impatient to see and talk to the guys, and find out what they discovered. I don't know how I'll wait the three hours until ten rolls around.

I dress and walk to the Commons House for some coffee. The place is quiet this morning. I pour myself a cup of coffee and sit down on one of the couches, hoping to clear my mind.

I check my e-mail on my phone and am surprised to see one from Kayla Fairmont. The subject line reads: *Important.*

Must be about my senior year or something. I open it and read it through a few times, trying to comprehend it.

Hi, Vivienne,

I hope you're enjoying Liberty Farms. You have such a great opportunity there to grow as an equestrian and I'm concerned you aren't taking full advantage of it.

I'd like you to call me as soon as possible so we can discuss this.

Kayla

Um . . . Okay. Now what in the heck does all that mean?

My hands are shaking and I really don't know why. I set the cup of coffee down on the table in front of me. As I stare at the e-mail again, I feel a surge of energy rush through my hands— and, oddly, it's a familiar sensation. When I touch a horse who is communicating with me, I feel this same kind of energy. I feel what I can only describe as a surge.

What does this mean? I know that I have to call Kayla, but I'm scared.

I look for her number in my list of contacts and in seconds I'm dialing her. It's very early on the West Coast, not even five o'clock in the morning, but I'm betting that she's awake. She's one of those people who tends to rise before the sun and get an early start with yoga or a jog. She's typically riding by seven.

She answers after one ring. "Vivienne, I knew it would be you. Did you feel it?"

"Feel what?" I ask with some trepidation.

"The signal."

"I'm sorry. I don't understand what you mean," I say.

"I was sending you a message, Vivienne. I was sending you the energy that we share with the horses."

I can't find any words to say.

She laughs. "Yeah. I know. Cat got your tongue. I told you that I knew about your gift. What I didn't tell you is that I, too, have the gift of communicating with our horse friends."

"W-what?" I stutter.

"I recognized it in you pretty quickly."

"You did?"

"Yes, and it's why I warned you to be careful before you left for the summer. It wasn't because I was trying to do you harm. I've been trying to keep you from harm."

"I'm really confused." Kayla Fairmont has just thrown me for one big loop. But what's new? I seem to be prime for them these days.

"I know you are," she says. "But here's the thing, honey, you are in danger. In my communication with the horses, I've picked up on something—that there is danger around you. One of the horses is putting you in harm's way."

"How do you know?"

"Well, that may take some time to explain. How much time do you have?"

"I have time. I need to know what you know," I reply.

"Okay then, let's talk."

"You have this gift, Vivienne, and so do I, and sometimes it can get in the way of accomplishing your goals."

"Can you back up a minute?"

"Of course," she says. "I'm sure you feel overwhelmed by this."

"Completely," I agree, and sit up. "First, when and how did you know you could, um . . . talk to them?"

She laughs a little on the other end of the line. "Probably when I was about nine or ten. At first I thought I was hearing voices when I would be at the barn and then I began to realize that it was the horses speaking to me."

"They actually speak to you?"

"Obviously not like opening their mouth and talking, but if you mean they transfer words to me, then yes."

"Wow." So I'm not going crazy then. Harmony is really using words with me.

"You don't communicate that way yet, do you? Probably only in images, like a movie reel, or in feelings that translate as waves of happiness, sadness, or anger."

"Actually, that's typically how I've been communicating, but just recently Harmony started using words." I can't believe that I'm talking to Kayla about this. My mom and I had made a promise that neither of us would ever tell anyone.

She laughs. "Good. Is she the only one?"

"Yes. The rest are still talking to me through images and feelings."

"They will all start talking to you before long. You'll see. I'm not surprised that Harmony is the first one. She's your girl and the two of you make a great team. I'm concerned, though, about what the others, and possibly even Harmony, might be communicating to you. There's something dangerous happening in the barn there."

"I don't understand."

"You may be receiving messages that aren't accurate. Remember this isn't an exact science. So it's entirely possible for the horses to mislead you; it's not conscious on their part, but it could still cause problems. To put it into terms that maybe you can understand better, think of the way rumors get started around campus. Once there is a miscommunication, things can start to snowball. Horses aren't always reliable."

"They've always been reliable to me." I'm kind of getting angry at her rhetoric and am wondering if she's trying to keep me from having communication with the horses.

"Don't be overconfident, Vivienne. I've been picking up on some communications between you and the horses that make me very uneasy. I don't want to see you get caught up in something you can't get out of."

"So, you're spying on me? I think I can handle myself."

"But these communications keep you from focusing."

"No, they don't."

"Are you sure about that?" she asks.

I sigh. "You just want me to be careful? Is that what you're saying?"

"Yes, and maybe to start tuning them out a little bit while you're there. Put all your focus on the riding goals. When you come back to Fairmont, I can teach you how to go deeper with the communication and help you from incorrectly reading them."

I don't know how to respond, because, the thing is, I don't think I've incorrectly "read" the horses I've worked with before. I'm pretty sure they've all been reliable. I've helped my mom heal hundreds of them who've told me in their way what is hurting them. Why Kayla might be trying to make me insecure, I have no idea. But it seems like too much trouble to fight her. I decide the best way to play this is to simply agree with her. I put on my best fake smile, even though she can't see me, and say, "That sounds great. I'm looking forward to that. And I promise to be careful."

"Please do, Vivienne."

I hang up the phone and the first thing I think about is how much I hate the way Kayla always says my name when she's talking to me. For some reason it seems like a put down. In fact, everything about that conversation made me feel demeaned. Her treating me as if I don't know how to utilize my gift is definitely not a pleasant way to start my morning. Besides, what the hell does she mean? If I can't trust the horses, my list of real friends is getting very short.

CHAPTER *twenty-seven*

Feeling a little shaky from the unexpected chat with Kayla, I grab some cereal and sit down to eat. I feel a little better as I start to get food in my stomach, and my thoughts become more practical. Is she right? Is there a horse here at Liberty who is giving me misinformation? I can't believe there's a horse here who would maliciously try to harm me. I know for a fact that Harmony would never do anything like that. I've had only limited conversations with Axel, and hardly spoken to most of the other horses here—except for Melody.

I almost choke on my cereal as the horse's name springs into my mind. Even I have to admit that some of her messages are strange and unclear. The one that reminded me of black smoke, and showed Emily, has thrown me for a real loop. I realize for the first time that during that conversation with Mel, I'd failed to get answers about why Wills had been petting her in a way that set off my inner alarms. The strange message she'd given me had completely distracted me. I need to go back to her for more answers. Maybe I'm getting closer to learning about what really happened to Joel the night he died. As I finish up and start walking back to the cabin, I think that maybe—just maybe—Kayla Fairmont gave me some great insight.

"There you are," Janna says when I open the door. She looks like she's been out all night, and not in a good way. For the first time, I notice bags under her eyes and I feel a pang of guilt as I realize I haven't checked in with her on the whole Chris Haverly thing. I'm still a little haunted by what Austen said about the way Chris treated her roughly. Then there's the fact that Janna has pulled away some—at least compared to the days when it seemed like my every minute with her was a personal inquisition.

"Quiet!" Emily hisses, rolling toward the wall. "Why are you yelling? Some of us are trying to sleep!"

Lydia is over by her bed, packing a bag for the pool party. She glances at me and says, "Looks like those two had some fun last night. I heard you come in around two."

"Shut up, Gallagher," Emily says and places the pillow over her head.

Two? That's about the time Riley and Austen texted me.

"Where did you guys go?" I ask.

"Oh, a little party that Chris invited us to. We tried to find you to ask you, but you weren't around," Janna replies.

"You should be careful. Sounds like rule breaking to me," Lydia says and tosses some tanning oil into her bag.

"I think there's plenty of rule breaking going on around here," Janna replies curtly and glances at me.

Whatever, as Harmony would say. But, what does Janna mean, exactly?

She clearly isn't going to explain further, because the next second she goes over to Emily and pulls the pillow off her head. "Get up. We've got another partay to go to."

"Ugh," Emily replies.

Lydia looks at me and rolls her eyes. Wait a minute, is she trying to bond with me? What is this? She's gotta be up to something. I ignore her.

"Chris is giving us a ride. Need one?" Janna asks.

"No. I'm good." I don't tell her whom I'm riding with.

I get ready and we all head out of the cabin around the same time. Although you can see Tiffany's house from the farm, it's still a distance and the road winds up and around to it.

I'm at Riley's Jeep before the guys are. When I finally see Austen, it takes all my self-control not to run over and throw my arms around him.

"Hey," he says as he makes it to the Jeep and smiles at me. He glances around, then leans in for a kiss. We're too paranoid to let it last, though. "Interesting night last night."

"Sounds like it."

A second later I spot Riley walking toward us.

We all get into the Jeep, with Riley behind the wheel. "Somebody better start talking about last night," I say.

Riley looks over at Austen.

"Riley was right," Austen says. "Those guys are all about drugs."

"Did he offer you any?" I ask.

"Not at first," Austen replies. "But Riley drove Chris so he had extra time in the car with him, and his story is different from mine. I figured we should both talk about what we saw firsthand, and then see where we're at."

"Good plan. You first." I knew they needed to be quick, though, because it wouldn't take too long to get to Tiffany's place.

"When I got there, Chris was kind of subdued with me," says Austen. "But he gave me high fives and all when I came in, and introduced me to his friend James."

"Paisley's boyfriend? I can't stand that guy," I say.

"Yeah, well Paisley isn't winning any charm awards in my book, either. She's a real freak."

"In what way?"

"Well, she's been fairly easy to deal with at the barn, I guess. Sure, she has weird mood swings, but she keeps out of my way and even acts all intimidated by me sometimes. She never says much. But last night, she was like a different person. She was all over James, and chatted me up like we were BFFs or something. She was telling me how much she loved Joel's horse, Melody, and that the horse should be hers but that her stepdad sold the horse to Fairmont Academy. She went on about what a jerk Joel's dad is—especially since he made her get a job as a working student this summer."

I shake my head. "Oh boohoo. I feel so sorry for her. Did she say anything about Joel?"

"Funny you should ask, because when she was carrying on about the horse, I finally said, 'Didn't your brother die?' Instead of what you'd expect, this funny smirk crossed her face and she said that he killed himself after a bunch of pathetic drug problems and a stint in rehab."

"I don't believe that! Is that true, Riley?" I ask.

"Not when I was around. You have to remember, though, that I wasn't close to him at all for two years prior to us meeting at Liberty, and a lot can happen during that time."

"I know, but don't you think he would have said something to you when he came to Fairmont? He was pretty forthcoming in telling you what had been going on around Liberty Farms with Chris, after all."

"Well," Riley replies, "maybe he didn't feel like sharing everything."

"I really don't believe that he was in rehab at any time. I just don't," I say. "It's a tactic to cover something up." Anger rushes through me and my ears start feeling hot. "I can't believe she's still being awful to Joel, even now that he's dead. I feel like killing her!"

"Easy, Viv," Riley says. "Don't get so worked up. Austen and I are for sure onto something, and you have to play along. You've got to keep your cool if we're going to make this happen."

"Sorry. Sometimes I just can't take her bullshit. But it's fine. What else?"

"Her boyfriend, James, walked up about that time and asked what we were talking about," says Austen. "She told him that we were talking about Joel. He eyed me and then said that we shouldn't be talking about morbid things and that it was time to move on."

"And Chris Haverly? What happened with him?" I ask.

"That's when it got interesting. Like I said, he was pretty subdued at first. I noticed Riley buddying up to him and talking throughout the evening."

"Yeah, man, at first you even doubted my motives," Riley cuts in.

"Look, Reed, you're one helluva actor. To me it looked like you were the best of buds. I had to ask you because I had to. You know that," Austen says.

"Vivvie once told me to keep my enemies closer than my friends. That's what I'm trying to do here. I had to play it up, and you have to admit that it worked," Riley replies.

"It did. It sure did."

"Oh God, can you two cut to the chase, please?" I plead.

"Chris offered us something called Big D," Austen says.

"Big D?"

Riley nods. "He didn't tell us where he got it, but he claims that the high is better than heroin, ecstasy, cocaine—anything out there. He told us that you can either take it in pill form or shoot up with it. And he said that it's making him rich."

"What? That kid comes from more money than God!" I say. "Why in the world would he need to pull in cash by dealing some kind of designer drug?"

"It's a game for him," Riley says. "I've known the kid since I was fourteen. Not well, but enough to know that he's seriously twisted."

"I don't even know what to say. It's just so stupid. Okay. Well, what did you guys do when he offered it to you?"

"I told him that I couldn't take it because, as an employee, I sometimes get drug tested," Austen says. "He told me that it doesn't show up in drug tests yet."

"What is it?" I ask.

"Dermorphin mixed with ketamine and a few other items that he referred to as 'secret ingredients,'" Riley replies.

"You mean ketamine, the drug they use on horses as anesthesia?"

"Yeah," says Riley. "It's used on people sometimes too. It's forty times stronger than morphine."

"It was being used on racetracks and going undetected until recently," says Austen. "Horses were running faster, not feeling the pain of their injuries, and finding the stamina to keep going. Chris told me that in humans, it makes you happy, high, and full of energy. It's the ketamine in the drug that makes people feel euphoric."

"Okay, so then what's dermorphin?"

"It's illegal on the track now, but there are all sorts of ways of getting around the rules."

"This is crazy," I say. "When he told you it goes undetected, what did you say?"

"I told him that I still wasn't into it, just in case," Austen replies. "But that it sounded interesting. And that is when things took a turn."

"Why?" I ask.

"He made me an offer."

"What kind?"

"He first basically said to my face that he knew I was pretty broke, since I was at Liberty as a working student. He suggested that if I wanted to make some extra cash that he could help me."

I shake my head. "No, no, no."

"Hear him out, Viv," Riley says.

"I told him that I'd be interested."

"Why?" I shout.

"Because it will get me in close," Austen replies.

Riley nods. "And as for me, he thinks I took the little green pill. I was watching Paisley and James the whole time, along with Janna, because I think all of them were on the stuff. I just copied what they were doing, and acted way overly friendly and totally blissed out—apparently I'm such a good actor that Austen thought I was becoming BFFs with Chris. Emily was the only one besides Austen and me who didn't get high. She was drinking. Don't know where the booze came from, but she had her own little flask, and just kept doing shots. If I had to guess, I'd say Haverly supplied it. Seems to get whatever anyone needs. The guy is connected, that's for sure."

"What's the next move?" I ask.

"Chris wants people using this stuff," says Riley. "He likes the money and the power. If he thinks he has me hooked, then I'll just buy it from him. And he will use Austen as a dealer," Riley says.

"He's right, Viv. He basically told me that selling this stuff to kids at Davis would make me enough money to pay off my student loans and have something in the bank when I graduate."

"You're making me nervous," I say. "Almost like you see the logic in it."

"Of course I don't," Austen replies. "But I'm sure some kids would."

"We're on to something, Vivvie," Riley says. "I do think Chris and James had something to do with Joel's death. Not sure what that is, but if we get in tight with these guys, I think we'll find out exactly what happened."

I bury my head in my hands as we pull into Tiffany's driveway, not sure if this news makes me want to smile or cry.

CHAPTER *twenty-eight*

My first thought when I walk inside the Parker house is that it seems more like a funeral home or an art gallery than a place where a family actually lives. The high ceilings, curving staircase, massive vases of fresh flowers, and paintings illuminated by track lighting add up to a place that looks expensive but not at all welcoming.

Austen, Riley, and I give each other a look that says "OMG."

"Oh good, you made it." Tiffany's frosted pink lips curve into a cold smile as she greets us. She's carrying a tray with sandwiches on it. "There's a group already outside. Drinks are in the cooler. Help yourself. Pool is that way." She points to two large French doors.

"Is Mr. Parker here?" I ask. "I wanted to give him my condolences about Joel."

Tiffany frowns. "No. He's not here. He's away on business. I'll pass that on, though. Go enjoy yourself."

As she breezes past us, Austen whispers in my ear, "Nice try, but you got the brush-off there."

We walk outside to where Chris, James, Paisley, and several other kids are already gathered. I spot Tristan and Lydia off in a corner of their own with some other Liberty kids who I don't know all that well. Tristan sees me and sort of smiles. I look away.

Down at the end of the pool, Emily and Janna are already on lounge chairs. I'm a little relieved to notice that they're not hanging around with Chris. Of course, the minute the jerk spots us, he waves and motions for us to join his crew. "You guys go," I say. "I need to use the bathroom."

"Hurry," Austen whispers.

I don't really need to pee, but the thought of putting my actress face on for Chris after what I learned in the car isn't something I'm ready for—not yet. I need a few moments alone.

Back inside the mansion, I look for a bathroom.

I walk down a long hall and see a handful of closed doors. I peek into them one by one, hoping I'll find a bathroom. No luck. There's a door toward the end of the hall that's cracked open, and I push it open just in case. I find myself walking into a large den, furnished with a leather sofa and a massive mahogany desk. "Oh," I say in surprise. Because standing inside the room in front of some shelving is Wills. He's holding a framed photo in his hand. "Sorry," I say. "I was looking for a bathroom."

He startles. "Oh jeez." I see him wipe his face and set the photo down. "Sorry. I didn't hear you."

"My fault. Guess I shouldn't sneak up on people." He tries to laugh. "You okay?" I ask.

"Sure. Yeah." He picks up the photo again and turns it toward me. "This is my sister. Anna."

I walk into the den and look at the photo. It's an aha moment for me. The photo is a little girl on a gray pony, with a slightly younger version of Tiffany standing alongside them. It's the pony Melody has been showing me for months—the dead one. I'm so surprised I go mute for a minute. Then I gasp, "She's so cute."

"Are you okay?" he asks. "You look like you've seen a ghost."

"I'm fine. Weird being here, I guess. Joel was my friend."

"I knew him but we weren't great friends or anything. My parents sold Melody to him after my sister stopped riding because of an injury."

"I guess your sister trained with Tiffany." I point to the photo. He nods. "Yep."

I already know the answer but want to see what Wills will say. "Does she still have the pony? Your sister?"

"No. He died."

"Oh no. I'm sorry."

Wills nods. "Yeah. Well, we better get out of here."

"Okay." I can tell he isn't going to elaborate on what happened to the pony, but all the same, at least this explains his connection to Melody. She was his sister's horse. Now that I know that, it seems less odd that I sensed something strange in his connection with Melody the other day at the barn. I'm not sure what to make of this new fact except to say that it's looking like Wills might be a far more complicated person than I imagined. And I think he has a skeleton or two in his closet.

CHAPTER *twenty-nine*

After finding Wills in the den looking at the photo of his sister and the pony, I wander down another hall until I finally stumble upon a bathroom. As I'm coming out, I bump into Tristan.

"We need to talk," he says and grabs my hand.

"No, we don't." I pull away from him and stare, hands on hips.

"Please, Vivvie," he says. "I just want to talk to you. This summer isn't turning out how I planned. I thought we would be together. I thought we would work through what went wrong," he says.

"I'm sorry it's not going as you hoped, but things change. And if you think I broke up with you because of Austen, you're wrong."

"What, so you broke up with me because of some stupid photo? You must have been ready to end it, because you never even questioned the truth of what you saw. You didn't even ask me to explain." He runs his hand through his sun-kissed blond hair—hair I used to love to run my fingers through.

"That's what you don't understand. The photo only made me wake up. It doesn't matter when it was taken. What it helped me realize is that I've never really known you. You don't share enough of yourself."

"You know me," he says.

"No, Tristan. I don't. You keep secrets. You work hard to hide what you don't want others to know. For me to be with someone,

I need to really know their fears, their secrets, all of it. Obviously you shared things with Lydia that you never seemed comfortable sharing with me."

"But I don't love her!"

I turn to walk away. "It doesn't matter."

He grabs my arm and turns me back around. Out of nowhere, he kisses me. It's so familiar that I linger a second too long, and then come to my senses and push him away. I glance behind me down the hall, horrified to think someone might have seen. But it's empty, nobody around.

As he pulls back, he looks at me pleadingly. "That matters, doesn't it?" he says.

"No." I shake my head. "It doesn't. "Especially not since I saw you and Emily coming back together one night from the barns. What are you two up to? And does Lydia know about it?"

He raises his eyebrows. "Seriously? For someone who doesn't care about me, you sure seem to be watching me. Look, forget about Emily, she was just having a tough day and wanted to talk. We were at Fairmont together for two years before you came along, remember? We actually have a lot in common. We're friends. Anyway, it doesn't matter. This is about us. Just say you forgive me. Please. That's all I need. If you won't come back to me, just let me know that you forgive me."

"Yes. I do. But there's really nothing to forgive. You were just being you."

"Vivvie," he says. "Stay."

I walk away without looking back, feeling more than a little shaken. Back out at the pool, the party looks to be in full swing. I notice Chris in a corner talking to Austen, who is nodding his head enthusiastically. Riley is in the pool playing volleyball tennis with James, Janna, and Paisley as if they're all the best of friends. Lydia is sashaying around, looking for Tristan, if I know her, and

Emily is passed out on a lounge chair. Tiffany is playing the hostess with the mostest. Wills is in the corner, and it looks like he's doing what I am—observing. He's up to something; I just don't know what it is. I have the unreal feeling that I'm in some kind of nightmare that I desperately want to wake up from.

CHAPTER *thirty*

Chris said he'll set up a meeting when he has the details lined up," Austen says as we drive back from the pool party. "Probably in a few weeks; he'll call me to solidify everything. I told him that I'm 'in,' and will sell whatever this Big D stuff is to kids on campus when school starts in the fall. He told me that I'll make about twenty grand a month and we'll split the profits in half."

"How are you going to get out of it?" I ask.

"Catch him before the summer is over. Prove he's manufacturing the drugs and is building a team to sell them."

"How's that going to help us find out what they did to Joel?" I ask.

"Now that I'm getting in so tight with him, he'll talk. I believe that," Riley says.

"He hasn't so far," I reply.

"We can do this," Austen says. "We really can."

"We've got to try," Riley says. "What else do we have? If we can get Chris and James to trust us, they might tell us if they were involved in Joel's death. That's what you want, isn't it?"

"Of course it is," I say. "But not at the expense of something happening to either one of you."

"Nothing is going to happen to us," Austen says.

"Everyone talks about how dangerous Chris is," I reply. "And you two are walking right into that danger, and I'm just supposed to stand back and let it happen?"

"No. You're the smart one," Riley replies.

"What does that mean?" I ask.

"I think he means that you have a way of figuring things out, usually better than we can. We can gather facts and piece some of them together. But, Viv, you have an analytical kind of mind. I don't how this will all come together, but I think you're the one who will figure it out," Austen says.

"Yeah, well, I think you guys give me too much credit."

We get back to Liberty Farms and park the Jeep.

"Hey, let's take a break from this for a few, okay?" Riley suggests. He looks at his watch. "Fireworks start in a few. I heard that we can see them well from the old farmhouse. Want to take a walk out there?"

"Sure," we both reply.

We hike on out to the old farmhouse with stars and the moon lighting the way. I want to hold Austen's hand. Heck, I want to throw my arms around him and kiss him, but we're here with Riley, so we maintain our cover of "good old buddies."

When we get to the farmhouse, I'm instantly a little creeped out. It's pretty dilapidated and the story about it being haunted is in the back of my mind, even though I know that's silly.

We walk up the steps of the porch and take a seat. There is a slight breeze, which is refreshing since even late into the evening, it's still quite hot and humid. It's funny, but I catch a whiff of what smells like expensive perfume, as if someone was recently here. I know it's not really worth bringing up to the guys, who will only make fun of me being worried about ghosts. I tell myself that it's only the scent of honeysuckle that the wind has carried our way.

I almost jump in surprise when I hear a loud pop, then laugh as I recognize the searing fizzle that follows—fireworks. The sky explodes in showers of blue and green light as we *ooh* and *ahh* at the sight.

Austen takes my hand. Riley is on the other side of me and doesn't seem to notice anything. I squeeze his hand and we continue to watch the splashes of colored lights brighten the sky— and I momentarily forget all my gloomy thoughts.

When the fireworks are over, we all walk back to our cabins. Riley and Austen leave me in front of mine. We must be putting on a good show, because Riley, who is fairly intuitive, doesn't seem to be picking up on our vibes. Like, how could he miss the fact that we desperately want to kiss each other good night? But the guy seems clueless.

"See you guys tomorrow," I say.

They both wave and head off to their own cabins.

At least I do get a *love you* as a text message when I get inside. He then texts me the smiley face emoji blowing a kiss, and I blow one back to him. The whole exchange makes me feel a little guilty about Tristan's kiss. Not that I was into it—I wasn't. But I wouldn't have wanted Austen to see us. I immediately type a text back telling him that I love him too.

CHAPTER *thirty-one*

The next morning I wake up early and meet Holden and Dr. Vermisio at Harmony's stall. I'm pleased James isn't with them. I'm not sure how well I would've held it together if that had been the case.

"Morning," Holden says, smiling.

I smile back. "Good morning."

"Ready? I'm ready. I bet you're ready. I'm sure Harmony is ready," Holden says.

I take a step back and look at him. He seems a little anxious, not like his assured, confident self. "I'm ready."

I pull Harmony out of her stall and put her in a pair of cross ties so Dr. Vermisio can examine her again. When he's finished, he goes back to his truck for the sedation and the laser. I whisper in Harmony's ear as to what's about to happen and that she'll be okay. I promise her that. She retorts with, *I understand.*

The vet puts a needle in her vein and she doesn't even flinch. That's my girl!

Holden rubs his hands together. "Let's do it. I know we're all ready to get this over with."

I look at him. He's being so weird. Everyone is weird around here. Forget about the drugs. Maybe it's in the water.

I'm relieved an hour later when the vet is finished and Harmony is coming out of the anesthesia. Holden has a stupid grin on his face. "What are your plans for the rest of the day since you have it off? Swim, hang out . . . ?"

"I don't know. I'll probably stay with her for a bit."

"Good. Good plan. Okay. I'll take care of the bill and you stay with Harmony."

"Okay." I shake my head at how strange he's being. Like I'd have scheduled anything besides spending time with my girl after her surgery. I check out Harmony's eye. The cyst is gone. I'm so relieved. "You can completely see again, sweet girl. You can."

No kidding, Vivvie. She then adds a thank-you.

"That's my girl, full of wit and sarcasm. You're welcome."

I wait a bit longer before taking Harmony back to her stall. Once I take the halter off, my phone rings. I see the call is coming from Kayla. I peer out of Harmony's stall and see that the vet and Holden are gone, so I take the call.

"Hi, Vivienne. We need to talk. Are you alone?"

"Yes."

"Good. I've been doing some long-distance work with the horses there and you're in trouble. You're being given mixed messages and I think they're coming from Melody. We need to do something about it."

"Okay," I answer, not knowing what else to say. Obviously this lady is like the voodoo queen of the horse communicators.

"This is about Joel, isn't it?" she asks.

Oh goodness, how do I answer this? I don't respond right away. I need to think about it. I decide that maybe the best answer is the truthful one. "Yes. It's about Joel."

I hear the pause on the other end. I guess it's probably funny to hear a pause, but I hear it.

"Sweetie, I need you to listen to me. You need to be careful."

"I am being careful."

"What has Melody been telling you? I can't get through to her. It's actually Harmony who has been telling me that she's afraid you're in trouble."

"Harmony? She hasn't said anything to me."

"She doesn't want to scare you. In fact, she's probably been a little curt with you lately. She's afraid."

I kind of feel betrayed that my horse has been carrying on a long-distance conversation with Kayla without including me. Especially now that I think about it and realize that, yes, she actually has been kind of short with me. I've been so focused on everything and everyone else that I haven't thought much about her brief communications. I figured maybe it was because she was now "speaking" to me, rather than just talking through images and emotions. She and I will have to have a discussion about it. "Okay."

"Tell me about Melody," she insists.

"She's been showing me clear images for months of a dead gray pony. That image always switches to one where someone is injecting Melody herself with something in the vein. Then she shows me crashing into a jump and a little girl on the ground." I don't tell her that I know this little girl is Wills's sister. She wouldn't even know who Wills is. "I think she knows even more. There's more she wants to tell me." I lower my voice, even though there is no one around us. "But since we've been here, her images have become blurry and confusing."

"Confusing as in you perceive something like dark smoke? And then see a rapid cycle of images, almost as if they're flash cards? And none of them make sense?"

I could ask her how she knows this and how she so perfectly put my recent experience into words, but again—who cares?—because the facts are she does know it. "That's exactly what it was," I say.

"She's been scrambled," she says, her tone of voice very matter-of-fact.

"Scrambled?"

"It means there is another communicator there who is messing her up."

"What?" I shout, then look around to make sure that no one is watching me. "Sorry. I didn't mean to yell. But, what do you mean there's another communicator here?"

"It may or may not be intentional, but Melody is talking and listening to someone else at Liberty Farms. Whatever the communication is, the horse has either become confused or is being used as a tool to send you scrambled messages."

"Seriously? Kind of makes me feel like we are a dime a dozen."

Kayla laughs. "Hardly. It's just one of those things. It's coincidence. But when you think about it, you're likely to find more equine communicators around horses than if you were just walking on the street."

"I guess that makes sense," I say. I'm absorbing the information that there is someone else at Liberty Farms who can talk with the horses. What I'm not completely absorbing is that whoever it might be is messing with Melody's brain. Or, is it possible that she's just confused by two different people speaking to her?

"Tell me what you think is going on," I say.

"If I had to guess, then I'd say, yes, someone could possibly be using the horses to get to you. Any one of the horses could communicate that you have been talking to them. You need to be careful. If someone is trying to manipulate Melody, and you really think that's the case, then they must have something to hide. I think whatever they're hiding is ugly—really ugly. The kind of ugly that could get you hurt."

"I think you're right, but I have to find out what Melody knows, Kayla. I have to know what happened to Joel—what really happened to him."

"I wish I could be there to help you, but I can't. I can help from here, though. You have to promise me that you'll be extremely careful. This is dangerous territory."

"I promise," I say.

"Okay then, I can teach you how to work with the horse. I can teach you how to unblock her."

"How?" I ask.

She clucks her tongue. "You're going to have to open up your mind, because this involves a little bit of magic. Are you ready to learn?"

"I'm ready."

As our conversation unfolds, my knees start to feel a little wobbly. Not only is Kayla Fairmont making suggestions that sound straight out of *Harry Potter*, but she's explaining a complicated procedure that has so many steps I have to sneak a pen and some paper out of the desk at the front of the Commons House to write everything down.

After we hang up, I look again at the scribbled to-do list in front of me. If Kayla's right, and this works, I might just get all the answers about Joel that I'm looking for—from Melody.

CHAPTER *thirty-two*

It's kind of spooky back behind the barns by myself after dark. I wish I were coming here to meet Austen. That's not the situation. Instead, I'm making good on Kayla's crazy suggestions for "unblocking" Melody so I can communicate with her more clearly. Yep, I've decided to go all *Harry Potter* tonight and try something with the horse that veers into, well, Hogwarts territory. Austen wanted to meet, but I said I had a migraine coming on and was going to bed early. I don't like lying to him, but I can't tell him about my gift. I don't want to risk messing things up—especially since tomorrow is his birthday and I want us to get some time alone. That has been in short supply lately. And if I explain that I'm trying to work magic on a scrambled horse, he might send me to the loony bin tomorrow instead of meeting me at the shed behind the barns in the evening, when nobody will be around to interfere.

I'm looking forward to celebrating with Austen, but not to the rest of what tomorrow will bring. I know from the schedule that I'll be working with Frank for the first time.

In the dark outside the barn, I double-check that I have everything that's on the list I scribbled down while talking to Kayla: all of Melody's favorite treats, a photo of Joel, a few pieces of Melody's tail, a pebble, a small piece of wood, and a string. I also have a white candle, some matches to light it, and, since I'll be sitting on dirt, I don't need the vial of dirt Kayla told me that I'd need if I planned to do the ritual inside.

I take one last look around to make sure I'm alone. Yep. All I can do is pray that nobody comes along,, because if anyone does see me, well, I can only imagine what they might think.

I don't go into the barn to see the horses even though I want to. Kayla told me that I shouldn't be in contact with any of them for a minimum of two hours before the ritual—and should wait at least two hours after it's finished to see them. So I'll have to wait until tomorrow before squeezing in any visits. When I'd left Harmony earlier, she was doing really well, and assured me that she was looking forward to going back to work in the morning.

Kayla had explained to me that the reason for leaving time in between being around the horses and doing the ritual had something to do with not wanting any of them to sense the energy around what I was trying to do, because, as I already know, horses not only communicate with people with my skills, but also they communicate with one another. I asked Kayla if it was possible that the block on Melody was being put in place by another horse. She said it was unlikely.

"People have been trying to get horses to do what they want for a long time, Vivvie," she'd said. "So most likely a person is the culprit."

Of course, I'd been racking my brain for who might be behind Melody's situation, but I had only one suspect in mind—Wills. I'd seen him with Melody. He'd acted strange. And he had a connection to her in that his sister had owned the pony who'd died— and she'd owned Melody before the mare was bought by Joel. That meant he would have had access to Melody in the past, to create a bond between him and the horse. He also appeared to be an observer like myself, a quality I associated with my empathetic gift. He'd spent time at juvenile hall, implying, maybe, that he was capable of dangerous things. And he had ties to Chris Haverly. Maybe Wills had "the gift," and he didn't want Melody to recall the pony . . . maybe he had something to hide. The only problem? I'm just not really sure if I'm convinced that Wills is a bad guy—someone who would intentionally try to manipulate Melody for some kind of sinister reason.

I walk a little way from the barn and sit with my back against a nearby tree. I take everything out of my backpack and light the white candle, after pushing it down into the ground pretty good so that it won't move. I take the piece of wood and, with a green string that represents Joel's competition color, tie to it the strands of Melody's tail that I cut off of her earlier in the day.

I set the piece of wood down in front of me and place the pebble on top of it. Then I set a row of Melody's treats out in a straight line—a carrot, an apple slice, a sugar cube, and a horse cookie. The final piece is Joel's photo. There's hardly any light, but I can just make it out: Joel holding up the second-place ribbon he won in Lexington while standing next to Melody and grinning from ear to ear. He looked so happy. He'd just been told that Melody was his to keep, because Kayla had bought her and gifted her back to him.

Looking at the photo reminds me of how certain I am that foul play contributed to his death. It also strengthens my resolve to finish this crazy ritual, even though I think it's a tad ridiculous. If it'll help find the answers that I know are here at Liberty Farms, then I'll do it.

I set the photo down and pick the pebble back up, holding it in my hand. Following Kayla's instructions, I close my eyes and picture Melody in my head. I hold the image of her as clearly as I possibly can. Once I have the image of the horse and feel comfortable that my mind is focused, I visualize a bright light above her. In my mind's eye, I enhance the light and make it brighter and bigger. I keep doing this until Melody is standing completely inside the light. I see my hands now in the image and I reach out to touch Melody's face within the light. I run my hands along her silken chestnut-colored coat. My hands stop at her heart, and I keep them there. I maintain the imagery and connection while I begin to send her feelings of joy, peace, love, and overall contentment.

I feel what I can only describe as a surge of energy travel from me to the horse. She tosses her head, agitated. I whisper the words, "It's okay. You're safe with me. You are safe." She calms at my voice.

I know that the next step could be tricky. Kayla warned me about it, so I take it as slow as I possibly can. I do the best I can to change my hands into Joel's within the image—it's hard, because I can't exactly remember what Joel's hands looked like. The one thing I do remember vividly, though, is a scar he had on the back of his right hand. He'd told me that he'd gotten it as a little kid when he picked up a wheelbarrow too quickly; it was lodged sideways under a cement mixer, and the sharp shroud of the mixer had cut him and left a distinct one-inch scar.

When Melody sees the back of his hand, she takes a step to the side. I again reassure her. "It's okay. It's Joel." I then show her an image of Joel and she stops moving; her ears prick forward and he begins to pet her. I can sense anxiety going through her because she doesn't completely understand what's happening.

She knows that he's been gone and I think she knows that he's dead, so this has to be somewhat confusing. But as I maintain the image of Joel's hands stroking her neck, her eyes close slightly and she relaxes. This is the state that Kayla explained I would want her in.

Then I say the words "*Concordia cum veritate*," which in Latin mean, "in harmony with truth." I repeat this over and over again, and with each time I say it, the light grows brighter and stronger around Joel and Melody until I can no longer see either of them. All I see is this blinding light—and then I see nothing as everything disappears and goes to darkness.

CHAPTER *thirty-three*

Voices wake me and I struggle to sit up. The candle has gone out. I have no idea how long I've been out.

Kayla did warn me that I might go unconscious briefly, depending on the intensity of the ritual, but I hadn't believed her. I'm groggy and my whole body feels heavy.

As the voices come closer—they sound male—I spring into action, gathering up my things as quickly as I can. Just in time, I duck behind a maintenance shed.

"What do you mean you couldn't get any more of it?" Now that they're closer, I recognize one of the voices. It's Chris Haverly.

"I tried. But he'd know if it were missing."

I can tell from the dour tone that it's James.

"We need some more of it, man. If we don't get it, we can't make the stuff and I promised we'd deliver on time. This is a big deal! The Russians, man!"

"I tried, Chris."

I see them pass the barn and pause beneath the tree where I'd just been sitting. I've got my body wedged in as tightly as I possibly can between the shed and barn. I can hear the horses moving around inside. My senses are on high alert and I feel strung out, almost as if I just drank five shots of espresso. It's a weird sensation. My heart is beating hard against my chest. I really hope they don't spot me.

"You tried?" Chris sounds like he's getting angrier by the minute. "You better try harder! I made promises to people who won't think trying is good enough, you idiot!"

"I'm sorry."

"Sorry won't cut it! Get the stuff so we can finish this!" Chris lights a cigarette and sits down right where I'd been. "What's this?"

I can see him picking something up and realize it's the photo of Joel. Uh-oh. *How did I leave that behind?*

"Shit, man, this is weird!" Chris says.

"What is it?"

"A photo of Joel and his horse." Chris hands it to James, who promptly tears it up.

"That's creepy," he says.

"Yeah. Kind of. Thing is, if you don't get what we need by tomorrow, you could wind up like Parker there."

"Screw you, Chris."

"I'm just saying, get what we need." Haverly stands up and walks away. James trails behind him.

I stay hidden until I can no longer see either of them. Then I walk quickly back toward the cabin. I check my phone now and there are five text messages. Three are from Austen, asking where I am and to call him, one from Riley, who also wants to know what I'm up to, and one—oddly enough—from Tristan, which just reads, *Hi. Thanks for listening the other day.*

Oh boy.

It's after midnight and I'm hoping no one is awake to ask me five thousand questions when I walk through the door. I had no idea I'd been out there for over three hours.

I text Austen and tell him that I'd fallen asleep, which is true. He writes back that he's happy to hear from me. I don't text Riley, because I'm sure he's asleep, and, as far as Tristan goes, the sentiment is nice, but he won't get a response from me—not tonight or tomorrow.

I'm thankful that everyone seems to be asleep and I don't even get undressed. I climb as quietly as I can into the top bunk, close my eyes, and try to process the night.

One thing I need to find out for sure is what Chris and James were talking about. What was it that Chris was insisting that James get? I think it's time that Riley, Austen, and I have another powwow.

CHAPTER thirty-four

My alarm goes off at six, and I make myself get up. I'm not happy about the early wake-up call, but today is a big day. I shower before texting the guys. I send Austen a Happy Birthday text and tell him that we need to meet for coffee. Then I send Riley a text that tells him to wake up and meet us at the Commons House.

Twenty minutes later I'm sitting with my guys over coffee and croissants. I want to hug Austen and kiss him and yell, "Happy birthday!" But no can do.

"What's up, Vivvie?" Riley asks.

I have to be delicate about this because of the lie I'd told Austen about having a migraine and falling asleep. "I heard something last night."

"What, like a bird?" Riley says.

"Smart-ass. No. I went to check on Harmony one last time and I saw Chris and James walking out by the barns so I spied on them," I say.

"She's like that Veronica Mars chick." Riley winks at Austen.

"Go on," Austen says.

I recount the conversation I overheard. They both stare at me, and then Riley's eyes widen. "Oh wow. That's how they get the mix—the ketamine and dermorphin. James works with Dr. Vermisio, right?"

"Yes," I say.

"Well, it makes sense that the vet would have the ketamine on board, but not the dermorphin unless he did some of his own illegal work on the side. You know, helping people drug their horses on or off the track," Austen says.

"Great. An unethical vet just performed eye surgery on my horse." I take a sip from the coffee.

"We don't know that," Riley says. "It's just a theory. But it does make sense."

"I'll know more when I meet with Chris to talk drugs," Austen replies. "I'll pick the guy's brain."

"I still don't like it."

"I know, but it's what we have to do."

I finish by telling them about what the two guys had said about Joel, leaving out the part about the photo of him. They glance at each other. "This is why we have to get in tight with them," Riley says. "And you need to be low-key, Vivvie. You do your thing. Ride. Ignore everything we're doing. Okay?"

"Easier said than done," I reply.

"Hey guys," says Austen, who's facing the window. "Chris is walking up now. Let's disband. Viv has made it clear to him how she feels. Might not look so kosher us hanging out together."

"See you at the barn." Riley stands up.

Austen leans in and whispers, "And I'll see you tonight." He walks away from me and back to the coffee as my cheeks flush.

Chris strolls into the Commons House and smiles at me. I look the other way. He heads over to where Austen is making himself a second cup and they start talking. I decide to head out to the barn and get the day started.

Harmony is finishing her breakfast and I take out my brushes and tack to prepare for the morning lesson. It's already hot and humid and, for the first time in a long time, I dread riding. I know it's because I'm about to face Frank again. I replay Austen and Riley's instructions to focus on my horse and try to calm down.

Frank comes into the barn while I put Harmony's saddle on. "Hi, Vivienne."

"Hello," I reply curtly.

He walks up to me. "I'm sorry about dinner the other night. I'm sorry that I told you in the way I did. Really, I'm sorry about everything. I do want to be here for you, if you'll let me."

"I don't know. Like I said, I think the best thing for us at this point is to work together as coach and student. I don't need a dad, Frank. I haven't had one in a long time."

He shoves his hands into his pockets. "You get a chance to talk with your mom yet?"

"No. She's still in Europe. I do plan to talk with her as soon as she gets home. But she's still traveling around the mountains."

"Good. That'll be good. When you can talk to her, I think it will all work out and be really good."

"I don't know how any of this is good. I really don't." I tighten Harmony's girth.

"I promise you, Vivienne, that we did things we shouldn't have, but they were done in order to protect you. Your mom loves you and I've always loved you."

I shake my head and kind of laugh. "You know, I'm tired of people trying to protect me." My thoughts turn to Tristan for a second. "I've discovered that if someone thinks they're protecting you, then they're usually lying to you, and I'm not sure what good can come of that."

"I understand. For what it's worth, I never meant for any of this to happen, and I'm sorry."

"See you in the ring," I reply, and watch him walk away. Under my breath I say, "Funny how everyone who thinks they're protecting me is always apologizing to me."

Harmony responds immediately. *I won't lie to you.*

"I know. I know you won't." I give her a hug before stepping up onto the mounting block.

We walk out to the jump arena. Lydia is there with Emily. I wonder how much Lydia knows about Tristan's apparently oh-so-supportive friendship with her. If she found out, that would be interesting. Then something strange happens—as if nothing strange ever happens to me.

Lydia comes over to me and says, "You know what, Vivienne?"

"What?" I wait for something nasty to come out of her mouth.

"I'm sorry about the other day. What I said about your dad and the scholarship and everything. It was wrong, and I'm sorry."

I can't even comment. The bizarre thought that flashes through my brain is, *Okay. What's Lydia Gallagher trying to protect me from?*

CHAPTER *thirty-five*

I look all around me before I enter the shed, my heart pounding because I'm so excited to finally be alone with Austen on his birthday. I don't see a soul. As soon as I walk in and shut the door behind me, Austen immediately grabs me around the waist and starts kissing me. I kiss him back—our hands are everywhere and my body burns as he picks me up off the floor and sets me on a worktable in the shed. I wrap my legs around him and run my hands under his shirt and over his strong, broad back. He moans a little bit at my touch and we press together even more tightly. We finally come up for air and I say, "Wow. Happy birthday."

"Yeah," he replies breathlessly. "I've been waiting and waiting to do that. Do you have any idea how hard it is to see you every day, have you so close, and not be able to touch you?"

"I think I do," I reply. "Because I feel the same way."

"It drives me completely bananas."

"I won't argue with you." I laugh. The kiss that Tristan planted on me at Tiffany's place pops into my mind, but I push it away. I've decided not to feel bad about it. All it did was prove that the only person I want to be kissing is Austen.

"I can't concentrate with you on the table like this," he says. "And we have to have an actual conversation."

"We do?"

He laughs and wraps his hands around my waist, lifting me up from the worktable and sitting me down on a bench. He puts an arm around me. "I wish we could stay here like this."

"Me too."

"How was today? With Frank?" he asks.

"It was all right. I kept it as professional as I could, but it's awkward. He's a good coach, though. You're right about that."

He takes my hand and kisses it. "That's good. Maybe something positive will come out of it after all."

"Maybe."

"You hear from your mom?"

"Not yet. I don't know when I will. She isn't back for two more weeks."

"I'm sorry you're going through all of this."

"What doesn't kill you makes you stronger. Right?" I lift his hand to my lips and kiss it, holding it tight.

"That's what they say. But I already think you're strong. And I know you're having a hard time with me getting in close with Chris and James, but you've got to trust me," he says. He runs his hands over my arms and then pulls me onto his lap. I inhale the incredible smell of him.

"I do trust you," I say, looking into his eyes. "They're the ones I don't trust. I'm afraid of what they could or would do if they find out you and Riley are duping them." I lean my head into the crook of his neck and he tightens his arms around my waist.

"I know," he says. "I do, but it's the only way."

"Okay, but promise me that as soon as you have some kind of proof of what they're doing we can go to the police."

"I promise." He kisses me again and I respond, and suddenly everything else falls away. I wish it could always be just like this— no worries, no cares, no drug dealers, dead friends, or parental issues. No interruptions. Just the two of us.

He takes my hand. "We better get back. Our time is short. As much as I want to spend my entire birthday night with you, I think that could get us into a lot of trouble."

"I suppose it could."

I jump off his lap and we both stand up. "I have to check the schedule for tomorrow and Faith said it would be up in the Commons House by eight. She's a drill sergeant—we have to have it checked off that we've read through the next day's schedule by nine every night. I just got a text from her before I walked in here making sure I would be looking at it."

"I don't know her very well," I reply.

"She's kind of one of those behind-the-scenes people. She doesn't do anything with the horses, just coordinates things. But she's been in the horse world a long time, and she's actually a smart, thoughtful person."

"We need more of those," I say. "Okay, well, I'll walk with you. Things seem quiet tonight and I don't think we can get into trouble walking together." He smiles and I put my arms around his neck. "I love your smile." I kiss him again and we spend another few minutes in that place of what can only be described as pure magic. Once again out of breath, I say, "We better stop while we can."

He spanks me lightly. "Not easy to do. Not at all."

"Come on, Romeo. Your schedule perusal awaits, and I'm sure my cabinmates are waiting up for me with baited breath." I haven't told him that I think Janna knows about us. I need to tell him but I don't want to break the spell of the moment.

Austen and I walk back to the Commons House together, making sure that no one is around as we play grab ass with one another. It's very quiet tonight at Liberty Farms, which is unusual. I wonder why.

"Only a month until your birthday," he says.

"I know. I'll be all grown up." I laugh.

"Look pretty grown up to me already." He reaches around my waist and tickles me.

We stop on the porch of the Commons House. "I better get back to my cabin."

"Wait. This'll only take me a minute. I'll walk you back. We've already determined that we can't really get into trouble walking together."

I smile. "Good point." I look around and, since no one is there, I kiss him on the lips as quickly as I can.

He kisses me back and then opens the door to the house and flips on the light.

"Surprise!" a room full of people shout as we walk in and the lights go on. Balloons are everywhere and a streamer that says "Happy Birthday, Austen" is hung across the threshold.

I'm as surprised as he is.

Janna walks forward and says, "Happy birthday."

Faith is right behind her. "This was Janna's idea. She heard it was your birthday. It was kind of impromptu, but we wanted to do something for you. Why didn't you mention it?"

Faith looks at me after she asks him the question and my stomach sinks. I'm pretty sure she has figured out our little secret. I glare at Janna; I could kill her right now.

Austen shrugs. "I don't do birthdays. I just don't think they need to be a big deal."

"Oh," Faith replies.

"But this is really nice." He turns to Janna. "Thanks."

"I love parties. Don't you, Vivienne?" Janna asks in that Southern accent, which had seemed so sweet and charming when I first arrived at Liberty. Now it seems more forced and definitely not so sweet.

"Yes. I guess I do. I'm curious as to why I didn't know about this one, though. Austen and I have known each other since we were kids. I would have thought you might have asked me what kind of cake he likes."

Janna laughs. "We just decided to put this together this afternoon. Sorry. I couldn't find you. And since you guys are such good friends, I was afraid that you might ruin the surprise."

"I wouldn't have done that," I reply.

"Get something to drink and eat," Faith says to Austen. "Janna, why don't you go with Austen?"

Austen looks at me, and I give him a slight nod.

Faith reaches out and taps my shoulder. I face her. "I'm sorry about everything going on here with Harmony, Vivienne. Holden has filled me in."

"Oh. It's okay."

"If you need anything, let me know."

"Okay," I reply.

"You and Austen seem to be really close."

"Yes. As you know, we trained with the same coach back in Oregon. He's, uh, he's like a brother to me." Those are hard words to say, because it feels like a really gross thing to say. The last thing Austen is like to me is a brother. The conversation feels forced and icky.

"And that's all?"

I take a step back. "Yes. That's all. Why?" Damn. She does have us figured out.

"Just asking. You two do seem very close and you do know the rules. I'd hate to have to send anyone home. And I see a lot of promise in you. I want the best for your career and I don't want to see it sidelined by anything."

I remember what Austen said about her being thoughtful, and I realize he's right. She's not trying to persecute me; she's trying to look out for me.

"Thanks, Faith," I say. "I definitely love what I'm learning here at Liberty."

"Good. Good to know. Listen, Vivvie, part of the reason I want to make sure your riding is a priority is because something occurred to me today when I was talking with Holden."

"What?" I'm not sure I like the idea of Faith and Holden having conversations about me.

"Well, I was telling him about a former Olympic gold medalist I know who's close to the University of New Hampshire, who just got in touch with me about needing a working student. Her name is Lena Millman."

"Oh my God! Seriously?" I'm in total shock. Lena Millman is legendary in the equestrian world. She's like eventing royalty.

"I'm not sure if you'd consider UNH for college, but it's got a terrific equestrian program. And if she could offer you a working position in exchange for room and board, it could be a great opportunity. I know some folks over at UNH who would be interested in an intelligent young woman like you."

All my worries about Janna temporarily leave my head at the sound of this incredible opportunity.

"Seriously? Would you recommend me?"

She smiles. "I'd like to. And with an additional letter from Holden, I have a feeling you'd shoot to the top of her list of potential candidates. And I am positive you can get into the university."

"I love the idea," I say. "I have a long list of schools to consider, and UNH has been on it from the beginning. For me, it's going to be a lot about where I get a scholarship. But having room and board paid for would really help."

"Well, then, let's do it," she says, smiling broadly. "I'll write up a letter and give her your contact info."

"That would be amazing," I say.

"Here's the thing, Vivvie." Faith's expression turns serious. "If anyone finds you breaking any rules, this opportunity will go away. Lena Millman isn't the type who puts up with nonsense."

I feel momentarily guilty but put on my best confident smile. "Of course," I say. "You don't have to worry about me."

"Great," she says. "Go get something to eat. Enjoy."

"Thanks." My mind is buzzing with excitement as I walk away from Faith. Then I spot Janna chatting away to Austen, who looks dumbfounded by her sudden chumminess.

I don't know what the Southern belle is up to, but I can say that I don't like it one bit. And now that I might have the chance of a lifetime to work for Lena Millman, the last thing in the world that I want is for this girl to mess it up.

CHAPTER *thirty-six*

During the birthday party, the annoyance I feel at Janna for pulling the stunt increases. By the time I get back to our cabin with Janna and Emily beside me I'm in a full-fledged rage. I don't know where Lydia is, but all I can say is it's a relief that she's not around to be yet another thorn in my side.

Emily is taking her turn in the bathroom when Janna says, "That was so much fun."

I blurt back, "What are you trying to do?"

"What? What do you mean?" she asks, playing the innocent.

"You know what I mean." I lower my voice. "You throw a surprise birthday party for my boyfriend and I don't even know about it?"

"Ah, so he is your boyfriend!"

My face is burning. I shake my head and roll my eyes. "Come on, don't act like you don't know. You've been trying to find out what our deal is since you laid eyes on him. Pretending to be my friend was clever. You knew."

"You kept denying it," she replies.

"At the very least, even if I was denying it, you knew that I've known him almost my entire life, and you don't tell me you're throwing him a party? You don't even know him."

She stumbles over her words. "I tried to find you. And that's the way I've been taught all my life. I'm from the South, Vivienne. We know how to be hospitable."

I cock my head to the side and laugh. "Right. You have my phone number. There's no text. Nothing. And hospitality? Please. I am so not buying it."

Janna clearly has another agenda. I can only assume she has eyes for Austen. I'm not sure what other reason she could have.

She turns red. "I didn't want you to spoil the surprise."

"I didn't believe you the first time you said that, and I still don't. Can you try being honest?"

"I swear. I was just trying to do something nice."

"Right. Something nice for my boyfriend?"

"Is that what this is about? You're jealous," she says. "Oh my goodness, Vivienne. You have nothing to worry about. I'm not trying to step on your toes. Austen is super cute, don't get me wrong, but I would never try and take a guy away from a friend. Besides, I'm involved already."

I stare at her. "That's a weird way to put it. I mean, you might as well just say it out loud. It's obvious the person you're involved with is Chris Haverly. Where was he tonight, anyway?"

"He had other plans. It was so impromptu."

"Hmm." I'm fuming. I really can't believe I was all worried about Janna and wanting to protect her. Clearly, she's got her own agenda.

"I didn't mean to upset you. Please. I am sorry. You're my friend. You really are."

"Is that what we are? Friends? I'm starting to wonder."

"You shouldn't."

I cross my arms. "I don't know what to think. I think there's something going on and I don't know what that is."

She laughs. "I think you're a worrywart. Nothing is going on."

"Oh yeah. I know you went to that rave. You and Emily. What's the story there?"

"Your boyfriend tell you that? Because he was there too."

"I know he was there. We don't keep secrets. Besides, it was obvious you went because of the hangover you two had the morning after."

"So I like to have a little fun," she says. "I doubt it would get me kicked out of here. Not like what you're up to. You and lover-boy think you're so incognito. Your cover may have been blown tonight, though, huh?"

The rage I'm feeling is threatening to boil over. I don't want to start a fistfight with Janna, but I'm getting close to trying.

I take a deep breath to calm down. "That makes a few of us keeping secrets, now doesn't it? I'm sure the staff here would be curious as to what you were doing at a rave off campus."

As I say that to her it hits me. Austen's birthday party wasn't about her trying to get his attention. It was about her wanting us to be found out. She wants me kicked out of here. Or maybe she wants Austen kicked out of here. Why?

"What does that mean?" Janna asks.

"Nothing. It means we all have secrets we don't want exposed."

Emily walks out of the bathroom and I walk past her and head in to wash my face. "Don't we, Em?" I ask, thinking of what Melody had shown me with Emily giving Joel that drink. I know Kayla said it might be misinformation, but it's still enough to make me suspicious. Not to mention Emily's thing with Tristan. I know it's wrong, but I'm sure Em has some dark secret she's keeping. Like everyone else around here, apparently.

"What?" she says after missing the conversation with Janna. "We all have secrets, don't we?" I repeat.

"Oh, those. Yep. Plenty. I'm not worried, though," Emily replies.

I shut the bathroom door behind me and wonder for the first time how Janna figured out that I'd be with Austen when he walked into the party. Had she followed us? Or was it just a lucky guess? Either way, she nearly got us 100 percent busted. I still don't even know if anyone spotted the kiss we shared before he opened the door.

I turn on the faucet and sigh. I'm pretty sure that Emily and Janna are having a powwow behind my back at the moment. Do they know each other's secrets? I'm not sure what they're both hiding, but I intend to find out.

ecrets, lies, and protection. Good God. I'm over it when I wake up the next morning. I want nothing to do with Janna or Emily. Oddly enough, Lydia is the one who is the least on my nerves at the moment.

I grab my morning wake-up call at the Commons House in the form of a steaming cup of coffee, and walk to the barn. I'm going extra early this morning in hopes of being alone.

What I'm craving is some quiet quality time with Harmony. If there is anything that can help me calm my mind and spirit, it's spending alone time with my horse. I need to sort out everything that's happened to me. There's my mom and Frank, everything I've learned about Joel, and now this new college opportunity that Faith mentioned. On the one hand, would I really consider moving across the country from my mom to attend UNH? New Hampshire is really far from Oregon. On the other hand, maybe some distance would be a good thing after all I've learned.

The other thing on my mind, of course, is what Kayla said about there being another communicator here at Liberty Farms. I need to have a talk with Wills. I'm just not sure how to go about it. "So, hey, Wills? Are you the evil mastermind who's been messing with Melody's mind in an effort to screw me up?" Yeah—probably not the way I should go about it.

All I can say is that I'm hoping that my little magic session has removed any confusion from Melody's mind.

I walk around the side of the barn and stop suddenly, taking a step back so I won't be seen. I need a moment to process what's in front of me. Melody is out in one of the back paddocks and she has company. And once I see who it is, I instantly know who the other communicator is. It isn't Wills.

I stare in surprise as I watch Paisley stroking Melody's neck. It takes all my willpower not to run over and rip the girl's hands off Joel's former horse. Poor Melody! Now I'm absolutely certain she has been manipulated on purpose. Paisley's been "talking" to Melody and I can guess why she's doing everything that she can to confuse the mare. Paisley knows what happened to Joel—and so does Melody.

I also realize that if Paisley is smart enough to block a horse's communication, she likely also knows that I've been trying to talk with Melody.

I see Paisley take a treat from her pocket and start to offer it to Melody. That's when I lose it and start running toward them. I hear myself scream, "No!"

Melody eats the treat and then, with ears forward, she looks at me. Paisley also turns to me with a smirk on her face. She takes a step back as I come charging at her. "What did you give her?" I yell.

"An apple cookie treat. Why? What's wrong?"

I freeze, unsure what to say. I can't just admit out loud that I've got this gift of talking to horses. Because, what if I'm wrong about Paisley? Maybe she isn't the communicator. My gut says yes, but what if she isn't? My mind races and I seize on the first thing that comes to mind.

"She can't have sugar," I blurt out wildly. "She has a thyroid issue."

"Really? That's the first I've heard of it, and I think I would know. The horse did belong to my brother."

"She's a school horse now, and Holden told me. And Joel was never your brother."

That smirky smile spreads across her face again. She crosses her arms. "Joel was my brother and he would want me to have this horse."

"No. No, he wouldn't."

Melody is tossing her head around and swishing her tail. I know she's uncomfortable with the obvious conflict that's happening. I can sense it.

"I know who you are," I say. "I know what you're capable of, and I'm going to prove you were involved in Joel's death."

She laughs. "People told me you were weird, but now I know you are definitely crazy. Joel killed himself. And as far as knowing what I am capable of, I don't know what you mean."

"Well, one of us is right. Either I'm crazy, or you're evil. I suggest you leave. And I suggest you stay away from Melody."

Melody has walked away from us and is standing in the corner of the paddock not eating, just standing.

Paisley laughs. "What are you going to do about it?"

I sigh. I see Melody's lead rope on the gate and go get it. I walk over to the mare and hook her onto the lead rope. "Since you won't leave, we will." I walk Melody past her. As I do so, I catch a whiff of her perfume and have a sudden memory. She's wearing the same scent I smelled sitting on the porch outside the farmhouse watching the fireworks! Paisley had either been there when we were, or had recently visited. But why?

I open the gate and turn back to see Paisley watching us, and I don't like the look in her eyes at all.

"It's okay," I whisper to Melody. "I won't let her near you."

Melody pulls back a little and I make a clicking sound with my tongue to get her to move forward. "Come on."

She doesn't budge. I taste bitterness in my mouth like I did when she showed me Emily handing Joel the drink. I feel sick to my stomach again. That dark smoke billows into view but then just as suddenly clears. Now I see an image clearly, and the mare is showing me something I haven't seen before. Waves of guilt wash over me as I realize that Emily has been innocent all along. And I feel sick with horror as I witness what really happened to Joel.

CHAPTER *thirty-eight*

I knew that Chris Haverly and his minions were bad. I'd known it from the moment I laid eyes on the guy. However, what Melody just revealed to me—and this time, I definitely believe she's communicating the truth—is far worse than I ever expected. Because what I've just learned is that Chris, Paisley, and James are killers. They conspired and carried out Joel's murder, and they got away with it. Now it's up to me to bring them to justice.

My hands are shaking because I'm also realizing that Joel's murder was premeditated. The three of them actually plotted it, and, to cover up the truth, Paisley was doing everything she could to mess with the horses' brains while we were in Lexington—she especially targeted Melody. Finally, now I know why my connections with the horses when we were at championships were so vague and confusing. The one piece that's missing is whether Paisley knows that I have the same gift as she does.

Another reason I feel so off-kilter is because everything I just learned from Melody is bringing back all my memories of the time around Joel's death. The thoughts tumble through my mind: Joel leaving the celebration party in Lexington kind of early; his decision to tell Emily the truth that he was gay; the obvious happiness he felt to know that Melody was going to be his horse forever, thanks to Kayla.

It's so horrifying and disgusting knowing what they've done. Of course, Melody didn't show me everything that led up to murder. She only showed me what she'd seen directly. Luckily, I can piece the rest together.

Everything that Melody just showed me is so awful, but I replay it again my mind:

"You said there was something wrong with my horse," Joel said. *"She looks fine to me."*

"Oh. Yeah. Well, I actually called you here to give you another chance," Chris said.

"No. I told you that I won't sell your stuff. I won't be involved in it. Not at all. You're twisted, man. I want you away from me, my friends, and my horse. I warned you that if you don't back off, I'm going to the cops with what I know."

Chris shook his head. "I don't like threats, and I don't like to have to be concerned about idiots like you and what you might go telling people."

That's when Paisley walked up.

"What do you want?" Joel asked.

As he turned and asked her this, Chris twisted Joel's arms behind his back, and Paisley stuck a needle in his neck. Almost immediately Joel went limp.

When Melody played this all out to me, I was stunned by the violence and cruelty.

"Did you bring what we need?" Chris asked Paisley.

She held up a handful of prescription bottles. "It's all here. We need to get him out of here."

"Where's James? Did you call him?" Chris asked.

"I'm here." James walked up to them. Joel was lying motionless on the ground. "What the hell, you guys? Is he . . ."

"Dead?" Chris said. *"He will be. He probably almost is."*

"What the hell?" James asked again.

Chris shook his head. "I don't like traitors. I don't like being told no. Joel here could have been a big problem for us."

"He'll be a bigger problem if you guys don't get him into his room and make it look like a suicide," Paisley said.

"You think you're going to get away with this?" James asked.

"Yes. We are. Get his legs and help me. Now, you idiot. Before we get caught!" Chris said.

Melody's communication had come to me along with a mix of confusion, sadness, fear, and anger. And at the very end of the communication, the last image she showed me was Paisley turning back to her and looking deep into her eyes. I'm betting that's the very moment that Paisley started messing with the horse's thoughts and memories.

I can't believe the way they killed him. I can't believe how heinous they truly are!

I'm also continuing to feel ashamed over my false assumptions about Emily. I was so ready to believe that she played a part in Joel's death, but did that ever really make sense? Kayla's condescending words in Kentucky about communicating with horses echo in my ears: *You don't have enough skill and insight yet to really understand how to handle it.* She had a point, but I was too egotistical to see it. This, plus everything else, has me on the brink of tears.

All I can think about is finding Austen—my voice of reason. He's been in this with me from the moment I arrived here.

I realize with a sinking feeling that I'm going to have to tell him how I know everything. I'm going to have to watch his eyebrows rise with disbelief as I explain that I've had this very special gift of talking to horses for as long as I can remember. Austen isn't the only one who needs to know, either. Riley does too.

I've got to figure this all out.

The rest of the day passes by in a fog. I take a lesson from Tiffany, then give Harmony a bath, but it's like I'm only half there.

The other half of me is obsessed with what I'll say to Austen and Riley, and whether or not Melody is safe. If Paisley figures out that I'm a communicator—and she must realize there's one here—then the horse could be in danger.

I take one last trip to the barn before dinner hour hits to give Harmony a treat and a kiss. I also give Melody a pat as I leave the barn. "We'll make this right," I tell her. I show her Joel's face in my mind and then scales, the symbol for justice. This horse knows like I do that Joel was murdered. She even witnessed it.

I feel certain that the injection Paisley gave to Joel was dermorphin. What else could knock someone out like that? Then James and Chris carried him back to his room and set it up to look like a suicide. The questions I have now are: Why didn't the autopsy report show the presence of that unusual drug? How had they gotten away with it? I couldn't count the number of people who'd told me about Chris Haverly's huge store of money and power. Could he have paid someone off? An intern in the coroner's office? It wasn't hard to imagine. He is a true sociopath or a psychopath—or both. I'm going with both.

I walk out of the barn and find myself wanting to throw up. Unscrambling Melody is something I should be proud of, because it helped me learn the truth. But all I want to do is cry.

I can't help myself, and tears spring to my eyes as memories of Joel run through my brain. Had he woken up after that first injection? Had he suffered? How scared he must have been! As I form a plan in my head to catch three cold-blooded killers, I'm becoming more and more convinced that my best friend and my boyfriend have to be let in on my little secret.

But how?

Before I change my mind, I send a group text to the two of them that says: *Need to see you both for dinner. I have a surprise for you.*

Then I go a step further to commit myself, and text: *I have a unique power.*

Now if I decide to back out, I'm going to have to come up with a really terrific story, because, let's face it, how do you backtrack on that statement?

Austen replies almost immediately, and my stomach sinks. *When and where? I wouldn't miss this for the world.*

A minute later Riley chimes in. *Intrigued. "A unique power." You are always full of surprises.*

"Yeah, I know," I say out loud as I brush away more tears. "Just full of surprises."

CHAPTER *thirty-nine*

I ask the guys to meet me in the parking lot and they're waiting when I show up. The plan is for Riley to drive us to the diner where we can have a conversation without a bunch of Liberty Farms kids surrounding us.

"Hey, Vivvie." Austen smiles at me.

Riley lifts me off the ground. "Unique power! What's this all about?"

"Let's head out and I'll tell you when we get there."

We all pile into the Jeep, and Austen asks, "You have a good day?"

"Yeah," I reply.

"Oh God, will you two cut the crap? I so know that you guys are together. I'm pretty sure everyone knows around here."

"She's just an old friend. That's all," Austen says.

"And you suck as a liar. Look, I may not have known Vivvie for as long as you have but I can tell when she's all into a guy. I could tell with Tristan after the first week. With you, I could tell the minute I saw you two together in the Commons House. All you had to do was glance at her and her eyes lit up."

"Riley!" I'm not as irritated at him for calling us out as I am at him for mentioning Tristan.

"Vivvie!" he mimics me.

"Vivienne?" Austen says, and I can tell by the way he says it that he's asking me if we should come clean or not.

"Yes. Fine. Austen and I are more than just friends. If you knew that, then you could've let us have a few moments alone on the Fourth. You know, fireworks and all that!"

"Ha. I was messing with you guys! But I knew it!" Riley says. Then he turns to Austen as he pulls out onto the main road. "Really. I'm sorry, man. Didn't mean to mention Tristan."

Austen shrugs. "His loss. Eventually we can let everyone know we're together, but for now we can't."

"Yeah. I get it. I know you risk being sent home and so does she. You've actually done a good job keeping it a secret. I liked the way you two tried to cover things up when you arrived at that surprise birthday party together. That was hilarious. And obvious. I'm really not sure how you didn't get busted by Faith."

"I said he was like a brother to me." My face heats up.

"Gross," Riley says.

"Kind of disturbing," Austen replies.

"I had to say something." Riley doesn't have the best filter and can drive me crazy, but I know, after all we've been through in the past year, that his heart is true. "It's obviously worked. We're both still here. Speaking of the surprise party, I've been forgetting to tell you guys something about that night. I think Janna set the whole thing up to get us busted."

"What?" Riley says.

"Yeah. I honestly think she knew that Austen and I would probably sneak out on his birthday to get some time alone. So she planned the party knowing we'd stumble in together. She's smart. If we'd been kissing when the lights came up, for example, Faith would have been forced to kick us both out then and there. It was close."

"Why would Janna want us kicked out of here?" Austen says.

"Maybe not you, like Vivvie said, but maybe her," Riley suggests.

"Why, though?" I ask.

"Chris finds out about everyone. I told you that. He wants Austen to sell drugs for him at UC Davis when he goes back to school. He sees that as a ten grand monthly paycheck. If he has ten guys making ten grand a month, you do the math."

"A hundred thousand," I say.

"Yes."

"What does that have to do with Janna wanting me out of Liberty Farms?"

"If Chris suspects that you and Austen are dating, you could get in the way of a good thing. You've told the guy that you don't like him. You've told James that you know Joel didn't kill himself. To those guys, you're nothing but trouble and could be whispering all sorts of these conspiracy theories in your beloved's ear at night."

I blush.

"Detective Reed might be onto something. Nice work," Austen says.

"Thanks," Riley replies.

"Okay, say I buy that. But doesn't that make it seem like Janna is working for Chris?" I ask.

"She probably is," says Austen. "Didn't you say that when you first got here you two were friends—fast friends?"

"Yes."

"But she went out right away with Chris. To that expensive restaurant, the first night you got here."

"Uh huh."

"And it wasn't long before you two stopped being so friendly."

"It's true," I say, remembering how she'd interrogate me, then sort of disappear and not talk to me for days.

"I told you guys that Chris is a mastermind at finding people's weak spots if they have them," says Riley. "He's not one you can keep a secret from. Maybe he got some dirt on Janna and used it to blackmail her into getting dirt on you."

"I think I'm following," I say. "So you're saying Chris got something to force Janna into keeping tabs on me."

"And her lightbulb has gone on, Sherlock." Riley glances at Austen.

"Shut up," I say. "That still doesn't explain how she knew we'd be together on the night of the surprise birthday party . . . Oh, wait a minute. My phone. She asked to use my phone the other day when hers was supposedly dead. I was heading into the shower. And the other day I couldn't find it when I got up. I was looking everywhere and found it on the floor. Near her bunk. I figured it had fallen off the bed, but maybe she'd grabbed it to read through my texts. I gave her my password so she could make her supposed call."

I smack myself on the forehead.

"Makes sense," Austen says. "Wonder what he's got hanging over her head."

"Must be big," I reply. I think of Wills, because I know that Chris has something on him too. I need to get to know Wills better and find out what happened to his sister's pony.

"If Chris Haverly knows everyone's weak spots, we need to figure his out," I say.

CHAPTER forty

Ten minutes later we are seated at the restaurant with drinks on the way, and both guys are looking at me expectantly.

"What?" I ask.

"What?" they both say simultaneously.

I sigh.

"Look here, Vivvie, you called us here to tell us something. Your text was pretty, um, I don't know—vague," Riley says. "And now that we've figured out what might be going on with Janna, it's time for you to tell us this big badass unique power thing."

Austen nods. "You did ask us to come to dinner because you have something special to tell us. I'm with Riley. What gives?"

"Okay. Here goes. You probably aren't going to believe me, and no matter whether I convince you or not, you have to swear on your life that you will never tell a single soul."

They both look at each other and then back at me. "Swear," they say.

"First off, I know for a fact that Chris, Paisley, and James killed Joel."

"I thought we all were figuring that out slowly, but have you found out something new that proves it?" Riley says.

I nod. "Yeah. I have. I mean, I know exactly how they did it. But I still don't know how to prove it."

A heavy silence comes between the three of us for about four seconds. Then Austen says, "What do you mean, you know how they did it, but can't prove it? If you know how they did it there must be a way to prove it."

"Yeah. So, tell us," Riley says.

"This is where things might get weird and unbelievable." I take a drink from my water and decide to jump in with both feet. "I have a gift. I've had it since I can remember. It's how I was able to find out who murdered Dr. Miller when I started my first semester at Fairmont. It's how I knew last semester that Harmony was sick." I turn to Austen. "It's how I knew that your pony, Harry, didn't like to jump when we were kids."

Both guys are looking at me but I can't tell what they're thinking. Now that I've dropped the bomb, everything could be ruined. But I have no choice. "I've had this gift for a long time. I can feel and hear horses' thoughts and emotions. They talk to me."

"What?" Riley asks.

"I talk to horses and they talk back. They show me things, like in a photo album, and they express feelings too. Oh, and in case you're wondering, the only other person who knows about this is my mom."

I don't want to tell them about Kayla yet, because I don't think she'd want me to. This is about me and not her. "I used to go out on vet calls to help my mom diagnose, because I was always able to tell her exactly what was wrong when a horse was sick. So, that's it. I talk to horses. They talk back, and Melody showed me exactly how Joel was murdered."

Once again that four-second bout of silence sets in between us; maybe it seems even more quiet this time. I feel like I'm in a black hole that's spinning in the middle of a restaurant filled with people. My stomach aches and I can feel my heart beating hard against my chest. I have just revealed my deepest, darkest secret and no one is saying a word.

And then Austen smiles and says, "Oh my God, I get it. You can. Oh, wow. I'm thinking about the time that my horse bolted on that horse trails at Rebecca Farms and tried like hell to get me off. You walked up to us and I can see it like yesterday . . . Oh holy crap! I so get it. We were like, what, *thirteen*?"

"Twelve," I interrupt. "We were twelve."

Austen nods. "Yeah. Twelve. Anyway, you were talking to him and petting him, and you looked at me and said that I needed to get my mom to call the vet over because you thought the horse was colicking. I thought you were crazy, but that's exactly what happened! No way! Really? Really! You can talk to horses? Vivienne!"

"Shh," I say. "Keep it down."

Riley still hasn't said a word, so I have no idea what he's thinking. I'm elated that Austen does really get it. But it's just as important to me that Riley gets it too.

Austen leans back in his chair and blows out some air. "This is awesome," he says. "Do you know what you can do with this? How many horses you can help? And people? If people knew you could tell them what was going on with their horses, your life would get crazy!"

Now, finally, Riley speaks up. "That's why she's never told anyone. She'd be exposed and everyone would try to manipulate her."

Tears spring to my eyes, because, like Austen, Riley also believes, and he really gets it.

CHAPTER *forty-one*

After I explain to Riley and Austen what Melody "told" me earlier, Riley pounds his fist on the tabletop.

"Those bastards," he says. "They really killed Joel." He shakes his head and tears form in his eyes. "We have to get them, you guys. We can't let them get away with it."

"I know," I reply. "But how?"

I glance at Austen, and his face looks more serious than I've ever seen it before. "Now that we're getting in deep," he says, "I think we should finish this talk somewhere else."

Riley and I agree, and after we pay the bill Riley drives us back to Liberty Farms and parks near one of the barns. We stay in the car to talk, just to make sure absolutely nobody will overhear.

"We've got to trap them," Austen says.

"They're effing killers!" Riley says and looks away. I get the sense, he's feeling his grief over Joel's death all over again; he's clearly upset. I want to give him a hug. I've had a few hours for the shock to wear off, but when I first found out, I was a mess. It's only been about an hour for Riley.

"You okay, Ri?"

He turns to me with a fierce look. "It's got to be me, guys," he says.

"What?" I say.

"I feel compelled, Vivvie. They killed Joel. I could have helped him. He told me before he left for Fairmont that Chris was threatening him, but I told him that he wouldn't have to worry now that he was going to live in California. I was wrong."

"But why kill him?" Austen asks.

"I don't know," Riley replies.

"I know someone who might," I say. "It's only a hunch, but my gut says it's a good one.

"What?" Austen replies.

"Do either of you have Wills's number?"

"Yeah," they both say.

"We need to talk to him."

"Why?" Riley asks.

I figure since I've already spilled my guts and come clean as to who I really am, I might as well tell them everything. So in one long rush, I explain what Melody has been communicating about the dead pony.

"That pony," Riley says, "belonged to Wills's sister. I remember them moving here before I left."

"The pony ties into this, you guys. I know it. Wills ties into this too. He spent time in juvie. I found him the other day in Tiffany's den looking at a photo of his sister on the pony. Melody fell while his sister was riding her, and I know that Joel said she never rode after that. What he didn't say was how badly the girl was hurt. I found Wills with Melody, talking to her and petting her. He seemed really sad. I think him winding up in juvie had everything to do with Chris, the pony, and Melody—and Wills's little sister."

Austen says, "I think we better find Wills sooner than later."

"I hate to be a broken record," says Riley, "but let's be careful."

"Now that I've seen how vicious they can be, I agree with you," I say. "I think Chris and his crew killed Joel for threatening to go to the police. Chris is willing to kill anyone who won't fall in line with his wishes. I think Wills knows firsthand about that. Now we just have to convince him to tell us about it."

CHAPTER *forty-two*

Unfortunately, Wills doesn't answer his phone, so I say good night to Austen and Riley, who plan to go track him down.

But the minute I get close to my cabin I freeze, unable to believe what I'm seeing. To the side of the front steps I see two people locked in a super passionate-looking kiss—and recognition slowly dawns as I realize it's Tristan and Emily. So *this* is the answer to what they were up to that night near the barn. Suddenly, it kind of makes sense; I always knew that Tristan was too smart and too good for Lydia. As the seconds stretch into a minute and I'm still staring at them, I have no idea what to do. I definitely don't want to interrupt them but I feel ridiculous just standing here like a statue. And clearly, I can't stay still all night—and their kiss looks like it might last that long. After another thirty seconds, I decide to keep walking and make my first step as noisy as possible, crunching over the gravel.

At the sound, they break apart. Even though I wasn't the one just caught in major PDA, I feel totally embarrassed as the three of us stare at each other in awkward silence.

"Hi, Vivvie," says Emily. I can see her blush even in the shadowy light.

"Um, hi," I say.

"It's not what it looks like," Emily says.

Tristan puts a protective arm around her narrow shoulders. "Actually, it is," he says.

I can't stop staring at the two of them in amazement. "Don't feel weird," I say. "Honestly, I'm happy for you."

Tristan smiles. "Well, that's a nice change."

I grin back at him.

Emily says, "You're not mad?"

I shake my head. "Are you kidding? I just can't believe I didn't guess."

"You're the one who told me everyone has their secrets," says Emily.

I smile. "I'm glad yours is a happy secret," I say. "Well, anyway. I'm sorry I interrupted. I have to get to bed and I know you two have to . . . um . . ."

Both of them laugh and call out at the same time, "Good night."

Maybe seeing happy people helps you sleep, because the minute my head hits the pillow, I'm out. When I wake up, it's early in the morning. The first thing I do is check my phone for new messages from Austen or Riley, but there's not a word from either of them. Worried, but knowing there's nothing I can do at this early hour, I do what I do every morning and get ready to ride. What other option is there? I'm trying to keep Chris's suspicion off of me, and I'm really trying to stay away from Janna.

The sun is just coming up as I walk down to the barn and I'm amazed at the beauty around me. As the first light hits the dew on the grass, everything sparkles, and the soft summer air smells fresh and clean. I have a sense of excitement to take Harmony out and ride her in the back fields. I'm reminded of Kayla's words, when she told me that I haven't been focusing on my riding the way I should out here. I've been missing out on my horse, and the beauty around me. The place is pretty amazing and if I take a moment to ride her on trail, I'll have a chance to breathe and think . . . God knows that there is plenty for me to be thinking about.

As I walk into the barn and head toward Harmony's stall, I spot Lydia brushing Geisha. I've never known her to be an early bird when she doesn't need to be, and I am really surprised. There's this piece of me that actually feels bad for her. Does she know about Tristan and Emily? It was weird enough for me to find out they were together. And I'm really happy for them. How about Lydia, though? She's been so into him for so long. If she doesn't know, what will she do when she finds out?

I breeze past her. She glances my way and gives a cursory, "Good morning."

"Hey," I say. I really don't know how to act so I just start patting Harmony's neck and giving her some love.

Lydia walks by me, heading to the tack room. When her footsteps stop in front of Harmony's stall, I turn around. She fixes me with a cold stare. "You know, don't you?"

"Excuse me?" I reply, but in my gut, I know exactly what road she's heading down. At the same time, there's something else going on—my ears are ringing as if fireworks just went off. I lean against Harmony for support, feeling dizzy. My heart quickens and I can feel it heavy against my chest.

"Tristan and Emily," Lydia says. "You know about them, don't you?"

Ignoring her, I leave Harmony's side and walk toward Geisha. I'm not sure why. I feel some kind of compulsion to do so. The feeling is like the day when the horses first arrived at Liberty Farms and Geisha was walked off the trailer—and I couldn't catch my breath.

I feel Lydia staring after me, so I nod my head, doing my best to seem normal. "I found out last night. I'm sorry." I don't know what else to say and my heart keeps beating harder and faster. I feel like I might pass out.

"It's okay. Kind of shocking, though. Right? Emily over me? I sort of got it when he chose you. You're pretty. I guess she's cute in a vampire sort of way, but she's kind of crazy, if you know what I mean. Over me?" She ducks into the tack room, shaking her head.

I touch Geisha and my heart quickens even more and I really feel like I might faint. The horse tosses her head. I know the horrible physical sensations I'm feeling are the same ones that are making her suffer. The symptoms remind me of a vet case I went on with my mom once, but I'm not an expert, so I can't possibly guess the exact problem. "Is it your heart?" I whisper.

Yes.

Oh, wow! Another horse is speaking to me.

She then shows me an image of the cross-country course, and I can hear a pounding heart that skips a beat. "Oh my God."

I go into the barn office and get a stethoscope out, then place it on Geisha's chest and start listening. As I listen to the rhythm of her heart, there is another skip—plain as day. This horse has a heart murmur.

Lydia walks out of the tack room, saddle over her arm, and says, "What are you doing?"

I pull the stethoscope away and I'm sure I look shocked. "Sometimes I take their vitals. You know, with my mom being a vet and all, and honestly something about her didn't look quite right. So, I thought I'd listen to her."

"What? You are just as weird as Emily. I guess Tristan likes the crazies. Get away from my horse."

"You need to listen. She has a murmur."

"No, she doesn't. My horse is totally healthy."

"Lydia, please. Please just listen to her. You can't run Geisha cross-country without having a vet check her."

Lydia stares at me. "You're serious," she finally says.

"I am."

She grabs the stethoscope from me and listens. She straightens herself slowly and her face goes pale. "I think that maybe I should call a vet."

She looks completely distraught, and I've got to say that I feel even worse for her now than I did a few minutes ago, when her biggest problem was Tristan and Emily hooking up. The facts are that if Geisha has a bad enough murmur then her eventing career could be over.

"I'm sorry," I say. "I mean, it could be minor. There are all sorts of murmurs, so don't jump to conclusions. But the only way you're going to know for sure is by getting her checked out."

She looks down and nods. When she glances back up at me, there are tears in her eyes. "I'm going to go make the call."

"Okay." I'm at a loss for words, because I know what the possibilities are and I can see how they're affecting her. On top of it, she's just lost her boyfriend to another girl, and I kind of know how that feels, considering I lost the same guy to Lydia not so long ago. "Think positive." I sound so lame saying that.

She walks into the tack room and I walk back over to Geisha and try and to listen to her again. I can distinctly hear the murmur without using the stethoscope now. And I'm getting a surge of feelings from Geisha that range from tired to stressed. I know that the murmur she has is no joke, and if I had to guess, I'd say that her career is probably over.

CHAPTER *forty-three*

It's been a weird week here at Liberty. Ever since I found out about Geisha's heart murmur, it feels like things have been in a holding pattern. Chris Haverly and his crew seem to be lying low, which makes me nervous. Janna hasn't mentioned them, and she's been keeping her distance from me too. As for Austen, we have been working hard to pretend like we're just friends. It's not always easy when we eat every meal together. When he sits next to me, feeling his leg brush against mine makes me want to jump into his arms. As for getting proof that Chris Haverly and his crew murdered Joel, we've got nothing. Our only hope is that Austen and Riley, who coaxed Wills into going on a trail ride with them next week, will find out something new during their time together.

"We have to be careful," Austen told me yesterday as we talked about the plan. "The last thing Riley or I want is for Wills to go tell Chris Haverly that we're asking questions about him. So we can't just interrogate him."

"What are you going to ask him?"

"We'll start by asking him about juvie," he said. "What it was like, and how come he was there. Maybe that will get him to start talking."

All I can hope is that they get something good. We need more information to help us expose Chris, Paisley, and James, because there's no evidence of their crime—not yet.

I'm a witness of sorts, I guess—but I'm pretty sure that if I went and told the police that I saw a murder through the eyes of a horse, then I'd be the one going to jail, or at least the psych ward.

I suppose that having a little peace and quiet hasn't been all bad. It has allowed me to spend some time concentrating on my riding. Finally! Harmony and I are feeling really in sync, and I know it's partly a benefit from the lessons we've been having here at Liberty.

Of course, just when I think nothing is going on, Emily finds me in the cabin when I've come back to change my clothes after a lesson.

"Hey, Vivienne," she says. "I was hoping to catch you alone."

"What's up?"

"It's just . . . well, I've been wanting to tell you something."

I almost feel like laughing. "If it's that you and Tristan are happy, no worries," I say. "No explanation needed. It's great."

"I wanted to thank you. Tristan told me that you saw us together at the barns before he even broke up with Lydia," she says. "I'm so glad you didn't tell her about it. That would have given her the wrong idea. That was before we'd even kissed. Considering she's my roommate, I'm just glad she doesn't think I was fooling around with her boyfriend before they broke up. We all know how mean she can be."

"You don't have to thank me," I say. In my heart, though, I'm glad to hear that Tristan broke up with Lydia before he kissed Emily. It shows he still has honesty, which, for a while there, I thought he'd lost completely.

"Well, anyway. The night you saw us at the barns was when things were just getting started between us. That was when we realized how much the two of us have in common."

I raise my eyebrows. "Like loving horses?"

She shakes her head. "No, like having truly horrible parents. Tristan said you know a little bit about how awful his dad has been to him."

I nod. "Yeah," I say, feeling suddenly kind of speechless. It's really not possible for me to forget that Tristan was abused by his own dad. It's such a cruel truth and one I wish I could erase for him.

"My mom hasn't ever hit me, thank God," she says. "But she's bad in other ways. She has never cared about who I am. My whole life she has been telling me that competitions are the only thing that matter. All I want is to eventually be a vet and have the chance to heal horses. I don't care about competing. But she never cared what I want. She just wants a kid who'll make her look good, who she can brag about in social circles. She's one of the reasons I got so depressed. She made me center my life on the kind of competitions I hate so much. That's why I learned to drink my way through things."

"That's awful, Em," I say.

"Well, once Tristan and I figured out we were both miserable, we started talking. And, somehow, we started planning."

I smile at her. "I can guess what came next."

She blushes. "Well, anyway, I wanted to be the first to tell you," she says. "Neither of us is returning to Fairmont next year. We're going to Ireland together. We found a great hookup to work at a horse farm. They'll pay us and our board will be taken care of. Just yesterday we both told our parents."

"Wow," I say. I definitely believe that Tristan getting out from under his father's thumb—or fist—is the best thing possible. "But what about graduating? And how did your mom take the news?"

"I hung up on her when she tried to argue. Tristan did the same with his dad. But they both called back. We told them if they wanted to ever hear from us again, they'd have to accept our decision. As far as graduating, we'll take our GED."

I smile and give her a hug. "That's amazing, Em. It seems really brave. Wasn't Tristan scared that his dad would just cut him off? And what about you?"

"We called Kayla beforehand, and she agreed to give us a loan if it came to that," says Emily. "Once she found out what Tristan, especially, dealt with at home, she wanted to support us."

"This puts Kayla on a whole new level of sainthood," I say. "I'm kind of surprised helping you guys wouldn't get her in trouble."

"Well, we have some leverage too," she says. "Tristan's dad would definitely want to avoid the scandal of his child being taken away by protective services. And my mom wouldn't want her friends finding out that she broke laws by paying a psychiatrist to start me on all kinds of meds. Plus, we'll both be eighteen within a couple of months, so there isn't much any of them can do, really."

"True," I say. "Well, Ireland sounds like an amazing plan. Now you probably can't wait to leave Liberty Farms."

"I just wanted you to be the first to know," she says. Then she smiles and heads back out of the cabin.

While I change my clothes, I realize that I couldn't do what Emily and Tristan are doing. I'm glad the choice is out there for them, though. I guess I get it. I've never been abused.

I've just been lied to. Something that I still haven't resolved. My mom is still on her trip, so there isn't much I can do until she returns in a week.

I have to question myself. Will I be as brave as Emily and Tristan when it's time to confront her? Will I really have the confidence to tell my mom how angry I am, and demand the truth about my paternity? I feel like it's my only choice if I want to get answers.

CHAPTER *forty-four*

Another week passes in the same quiet way. Of course, there's a little teasing from Riley and Austen about my "power"—but only when we're alone, since they realize it would be no joking matter if anyone else found out, especially someone like Chris Haverly. But they definitely see the lighter side of it. Austen keeps asking if I can eavesdrop on his thoughts about me through his horse, Axel. I wish!

After a long day of lessons toward the end of the week, I put Harmony away after flatting her for a while on my own. As much as I enjoy lessons, sometimes the best thing a rider can do is focus on what she's been taught, rather than being taught in the moment.

As I walk out of the tack room, I nearly bump into Lydia. She looks like she's been crying.

"Hey," I say. "Are you okay?"

She shakes her head. "No." Now she starts to cry.

This is a real first for me.

"I owe you a thank-you," she says.

"What? For what?"

"You probably saved Geisha's life."

Then she does something so completely out of left field and hugs me. "I don't understand," I say.

"If you hadn't listened to her heart and detected the murmur, she could have dropped dead at any point out on the cross-country course. The murmur is significant and she has heart disease."

"Oh no. I am so sorry. I really am." I hug her back. I mean, I know we've never been the best of friends, and have even been sworn enemies, but learning this has to be one of the hardest things she's ever been through.

"No. I don't want you to be sorry! You should be glad, because you pretty much saved her life. I'm going to talk to Kayla and see if Geisha can stay at Fairmont on the grass. Yeah, it sucks that I'm going to have to retire her, but at least I found out in time. If you hadn't realized the problem, she could have died. We just came back from the vet hospital where they did her echocardiogram and it revealed that she has a closed valve, which means she's not getting the blood and oxygen she needs during exercise."

"I really don't know what to say. I can't even imagine. I just . . . All I can tell you is how sorry I am."

She shrugs. "You know what, there's that thing about karma. I guess maybe it's come back to bite me. First Tristan breaks up with me, and now this. I know I haven't been the greatest person in the world. I know that I've gone out of my way to make your life a living hell, and I'm really sorry."

"It's okay. It's all behind us," I say.

"But it isn't okay. I need to make some changes and I want to start with you. Can we maybe call a truce?"

I nod. "Yeah. I think that's a great idea."

"Then I have to admit something. You know the picture that was texted to your phone that showed Tristan in my bed? Well, this might not surprise you, but it was from me. I set my phone so it would show up as a blocked number."

She's right. I'm not surprised. "I don't think I need to ask why," I say. "I know you always had feelings for him. And he clearly had feelings for you."

"Oh, please, Vivvie, he was so into you. He never would have cheated on you. That photo was from the year before you showed up at Fairmont. It was the first—and really, the only—time that Tristan and I got really drunk together. We started fooling around and then I went to the bathroom. When I came back, he was out of his clothes and passed out cold. He looked kind of irresistible, so I snapped the pic."

She's being so honest that I can't get mad. Especially because, in some ways, that photo helped me find my way into Austen's arms.

I reach out and touch her arm. "Honestly, Lydia, don't worry about it."

She wipes her tears away and we start to walk back to our cabin together. Pretty soon she's recovered and starts getting chatty again.

"You know, I still just can't believe Tristan and Emily. Honestly, I would rather it be you. I still think Emily is a little bit off."

I kind of laugh.

"But maybe they're good for each other," she says. "It's not like either one of them have super fun family lives. Tristan's dad is horrific. I mean, he beats him and is totally emotionally abusive. Plus, he's bad news in other ways. He's into some illegal stuff, and I've always wondered if he'd try to get Tristan involved."

I nod. "I sort of figured. Tristan and I touched on it, but he never went into detail."

"Yeah. You don't want to know. It's an ugly situation, so I was happy when he told me that they're going to Ireland next year. You probably heard that too, right? Since they'll both be eighteen by the fall, he told me that they're leaving Fairmont to go work at a big jumper barn out there."

"Yeah, Emily told me," I say.

She shrugs. "That's what he said and I think it's kind of cool and probably good for both of them."

"Yeah. Maybe. Emily's mom is also pretty obnoxious. I think it's why Emily sometimes checks out with drinking. She's got good reasons to leave too."

Lydia sighs. "It's shaped up to be quite a summer."

"Yes, it has." I can't tell her the obstacles that I've been dealing with over trying to find Joel's killer, of course, and I'd never trust her enough to explain my gift with horses. "But I guess not a terrible one."

"I suppose if anything good comes of it all, it's that you and I have made amends. Maybe we'll even become friends," Lydia suggests.

"You know, stranger things have happened."

Later that evening, I head down to the barns for a long-awaited meet-up with Austen. He whispered to me the day before that he had "something to say."

"So?" I kiss him. "What do you want to tell me?"

He kisses me back, then pulls away and looks at me with soulful eyes. "I know this might seem crazy . . . but, Vivienne Taylor, I want to imagine a future with you. I'm crazy about you and have been ever since I can remember. I know in my heart that what we feel for one another is not some kind of teenage game, or silly little romance. What we have is real. We're supposed to live the rest of our lives together."

I'm staring at him.

"There," he continues, "I said it."

I give him a long kiss filled with passion. When I pull away, I say, "You're my soul mate and I can't imagine my life without you. So, what are we going to do about it?"

"I was thinking maybe you'd want to come to UC Davis," he says.

I feel a stab of guilt as I recall the excitement I felt when Faith had mentioned the offer at UNH. I don't know what to say. Then I realize that I owe Austen nothing short of honesty.

"Would you ever consider becoming a junior transfer?" I say.

"Vivienne," he says, pulling me close. "Is there something you haven't told me?"

"It's just an opportunity," I say. "But it might be a good one. A chance to get room and board paid at UNH and work for an Olympic gold medalist. For Lena Millman."

"Well, that does sound amazing," he says.

"Look, I still have a lot of things to figure out," I say. "But the one thing I already know is that you are the one piece of my life that makes sense. If I end up going, maybe you could come join me?"

He pulls me close. "We'll find a way to be together. I know we will."

CHAPTER *forty-five*

It seems to be turning into my routine to go to bed early and wake up before the sun is really up. Maybe it's my way of avoiding my roommates in the morning. After all, Lydia is still bummed out about Geisha, and probably Tristan, not that she'd admit it—although of course she still looks like a perfect Barbie every morning. Emily is glowing with happiness. They pretty much ignore each other. Janna seems withdrawn, and there's a big part of me that wonders why. After the surprise birthday party stunt for Austen, I'm just waiting to see what she'll do next to try to get us in trouble.

I toss on some clothes and head down to the Commons House for my usual early bird breakfast. I'm always the first one in there, but it's kind of peaceful. I'm surprised as I'm making a cup of coffee from the Keurig to hear someone come in—lately I've been the only person up around here at this time.

Thing is, when I turn around to see who it is, I'm shocked to see it's my mother.

"Mom?"

"Hi, Schnoopy. I just got in late last night and didn't want to wake you. I was told you'd be down here first thing in the morning."

I stare at her and feel my face turning red with anger. "It's true, isn't it?"

She comes closer to me and I can see tears in her eyes. "Yes."

I feel like I've been sucker punched and the wind knocked out of me. I turn and start to stir my coffee. My body is shaking. Why didn't anyone warn me she was coming?

"I don't want to talk to you right now," I say.

"Schnoopy, please. We need to talk. I have to explain."

I turn to face her. I speak as calmly as I possibly can, but I can hear the shaking in my voice. "What do you need to explain? You've lied to me my entire life. I don't see how that needs an explanation. And do not call me Schnoopy ever again."

"Vivienne," she says. "We have to talk. You can't walk away. You don't have the whole story. I'm not even exactly sure what you were told by your dad."

I let out a sarcastic laugh. "My dad. My dad? My dad! Come on! You mean Frank, don't you?"

"Will you please give me a chance?"

"Sure. Go for it! Tell me why you've been keeping the deepest, darkest secret that you could from me. Tell me why I've thought forever that Frank is my dad! Then tell me why, if you were keeping this secret all this time, you couldn't have at least told me when he left us that he wasn't my dad? Maybe then . . ." I can hear my voice rising but I don't care. "Maybe then I would have sort of understood. Maybe then I wouldn't have wondered for the last almost eight years why my *dad* left and why I was not worthy of his love any longer!" Hot tears sting my eyes and face.

She doesn't say anything for a moment.

"I'm sorry, sweetie. I'm so sorry about all of this."

"Okay." I mean, what does she want me to say? That it's all good? "That doesn't change anything."

"I don't expect you to forgive me. I don't expect you to accept my apology, but I think if you hear me out then maybe you'll understand better."

"I am hearing you out, Mom. Right here. Right now."

She sighs heavily and starts in. "I met Frank after I had met another man. I fell madly in love very quickly with the first guy. I was twenty years old. He was my first love, I guess you could say. It didn't last long and we lived in different countries. I met him at a riding clinic in California while on a break from college."

"Okay."

"I went back to Oregon after a month of being in California, because I needed to go back to school. We tried for a few weeks to keep in touch but he moved on, which forced me to move on."

"True love doesn't do that," I say sarcastically.

"Maybe. Maybe not. We were both only twenty. Young people do stupid, impulsive things. I did. He did. I did love him, and I think that maybe he felt the same way about me. But he had a riding career ahead of him and I knew I wanted to go to vet school. Then I met Frank. He was cute, nice, smart, funny, and he cared about me."

"More true love." I look away from her.

"I learned I was pregnant a month after I met your dad. I mean, Frank."

"Jeez, Mom, what were you? Sounds like you got around."

She turns red and shakes her head. "No, Vivienne. Not really. Actually, I've only slept with two men in my life. The first one because I was head over heels about him. The second one was to forget the first one."

I nod and look down, stirring a spoon around in my coffee cup. Her comeback does make me feel bad. I know in my heart that my mom isn't a slut. She hasn't dated since Frank left—not really. She's been busy trying to support my brother and me.

"When I found out I was pregnant, I really didn't know who the father was. But when the doctor gave me the due date, I knew it wasn't Frank."

"Why didn't you just call the other guy and tell him, then? Wouldn't that have solved all of this?"

"No. I actually tried, but he was in Europe competing. That was where he was from. He'd been over here on a visa. I wanted to tell him, but I saw media photos of him with another woman and they looked happy. And Frank wanted to marry me. I was scared, Vivienne. I was twenty years old. I wanted to have you, and I wanted you to have two parents, and I knew Frank would be a good dad."

"But he wasn't, was he? He left us after all."

"That was my fault too."

"What? He told me he had an affair after he found out about me."

She nods. "He did. We discovered that Frank couldn't have kids and that's when we did in vitro with your brother using a sperm donor. After the doctor told him that he had likely been sterile his entire life, he started to put two and two together. I had to tell him the truth then. It was horrible and, trust me, I have such regrets. I've tried for years to focus on the positives of this, and they are that we do have your brother, and that the three of us got to stay together as a family."

"Maybe you had regrets but you didn't try to come clean," I say. "Obviously."

"Look, the point is, I got to focus on you and your brother. You know I'll do anything to make your dreams come true. Same goes for him."

"Why? Out of guilt?"

"No. Because I really do love you. I know what I did was stupid and using my age then probably sounds lame. But, trust me, I thought it was the best, and I only wanted to do what was right for you."

I look into her eyes and I know she means what she says. My heart softens some because, no matter what, she's my mom and I do love her. That's why this is killing me so much.

"Why didn't you tell me the truth after Frank left us? Why did you keep hiding the facts from me?"

She shrugs. "Probably because I didn't know how you'd handle it. I didn't know what to say. You were only ten."

"Okay, so why not tell me later, like when I was thirteen, or something? When I could understand."

"Maybe I should have. But over the years, you've become so well-adjusted. You have the horses and your future. And we have always been close. I guess I was scared that if you knew the truth that maybe you'd search for your birth father, and we would lose what we had together."

"That's so selfish, Mom."

"I know. I know it is."

"But, strangely enough, I kind of see your point."

"You do?" she asks.

"Yes."

"I wanted you to stay focused on your dream of going to the Olympics one day. If you set out on another mission, my fear was that it would take that away."

"Maybe. I don't know. But you're right. I want to . . . I *need* to know who my real father is."

Just then, over my mom's shoulder, I see Lydia and Janna walking into the dining room. Both of them look surprised to see me with someone. They walk over to where we are at the coffee station and stare at us.

"This is my mom," I say, stating what's probably obvious. "She got in last night."

"Nice to meet you," says Lydia.

Janna smiles.

My mom turns back to me. "Vivienne, I'd really like to finish our talk," she says.

"Fine," I say. "Go ahead. I've got nothing to hide."

Lydia catches my eye and gives me a supportive look.

My mom shakes her head. "Not here. Let's go somewhere private."

I feel myself starting to shake with anger again. My emotions are clearly on a roller coaster, so maybe my mom has the right idea. I reply, quietly, "Fine. Let's go outside."

We walk out of the Commons House just as Austen comes up the steps.

"What a surprise," he says. "Hi, Dr. Taylor."

It sounds so funny when he says it, because it hits me that my mom never changed her last name from Frank's—mine either, for that matter.

"Hi, Austen," she says.

Then Austen turns to me and looks deeply into my eyes and I know he's trying to tell me that he cares. Everything about his look is trying to remind me that things will be okay, that I need to breathe and all of that . . . and I know that is what he's saying. But right now I don't want to do any of those things.

All I want is the truth, and I really hope I'm going to get it.

I lead the way and my mother and I walk out onto the path that leads to the cross-country course. Neither of us says anything. It's already starting to get hot, which only adds to the misery. We pause when we reach a big tree that offers shade and a patch of grass, and my mom tries to take my hand, but I don't let her.

She sits down. I'd prefer to stand but I sit down too, cross-legged, and I face her. "Well. I'm here. We're alone. It's private. Not that it matters. Everyone already knows what's going on."

She doesn't say anything for a long time. Then, finally, I break the silence.

"Well, are you going to tell me? You said he lived in another country. Where? You said that he rides. What does he do?" Suddenly, I'm fascinated by who this man is, and I have a ton of questions. My mind is abuzz.

Her eyes soften. "You already know him."

I cock my head to the side. "What?"

"Yes. You know him really well. He lives here now."

"Mom?" Oh God, here comes that sick feeling again in my stomach. "What are you talking about?"

"Your dad is right here. He's actually right over there."

I look to where she's pointing and I feel like I'm going to pass out as I spot Holden Fairmont walking our way.

CHAPTER *forty-six*

uddenly, the warm, humid morning feels unbearably hot as prickles of sweat break out all over my body. I stare at Holden as he walks closer.

"Does he know?" I ask.

"Yes," she replies.

"What? For how long?" I'm stunned as I try to wrap my brain around this new revelation. There is this part of me that wants to get up and run as fast as I can, but my legs are like Jell-O and there is no way I can move.

"Since you were hurt and went to the hospital last December."

"What?"

Holden slows as he approaches us and looks from me to my mother. "She told you." It's definitely a statement, not a question.

"She did." I hear the words, but question if they're coming from me. I find myself in this strange state of confusion mixed with anger and amazement—I really don't know how to describe it. I really don't know, because I have never felt anything like this ever before. Holden is my father. UNEFFINGBELIEVABLE!

I also find myself studying his face like I never have before. Oh my God—his eyes. I think we have the same eyes. I really do, and I touch my face. Do we have the same nose? Same cheekbones? I always thought I looked like my mom.

He sits down on the other side of me, his long legs stretched out in front of him. "Kind of crazy, isn't it?"

"You could say that," I reply. "I've heard Frank's story, and now my mom's, so what about yours?" I want answers. Maybe I am as brave as Tristan and Emily.

"I suppose you deserve to hear my side of the story," Holden says. "I'm sure your mom told you that we had a love affair."

When he says that, I kind of find myself cringing. I mean, my mom and Holden? I think of him as my mentor, my coach—and now I've just found out that he's my dad. Who was once together with my mom. It's weird.

"Yeah. She told me."

"I didn't know she got pregnant. And after speaking with your mom last December, I understood why she never told me about you. I really do understand. I can't say that I'm happy about it. I want you to know that if I had known, I would have been there. To know you now and know what a wonderful young woman you are, I'm honored to be your father."

"Then why, if you've known for seven months, didn't you tell me this?"

He looks at my mom and she answers. "We planned to, but you were going through so much at the time. New school, being hurt so badly, catching a killer—all of it. We felt it was best to wait."

I shake my head. "When did you plan to tell me?" I'm feeling that raging anger start up again.

"It wasn't all her idea," says Holden. "I also asked your mom to wait. I wanted to finish things neatly with Kayla before we told you."

"What?"

"Kayla and I are divorcing. She wants to be with Christian. It's a long story, but it's the right thing. When we told you, I wanted all of that taken care of, so it wouldn't distract me. I wanted to be as available as I could possibly be for you. I knew that this would be an entirely new relationship for us. And I liked the idea of doing it away from Fairmont, after your first year was over. You had such a big adjustment starting school there, coming in on scholarship like you did, and being forced to hold your ground as the new girl . . ."

"What do you mean?" I ask.

"Not much gets past me, Vivvie. I cofounded Fairmont with Kayla. We've always known about the mean-girl problem. We knew they'd see you as prey. Luckily, it doesn't look like that worked for them."

I actually smile when he says this. "I kind of did give it back to them."

"I figured," he replies.

"On top of you dealing with that adjustment, you had the Newman Becker thing," he says, referring to a big-time trainer I helped put behind bars for murder, with Harmony's help. "And you got hurt. After that it was Martina's disappearance," he reminds me, referring to when my roommate went missing at the beginning of last semester. "And then there was Joel's death after the championships in Kentucky. You've had a lot on your plate, and your mom and I both agreed that the timing needed to be right."

"I'm not sure that the timing could ever be right in a situation like this," I reply quietly.

"Yeah," he says.

My mom takes my hand. "I'm sorry, Vivienne."

"I am too," Holden says.

I sigh heavily. What do you say? How do you react? On one side, I can see their point. I mean, I've never been a parent, but I know how I feel about my horses, and I'd probably do just about anything to protect them. I've had a lot happen in this past year, and maybe—just maybe—I'll eventually understand. On the other side, there's the way my mom, of all people, has acted after continually telling me to be honest. And to find out that she's lied to me my entire life by omission? It's a lot to swallow. And now I find out that Holden has been harboring this secret for more than six months. I finally say, "If it's okay, I really need some time alone, some time to think."

"Of course," they both reply in unison.

I stand and walk away with this foreign but true thought crossing my mind, "I'm walking away from my parents."

CHAPTER *forty-seven*

I'm lying on my top bunk staring at the ceiling when a text from Austen pops up on my phone, then one from Riley. Having seen me leave the Commons House with my mom, I'm sure they're wondering how our "talk" went. I just respond the same way to both of them: "Meet for coffee?"

I don't really want to talk about it. Because I'm not actually sure what to think. I'm feeling understanding and compassion and hate and anger toward my mom, all at once. And that's confusing.

She has called three times. Holden twice.

At the same time, I can't just stay on my bunk in isolation all day. It seems weird to keep such big news from the two people I'm closest to. Ten minutes later, the three of us sit in the mostly empty dining hall with cups of coffee as I tell them the news, and watch their expressions stretch in amazement.

"Holden is your dad," Riley repeats, his eyes wide.

"Yep," I say.

Austen seems more shocked about my mother's behavior. "She always preached honesty even about things like stealing from the cookie jar," he says. "It's so surprising."

"I'm not forgiving her yet," I say, looking down at my cup.

"Are you okay, Viv?" he says.

"Honestly, I don't know," I say. "I just need time to think things over."

"That's completely understandable," Austen says and he eyes Riley, who nods.

"Yeah, it is. But we are here for you," Riley adds.

"I know. That's why I called you both." I look down at my phone on the table and see the time. "I've gotta go. I have a lesson with Bernard."

"Good. Take your mind off of all of this. The best medicine is your horse," Austen says.

"Thanks." I stand up and they both get up and give me a hug. I recognize concern in their eyes. "I'll be okay," I add.

I head to my lesson and afterward go back to the cabin, feeling exhausted. Harmony is probably feeling neglected by me right now, but I just want to crawl in bed and hide. My brain is short-circuiting from the news I just learned about my parents, and I actually fall asleep. When I open my eyes, it's getting dark. I didn't mean to nap, but clearly I'm wiped out. Hopefully the rest will do me good. I reach for my phone and see that Austen texted me again.

It's going down tonight. Didn't want to bother you with it earlier. Don't worry. Ri and I have this.

What the hell is he talking about? I call him and get no answer. I call Riley and there's no answer. I don't like this at all.

Besides, what exactly does he mean that something is "going down tonight"? I realize with rising worry that it must be the meet-up where Chris is going to tell Austen all the details about distributing the drugs. I feel panicky as I grasp the idea that my two guys are about to get into the thick of things with that vicious trio. Especially because neither Austen nor Riley has filled me in on exactly what they plan to do—or how they might get Chris, Paisley, and James to implicate themselves in Joel's murder.

How could they leave me out? Jesus! Then it occurs to me: maybe I seem like a liability. With everything else I've been dealing with, maybe they decided I was better off working through my parental crap than putting Chris and his two followers away.

My hunch about Wills had turned out to be a dead end—because the kid was a vault. Even on the trail ride, Austen and Riley hadn't been able to get him to provide details about why he'd landed in juvie or tell tales about Chris Haverly. I'd tried to further befriend Will over the past couple of weeks as well, with no luck. He'd grown into less of a joker as the summer had progressed, although that "observer" quality I'd noticed at Tiffany's house on the Fourth of July was still discernible. Wills had something brewing in his mind, but what that was, none of us had a clue.

I pound my fist on the mattress in frustration. Dammit! Why didn't they bring me in on the plan? I know the first thing I have to do is immediately track them down.

In seconds I'm pulling on my shoes to head down to the barn. My gut tells me to do this, because it's the one place that I seem to find answers—thanks to the horses. It's getting dark when I step outside and, for a moment, I pause and consider getting backup. But who? I mean, how do I explain any of this? It's not like I can just go find Emily or Lydia and be like, "Hey, so, care to join me on a quick errand to collar some killers?" Nope. There will be no backup.

I text Austen again. I try calling as well but the call goes straight to voice mail.

The same thing happens when I try Riley.

Yeah—something is very off. But the dumb side of me ignores that obvious fact and I forge on alone. I find comfort in Harmony's stall. She comes in from outside of her pen and places her head on my chest as usual. "I'm so happy that you can see all the way again," I say.

Me too.

"And I'm so happy you can actually talk to me, tell me things. I have to tell you that I'm scared right now, because I can't find Riley or Austen."

She lets out a low nicker and shakes her head from side to side. She doesn't say anything but the next image she shows me makes my heart stop beating: It's Austen. He's facing Axel and giving him a carrot. Chris walks into the barn next to him. They share a friendly high five, but then Chris's smile fades. "I know what you, your pal Riley, and your little girlfriend have been up to, and I don't like it," he says. "I don't like being lied to, man."

"I have no clue what you're talking about."

"Sure you don't." Chris swings a punch at Austen. There's something in Chris's hand. Oh my God, it's a needle! The punch connects and the needle plunges into Austen, who reaches his hand up to his chest where the syringe is sticking out. He goes to pull it out, but wobbles. Chris takes this second to lurch after him and press down the syringe. Austen lets out a cry of pain. He stumbles further and then falls to the ground.

"Oh no, no, no!" I yell. "No!" Did I just see Chris give Austen the same deadly drug that killed Joel? Oh my God. What if . . . No! I can't believe he's dead. I have to find him. I have to find where Chris has taken Austen.

I put my hand on Harmony's neck and start petting her, tears streaming down my face.

She continues with the images. "He took him," I say.

Yes.

"But you don't know where."

No.

Then I have an idea: The farmhouse that smelled like Paisley's perfume. That's where they've taken him. I know it.

"I have to go find him," I tell Harmony.

As I shut the stall behind her, she lets out a shrill whinny, and I realize as she does this that I'm in some trouble.

"Talking to yourself, Vivienne?" I whirl around to see James right in front of me. And the first thing I notice is that he's holding a hunting rifle in one hand. Behind us, Harmony is going berserk. She knows that I'm in danger. We've been through this before.

"You have Austen, don't you?"

He smiles. "You need to come for a walk with me."

"I'm not going anywhere with you," I say. "You're going to tell me where Austen is and I'm going to call the cops."

"Oh, I don't think you will. You don't have a leg to stand on, Vivienne. Now come with me right now or we can do things the hard way, and I'll shoot your pretty little horse in the eye—really blind her—before we go."

"You son of a bitch."

"Names don't bother me. Now come on, Vivienne, let's go for that walk."

CHAPTER *forty-eight*

I walk ahead of James on the path that I know leads to the old farmhouse. "What are you doing?" I ask.

"You know what, Vivienne Taylor, I don't think you're in any type of situation to be asking the questions. We do have questions for you, though, and we want answers. You really, really should've minded your own business and life would've carried on status quo. But you and your little boy toys had to get all hot and bothered about seeking justice for Joel. Come on now, Joel was a tortured soul. Couldn't you have just left that alone?"

"You guys killed him."

He sighs heavily. "Keep walking."

"Where are Riley and Austen?"

"Like I said, you're not in the position to be asking the questions."

We make it to the front porch of the old farmhouse—and it's just as I figured. This is their meeting place. The house is dimly lit inside. I'm afraid to find out what is on the other side of the door.

"Go on. Open it," James insists. "Don't make me make you do it. That would suck. I want to be as nice as I can for as long as I can. Who knows, maybe you'll get to live tonight, Vivienne. That is, if you play by our rules. Open it!"

My hand is shaking as I turn the knob. I have no idea what he means about their rules and playing by them, but I know that regardless of all the crap I've been through lately I like my life a whole lot and I want to live.

When I open the door, I see Riley tied in a chair and clearly unconscious. Janna is in a chair next to him, also tied up and gagged. Her eyes are wide with fear. I run to Riley and kneel down. I reach my hands up and touch his face. "Riley! Riley!" I yell. He's out cold and I don't know what's been done to him. My nerves are racing as I realize that I'm not even sure he's breathing.

I hear clapping and turn to see Chris Haverly walking into the room. He comes forward into the light. "How touching. You running to your gay boy. Such good friends."

"What have you done to him?" I scream.

Chris shrugs.

I hear giggling behind him and then I spot Paisley. From the wild, cruel look she has, I come to the realization that all three of them appear to be high, meaning that we are in some real trouble here. "Where's Austen?" I yell.

Paisley laughs harder and then mockingly cries out, "Where's Austen? Poor Austen. Poor Riley. What about poor Janna? Don't you care about her? Oh yeah, why would you? She was helping us. She was in way over her head, of course." Her smile falls away and she looks at me in disgust. "What, little Miss Do-Gooder is surprised? Well, let me tell you, she dug her own grave. Back at the championships in Kentucky, Chris saw her doing the nasty in the barns one night with—can you believe it?—the jump coach from her school; yep, kind of a famous guy who apparently likes his girls young. Very young. Anyway, Chris snuck a couple photos of them getting it on, sight unseen. Then he befriended her, just for fun. When her name popped up on the list for this summer, we knew we had her. She'd *have* to work for us. And wouldn't you know it, once she saw the pictures Chris had, she promised to do anything we wanted if he'd destroy them. We plan to release them anyway in the fall, of course. Imagine how much the horse world will love a juicy scandal like that. Her reputation as a slut will go national." Paisley gives a high-pitched, awful laugh. "Too bad she won't be around to see it. Poor girl, though. That jump coach took what he wanted and left her high and dry. She was looking for love again, or so she told Chris. It's amazing what girls will tell him after he gives them a little bit of the Big D. Good drug, my friend. Most pathetic part is how badly she wanted Chris to be her rebound."

Paisley stands up and walks over to me, hands on her hips. She opens her palm and slaps me hard across the face. It stings immediately. "And poor, poor, Vivienne," she says in a cold voice. She brings her arm back and backhands me on the other side of my face. "You're the reason Melody isn't mine. You're the reason that my summer has been ruined worrying about your nosy little questions. We kept thinking you'd forget about Joel—move on. But nope, you're an idiot and now you and your boys will pay for it."

"Where is Austen?" I ask again, and this time I surprise myself, because the way it comes out of me, it's almost like a growl, guttural and instinctive. I want to hurt this bitch.

"I'm already bored with her," says Paisley. "Tie her up and let's get this started."

Chris comes on one side of me, and James the other, each taking one arm and pulling me roughly off the ground.

"No," Paisley says. "On second thought, since we're going to have to kill them, might as well let her see her pretty boy one last time. Let her die with him. He should be awake by now. You didn't give him enough to kill him. Just enough to get him here. Useless, though. I figured maybe he'd tell us something we didn't know. But, he isn't talking. Hopefully he hasn't told anyone else about us."

My stomach sinks rapidly. I don't know what they have planned, but it's apparent they also have Austen here. Chris and James flank me as they drag me back farther into the house. There's a small room off the hall. The door is closed. Chris opens it and shoves me inside. I see Austen in a chair, tied and gagged just like Riley and Janna. At least he's awake. He's bruised and I can see dried blood on the side of his mouth. Tears burn my eyes at the sight of him. What have I gotten us all into? I run to him. "I'm so sorry."

He shakes his head and he also tears up. Chris grabs me by the back of my hair and shoves me into a chair. I'm quickly tied. I start screaming as loud as I can. Paisley walks in and slaps me hard again but I scream some more. I bite Chris's hand as he goes to tape my mouth shut. "You little bitch!" he yells. He hits me now, and it's with a lot more blunt force than Paisley. I feel nauseous and dizzy, like I might go unconscious.

I hear Austen making noises from his chair.

I'm now tied and gagged and facing Austen. I can't believe this is happening.

"Go ahead," Paisley says. "We have a rave to be at in an hour. Money to make. And since our James came through for us yet again, we are going big time. Thanks to the help of the Russian mob."

James walks out of the room and comes back a moment later. He has a gasoline tank and he begins to line the room with gas. I stare in disbelief as I try to process that my life is about to end. And not just that. This is going to be the end of Riley's life, and the boy I've loved since I was eight years old is also going to die. I would take it all back if I could. I stare into Austen's eyes and know he's trying hard to convey some kind of comfort to me through them. I can see it, and I can feel it. I try to return it. But I'm so scared.

"Good money in what we do," Chris says. "Not that we need it. But all of you do. I just don't get it. Joel's job was going to be so easy out there in Cali. Selling drugs to rich kids is like shooting fish in a barrel—I would know. But nope, the loser wouldn't do it. He left us here high and dry and refused to sell the goods like we told him to. And then, Riley, wow . . . what a disappointment. Could have made some real cash. He could've made enough to move his gay ass away from his parents. That's all the kid ever wanted. But no. You three had to try and do the right thing. Bet you're sorry now."

"Come on," James says. "All we have to do is light the match. Paisley is in the car. Let's go."

"Wait," he says, his cruel gaze stuck on Austen and me. "I can't go without reminding you all that you could still have a long, happy life ahead of you if you'd just done what we wanted. You could have been—like Wills! There's a good kid. Not at first, of course. At first, he wanted to take the high road like you. That's when we killed his little sister's pony as a threat. Can you believe? He still kept refusing us. That's when we shot Melody full of some Big D. It's good shit. It can take down a horse, no problem. Too bad his sister was riding when it happened. Poor little Anna got hurt. But Wills kept his mouth shut. Even when he got caught selling dope. But he didn't say a word even in juvie, and he's still keeping his mouth shut. He does everything we ask him to. That's what I insist on from all the people who work for me. Loyalty! Speaking of that, Austen, you really didn't fool me." Chris pretends to rub his eyes like a crying little kid. "Boohoo, you acted like my friend, but you didn't really like me." His mouth twists. "As if Vivienne Taylor's little boyfriend could ever get into my inner circle."

"Chris, let's go," James says, just as Paisley appears in the doorway. My mind scrambles frantically as I try to make sense of why she's carrying a brick.

"James, honey, I'm afraid you're staying," she says.

In a lightning-fast moment, Chris takes the brick from her hands and hits James on the side of the head. Austen and I watch helplessly as he goes down like a bowling pin, his body hitting the floor with a sickening thud.

Paisley casts one last look over our little assembly. "Great knowing you," she sneers.

"Not," says Chris. Then he lights a match and throws it on the ground. He reaches for Paisley's hand and the two of them walk out of the room like they're leaving some meet-and-greet party instead of the room where Austen and I, not to mention James, are clearly going to die.

CHAPTER forty-nine

The sound of someone calling my name pulls me back into consciousness, but as I open my eyes I feel only half awake. In a slow, dull moment I also hear the crackling of flames and realize everything around me is searing hot. Panic floods my body with adrenalin as a voice screams right behind me, "I found her!"

Reality sets in as I see red flames licking the walls. I can't breathe. My chest hurts.

"Say something, Vivienne." My arms go limp as the ropes that Chris and James tied me with fall away. It's Tristan, I realize from the voice, who just freed me, but I can't catch my breath enough to talk. I feel hands cup under my armpits and lift me up.

"Is he free?" Tristan yells as he starts carrying me toward the exit.

A girl's voice replies, "Yes, but I can't move him!"

"I'll get him," Tristan screams. "Come help Vivienne!"

It's like a nightmare where nothing quite makes sense. I feel like a bag of sand as Tristan puts me down and another set of arms support me from behind. I'm moving and being guided but I can't see a thing. I can't feel a thing and my mind races in a whirl of confusion.

Glass shatters somewhere. "Go first!" Tristan yells. "And then, you'll have to help them out after I get them through the window."

I'm trying to comply. Then all the pieces of what's happening come together and I suddenly escape the trap of confusion. I'm escaping a fire.

Hands on me and I'm sliding through the window and down onto the cold, hard ground. I lie there trying to breathe. Where is Austen? *Where is Austen?* Oh my God—where is Riley? And Janna?

I hear more glass breaking and a moment later I'm being dragged across the ground. I start to cough profusely, and a few seconds later I hear someone else coughing.

My eyes are open now and I can see smoke swirling. I hear the crackling of fire and I start to sit up.

"No, no. Lie back. Help is on the way, Vivienne."

I look into the face of Emily and I'm surprised it's her.

"Where is Austen?" I ask. "Riley? Janna? James is in there too."

I hear the words, "Over here, baby."

My heart pounds heavy against my chest at the sound of Austen's voice, then I begin coughing again. I finally catch my breath and then I also hear Riley. "I'm here."

They are on either side of me.

Then I hear screams and I try to focus on them. Fire! Oh my God! Tristan is running away from the house but he's on fire! I see him drop to the ground and roll. Emily is also screaming. My own scream dies in my throat as I start to retch again. I hear sirens in the distance.

I see Austen struggling to get up and go to Tristan. Riley is trying to crawl over the ground, but I can't move.

I see red-and-blue flashing lights across the lawn as the first emergency vehicles arrive. I start to cough again, and an EMT bends down next to me and asks me my name. I start to say, "Viv . . ." and then everything goes dark.

CHAPTER *fifty*

I wake up inside the ambulance. I hear the screaming siren. "How are my friends?" I keep asking, taking the oxygen mask off my face.

"It's okay, sweetie. Just relax. We're giving you something to help you breathe and also relax. You can't take off the oxygen mask. You've got to keep it on."

I look up and see a man sitting on the ambulance bench next to me. He looks to be doing something with tubes but I can't make sense of it. I take off the mask again. "My friends? My boyfriend?" I repeat.

"Keep the oxygen on, please, Vivienne. We need you to do that. Okay?"

I try to nod in agreement and act like I understand why he wants me to follow his directions, but at the same time, why won't he answer me? I'm feeling drowsy again and I drift off—away from this ongoing nightmare and the vision of Tristan emerging from the house on fire.

The next place I find myself awake is an emergency room. I've been down this road before. Nurses are taking my vitals, and a conversation that I don't really understand is taking place. I'm groggy from whatever they gave me, which I'm guessing was a sedative. The oxygen mask is still on me.

I'm not so concerned about what's going on in the small space, because I sense that although I've suffered some, the doctor and nurses aren't extremely anxious. What I'm concerned about is the yelling I hear going on next to me.

I turn my head to the side and open my eyes. I see nurses and doctors surrounding Tristan. He's facing me, and his eyes are open. I can tell he's in shock. I can see that he recognizes me, and as he does, a smile crosses his face. Then his eyes close and I hear someone yell, "Pressure is dropping."

A nurse sees me and shuts the drape between us as I begin to cry.

CHAPTER *fifty-one*

The next two weeks pass in a blur. From what other people have told me, I stayed in the hospital for a day suffering from smoke inhalation, as did Austen and Riley.

Thankfully, Tristan survived that fateful night, but not without consequence. He's still suffering from third-degree burns over 15 percent of his body. They are mainly on his arms and chest. I have not been able to see him, as his parents transferred him to a private burn center fifty miles away from Liberty Farms. I've tried calling and e-mailing, but with no response. I've spoken with Lydia, but she hasn't been able to reach him, either.

What's still hard for me to process is that Janna didn't survive the fire. It's sad and horrific, and I realize I never got to really know the true Janna. Even though she was doing Chris Haverly's bidding, I believe that she was a good girl. I saw that when I first arrived at Liberty and she greeted me so kindly. If Chris hadn't gotten his hands on her . . . if he hadn't found something to blackmail her with back in Kentucky, her future would have turned out so differently. Losing her still feels like it's out of a nightmare, and I feel incredibly bad for her family. I spotted a woman who must have been her mom leaving the cabin with Janna's things packed up in a suitcase, and her face was the saddest thing I've ever seen.

Of course, the more I learn about the whole night, the more I realize that it was a tragedy on a large scale—it's like that night was the end of what Chris and Paisley started when they killed Joel.

I know when the craziness started for me—when I couldn't reach Riley or Austen. Of course, Harmony showed me how Chris had drugged Austen.

And now I know what happened to Riley; he'd been lured into the situation easily enough. Paisley had texted him to say that she wanted to talk to him in private—and tell him something about Joel's murder—before he met with Chris and James that night. She said she wanted to keep Riley from falling into their trap. She told him to meet her at the farmhouse. As soon as Riley walked in, Chris had him on the ground and then tied him to a chair.

Now, I love Riley dearly—I really do—but I have to admit that I've so wanted to give him crap for being such a sucker. I mean—really? Who would have believed that line from Paisley? It's like straight out of the what-not-to-do handbook. But maybe that's why I love Riley so much. He's trusting and in many ways still pretty naïve. I made him promise that he'll never go off alone if we're trying to get to the bottom of a murder.

"How about I promise you that we never get involved with another murder, period," he replied.

"Good point," I said.

Once they had the guys, I was obviously the next victim. They'd gotten Janna easily, of course, by simply telling her she had to join them—with the awful photos Chris was using to blackmail her, she didn't resist one bit. They all knew I'd go looking for Austen and Riley, so after James had brought Austen to the farmhouse, he'd gone to watch the cabin and followed me to the barn where I became easy prey.

The rest of our survival tale is mostly about lucky breaks. Because, honestly, Austen, Riley, and I got lucky. I mean, we got really, really lucky, thanks to the unlikely hero and heroine who saved us—Emily and Tristan. It was kind of incredible for all of us at the farmhouse that they'd planned a romantic nighttime walk around the property, hoping to get some quiet time together. They'd been the first to smell smoke, and started running to investigate. On the crest of a hill, they'd seen the blaze and immediately started to panic that someone might be inside the burning house. That's when Tristan had called 9-1-1.

I still don't know how any of us can ever thank them enough. Although, to tell the truth, there were actually two more people involved in saving us: Kayla Fairmont and Lydia Gallagher.

Three days after coming home from the hospital, while I was in Harmony's stall reassuring her for the millionth time that I was fine, my phone rang.

"Vivienne?"

"Yes."

"It's Kayla."

"Hi," I said.

"Hi, honey. Are you okay? I've been really worried about all of you."

"I'm doing okay," I replied. "I'm just really worried about Tristan. I don't know what's happening with him. It's so sad. He and Emily had so many plans."

"I know," she said. "They told me about their plans to work in Ireland. Maybe they'll still be able to spend part of senior year there together. Right now, though, he has to heal physically. In a more emotional way, so do you and Riley and your friend Austen."

The way she said *friend* when she referred to Austen led me to believe that she knew we were more than friends. When I didn't say anything, she continued.

"You need to know something. You need to know that Harmony helped save you guys on that night of the fire, and so did Lydia."

"What?"

"I'd been checking up on you pretty often through the horses, especially Harmony. I've known her since she was four years old, and have an especially strong connection to her. Through her, I got the sense that you were putting yourself in harm's way trying to find out who was behind Joel's death. Over the last month, I was feeling increasingly frightened for you. That's why I suggested you back off from asking so many questions. My instincts were right. You were almost killed."

"I know." I sighed. "But we also put the two really bad people in jail. I know they're getting locked up for Janna's murder, not Joel's, but at least in my own mind I know there's justice for his killing. There's justice for a lot of people."

As I say this, I'm thinking of Wills, who did finally escape from under Chris Haverly's cruel thumb, and saw justice served for the crime against his little sister, Anna.

"I agree. But it was very dangerous."

"Did you know who murdered Joel all along? His horse, Melody, must have told you, since you've had long-distance communications with the horses all this time."

"Being so far away, I was never able to clearly get into Melody's thoughts," she says. "I can only manage long-distance conversations when I know the horse incredibly well. With Harmony, I have a strong bond. Melody, on the other hand, was raised on the East Coast. She was Joel's horse when he was alive, and I never really got to know her. So, to answer your question: no. I had no idea what really happened to Joel. If I had, I would have made sure that Chris and Paisley were arrested immediately. I would've figured out how to make that happen."

"I wish that had happened. Janna would still be with us. Nobody would have been hurt."

"I wish that too, but it just wasn't possible. Thankfully, Harmony came through for us. I was just getting ready to go to sleep in California on the night of the fire when I took a minute to check in with her emotionally. As soon as we connected, she showed me the image of James taking you from the barn at gunpoint."

"You must have been horrified."

"I was. But I couldn't call the cops. How could I possibly explain that I saw you taken against your will through the eyes of a horse three thousand miles away from my home in Southern California? I tried calling your cell and obviously you didn't answer. So, I called Lydia. I'd seen the roster and I knew you were sharing a cabin."

"Lydia?"

"Yes. I couldn't tell her the facts, but I told her that I was worried that Chris Haverly and his crew were bullying you. I didn't know what else to say. I was amazed at how quickly she agreed to help me. In fact, she said she'd do anything to help me find you. Lydia actually told me she'd never forgive herself if something bad happened to you."

I have to admit that I was a little bit surprised to hear this. I mean, I know that we'd agreed on a truce after I'd helped find Geisha's heart murmur, but this showed that her concern for me was more than a truce. She actually cared. That is what I would have to call turning over a new leaf.

"She said she'd call around to try and find you. Of course, I couldn't alarm her and tell her the details of what I knew. I hung up and kept checking in with Harmony, and once she smelled smoke, I did too. I feared the worst. So I called Lydia back and told her to call nine-one-one and report a fire. I also asked her to trust me enough not to ask too many questions and cause delay. She handled it beautifully."

"Oh my God. You and Lydia saved us too. I bet she reported the fire even sooner than Tristan did."

"I think so," she said. "Yeah, she handled it well. I just wish Tristan hadn't been hurt. Then there's Janna, and her death is tragic."

"I know, but you can't blame yourself," I said, even though I was busy blaming myself.

We hung up the phone after agreeing that when I return to Fairmont in the fall, we'll get together so she can help me with my skills. I have to say, I'm already looking forward to it. When the school year ended last year I didn't think I could trust Kayla at all. Knowing that she played a vital part in saving our lives, I have to say that I really do trust her now. Especially given the support she showed for Tristan and Emily. How ironic is that? Kayla, the one woman I wasn't sure about, has turned out to be incredibly honest and wonderful. And my mom—the one person I thought I could always trust—turned out to have told some whoppers.

But we're not giving up on each other. Not at all. My mom hasn't left here since she broke the news about Holden. I guess there is something to be said about a silver lining, right? We've been able to talk about everything, and surviving a second maniacal killer in a year's time has made me take a good look at life. A real good look, and what kind of person would I be if I couldn't forgive a mother who has loved me, adored me, and always tried to protect me? Then there's Holden. He wants to become more of a dad to me. We've had a few of our own heart-to-hearts. And you know what? I want him to be my dad.

As far as Frank goes, I don't think I need much from him. He did really choose to leave. Sure, my mother played a part in it all, but at the end of the day, it was his choice. He has another family now. I can learn from him as a rider, but as a daughter, I don't think so. But the way things have played out has made me so much less angry at him.

What's really interesting—and I find I don't object to it—is that I've noticed my mom and Holden have been spending time together, walking around Liberty Farms and eating dinner, just the two of them. The three of us have also spent some time together.

It's kind of weird, but for the first time in almost ten years, I feel like I might have a whole family. It's different. It's unique, but we are a family.

CHAPTER *fifty-two*

oday is my eighteenth birthday. We have to leave Liberty Farms in less than a week. My mom is going home in the morning. She knows that I'm okay and she really needs to get back to my little brother, grandmother, and her vet clinic. But she is refusing to leave until she throws me a party, which is planned for tonight. I have to admit, I'm kind of looking forward to it. Eighteen. It's a big day. I won't have to hide my relationship with Austen anymore.

But it's still morning, the party is hours away, and I'm out on cross-country for a lesson with Frank, alongside Lydia and Emily. I try to ignore everything but his instructions, because I feel terrible for both girls. Lydia is riding one of the horses from Liberty Farms, knowing that when she returns to Fairmont, Geisha will be retired to pasture. Emily hasn't smiled since learning that Tristan was being placed in a private hospital. I know that she hasn't seen him.

"Okay, girls, we're going to work on down banks and drops into the water today. So, let's warm up with the down bank. Who wants to go first?"

I decide first is better than last. "I'll go," I say.

"Think choppy strides, nice and collected on the approach. Ride the middle of the horse over the jump, and put her on a loose rein," Frank says.

I take the instruction, reminding myself that he's only a coach to me at this point.

All three of us school the down bank pretty well, and Frank has us move onto the down bank into the water.

"What's different here," Frank says, "is that your horse can't see the water that's coming up, so you need to really ride to the base, keeping your leg on, eyes up, and coming out of the jump keep riding the horse and then jump the cabin, which is a four stride."

Emily goes first and instead of loosening her reins to the buckle, she actually pulls on the mare, who chips in, taking an awkward stride close to the fence. It's definitely ugly and she's lucky the horse is honest, because the mare almost hangs a leg. Fortunately, Emily greased the horse's legs and that's what helps her slide off the jump. It wasn't the horse's fault at all.

"Damn!" Emily says.

"Okay, you need to do that again," Frank says. "And this time, ride it on that loose rein. You pulled back and your horse stalled. It's like braking. Come on. You can do it."

Emily rides the exercise correctly this time around, and fortunately, so do I. Lydia also nails it. I have to say that it's been a decent schooling.

When we're through, Frank calls out to me before I take Harmony back to the barn. "Whoa," I say to Harmony. She halts and Frank walks up to us.

Emily and Lydia walk on ahead. It's nice to see them handling each other well now. They're no longer giving each other the silent treatment and they even seem to be friendly. I have to say, Lydia really has come a long way. I do think that knowing that Tristan got so hurt has allowed each of them to get past any animosity they may have had. Traumatic events tend to make people see what is really important in life, and not care so much about the small, stupid things.

"Good riding today," says Frank.

"Thank you."

He smiles up at me and there are actual tears in his eyes. "Happy birthday, Vivvie girl."

I swallow back my emotion. He always called me that when I was little. All I can muster is another, "Thanks."

"I'm here. I really am. If you ever need anything at all, I'm here. I won't abandon you again. Maybe someday we can have a relationship. I had no idea your dad was Holden. But I'm happy it's him. He's a good man. And maybe I can't ever be your dad again, but hopefully I can one day be your friend."

I smile as much as I can back at him and say, "Yeah. Maybe that would be good someday."

I don't cry. But boy, does this hurt. I take Harmony back to the barn. She tells me that she loves me. I reply with, "Dammit, don't make me cry."

Sorry.

Lydia and Emily are busy putting their horses away. Wills comes in after his lesson with Bernard. Tiffany has taken a hiatus, which makes sense, considering that Joel's dad is divorcing her and she's trying to help her horrible daughter deal with the trial. I wave at Wills.

"Hey, Taylor, how's it shaking? Eighteen now? Oh, you and your boyfriend are finally legal. You guys want to party with a minor? I'm available."

"You're funny, Wills. Funny." It's a relief to see Wills back to his jokes and banter. Clearly, having Chris Haverly behind bars has improved his outlook on life. "Are you all healed up?" I ask. He'd been pretty banged up after the night of the fire. Yep, Wills had gotten involved in the chaos too. He'd actually played a major role in the plan hatched by Riley and Austen, because, unbeknownst to me, he'd finally revealed his whole story to them on the very same day that my mom had showed up and dropped the bombshell about Holden.

While I'd been napping off the trauma of discovering my dad's true identity, Wills had been bringing Riley and Austen up to speed on all the ways Chris had bullied him into drug dealing.

He'd told them all the details: like the fact that Chris had killed Anna's pony and drugged Melody. What I didn't know until later was that they'd drugged Melody as a warning to Wills to do right by them, and that Wills's sister, Anna, had been permanently paralyzed from the waist down because of it. Wills wanted his own revenge.

That night of the fire, Riley was supposed to contact Wills to let him know where they'd be meeting Chris Haverly. The original plan was that Wills would hide out nearby the meet with a recording device on him. Wills had a hunting rifle and was going to pull it on Chris once they got the evidence on tape.

In the end, however, Chris had pulled the plug on the "official" meet-up. Instead, he'd followed Austen down to the barn and attacked him with the syringe.

When Wills couldn't reach either Austen or Riley, he got into his car with the idea of driving around to look for them.

Then he saw the flames from the farmhouse and knew something awful was happening. He turned his car back that way just in time to see Chris and Paisley drive past him. He called 9-1-1 for backup, explaining he was following two people he thought were responsible for arson, and then pulled a U-turn to follow their car.

Of course, they'd been going to a rave. Wills had confronted Chris in the parking lot of the rave and started a fight, buying enough time for the cops to show up and take all three of them into custody.

At the station, all three were questioned, but by then, the true story was becoming evident as those of us at the farmhouse were being rescued and starting to explain the sequence of events.

And now, Chris and Paisley await trial. And because they are eighteen they could face the death penalty for Janna's murder. Here's the most incredible part: There's no way they can get out of the charges, because James also survived the fire. He'd apparently been capable enough after that blow to the head to crawl out, because the rescue workers found him on the scene and brought him to the hospital for smoke inhalation along with the rest of us.

James got immunity for himself by agreeing to give details about the case—how he'd stolen the drugs from the vet group to make Big D, and how Chris was masterminding a plan to create a larger drug ring with the Russians.

I have no idea if James is going to inform on them about Joel's death. Proving they killed Joel would be another story. At least I'm sure they will go to jail for Janna's murder. Plus, they are also being charged with attempted murder for the rest of us!

I'm just happy that everyone now knows what I knew all along: Chris Haverly is a sociopath who thought his family's fortune could save him from anything. I still can hardly understand why he did it. I guess it was greed, and the desire for power. The most horrible thing about it all is that he didn't need the money. He is a spoiled rich kid who gets everything his heart desires. Yet control was what he really wanted. As for Paisley, I can't decide if she's more or less evil than Chris. One thing for sure is that she was so in love with him that she did everything he wanted her to. Yep, it became clear right away that she'd only been using James for his drug connection all along. She and Chris had been pulling the wool over his eyes for ages.

I don't believe that Tiffany knew any of the details of what her daughter was up to. But I'm content in knowing that she's probably not going to be living the happy life any longer. Apparently Joel's dad made her sign a prenup. Now that he's divorcing her—don't think he's the type to stick around through the "hard times"— she's got practically no resources. Luckily for her, she can always make money as a trainer. Besides, knowing her ability as a gold digger, I wouldn't be surprised to hear she was marrying Donald Trump next.

I'm washing Harmony in the cross ties when Wills puts his gelding, Luke, in the wash rack next to mine.

"How are you really? You good? No joking. We can do that at my party tonight," I say.

His face is black and blue from the fight he started with Chris in the parking lot of the rave. "I'm good. I really am. I'm happy that Chris and Paisley got theirs, finally. I wish I'd known that all of this time we had the same agenda, Vivienne."

I nod. "I know. But, I didn't know who I could trust. I had to be careful. I even had my doubts at times about Riley, but he came through for me. I just wish that Haverly didn't manage to intimidate everyone. Joel might still be here."

"He's a scary guy and his family is even scarier. There's a lot of money there, and a lot of power. I mean, the guy's dad owns Haverly watches, his uncle is a senator, and his other uncle is a judge. I'm afraid he could be out before he ever spends much time in jail."

"I hope not. Justice can't ignore the facts on this one, since James is giving testimony. Besides, there's evidence they murdered Janna, so I seriously doubt they'll be getting out of this."

"I hope you're right," he replies. "For Anna, for Joel, for Janna, and for anyone else they hurt."

"You know what I don't get?" I say, turning on the hose and spraying Harmony down.

"What's that?"

"Why do kids who have grown up with so much, who could really have anything they ever dreamed of—especially Chris—bother with such a scheme?"

"I know what you're saying, but I think it's entitlement. I've thought a lot about it. Chris Haverly always viewed himself as above the law—and all he wanted was to control other people. He's seriously disturbed. He doesn't care about anything at all, except what he can gain, which is power."

"It's hard to understand that kind of evil."

"It is, but hopefully it's over now and Joel can rest in peace. I even got my sister to say she would get on a horse again." He smiles. "She's willing to try some therapeutic riding."

"That's great news," I reply.

"It is." He sponges down Luke. Then he stops, turns off the water, and comes over to me, putting an arm around my shoulders. "I'm glad we met this summer . . . I'm happy we're friends. And I have some news. I'm thinking of transferring to Fairmont for my senior year."

I raise my eyebrows. "They don't let in jokers, you know." He smiles and I lean my head on his shoulder. "That's great news. I couldn't be happier to hear it."

CHAPTER fifty-three

The candles are lit and Austen is at my side. My parents are at the end of the table. Yep—my parents: Mom and Holden. They're filming this thing with their smartphones.

The night couldn't be any better. Riley is mixing the music and I haven't seen him this happy in a very long time.

He called me when I was getting ready for the party. He sounded out of breath and stressed. But it wasn't stress! It was excitement.

"Vivvie! You're not going to believe it!"

"What? You okay?"

"Yep. I am good! Kayla freaking Fairmont is a freaking saint!" he said.

"What are you talking about?" I laughed.

"Melody! Melody is mine. Kayla just called me and told me that she wants me to have the mare. She also told me that Santos can retire at Fairmont and live there the rest of his life. She said that she wants all of us to be living our dreams and that she thinks Melody is the perfect horse to live out mine with. Oh my God, do you think she knows about me wanting to go to Europe?"

"I don't know, but I believe her when she says that she wants us all to live our dreams. I would agree that Kayla is a saint." We laughed and I tried not to cry, because I didn't want my mascara to run. But hearing the joy in his voice and knowing that Riley might still have a chance to go to Germany was some of the best news I could have ever been given, and on my birthday no less!

I look around the room and see a wonderful sight. Tristan is back. He's at my party! He was released from the hospital this morning, and before his dad could get there, Emily had borrowed Austen's car and driven up to get him. She's smiling from ear to ear.

He's bandaged around his chest and there are scars on his face, but he's here. And the way he and Emily look at each other is proof that something real is happening between the two of them. I'm getting the distinct feeling that Emily has found a cure for her unhappiness that has nothing to do with alcohol or pills. Clearly, their idea to escape their horrible families by working at a horse farm in Ireland is giving them a future—although the plan is up in the air, given Tristan's injuries. But looking at them now, sitting so close, with such happy expressions, I think the two of them are even closer after having rescued us the night of the fire. They seem bonded in a way that I recognize. Some bonds can't be broken— like the one between Austen and me.

I even see Lydia having a good time. She's been chatting with Wills off and on, and now he's sitting by her and the two of them are laughing about something.

As my friends and family finish singing to me and insist I make a wish, I do so.

My wish comes true. Austen kisses me in front of all of them. When we pull apart, I look up and say, "I'm eighteen, everyone, I'm eighteen!"

The room busts out laughing, although I can tell my mom is crying a little bit. Holden puts an arm around her. I wrap my arms around Austen and we kiss pretty much like we've never kissed before. There is something even more permanent and real in this kiss, and I know my future. He is right here next to me.

Obviously, we aren't absolutely sure about what the next few years hold, but I believe in what we feel for one another. I've heard people say that you should never commit yourself to one person at such a young age. Maybe that's true for others, but for us it isn't. Austen is the one—the only one.

Holden walks over to me and hands me an envelope. He's smiling wide. "I have something for you too," he says.

"What's this?" I ask.

"Open it."

I do so and I have to read it over a few times. I look up at Holden—my dad—and say, "Really? Really?"

He nods. "She's all yours. Kayla and I agreed. Your mom agrees. Harmony belongs to you."

I read the transference of ownership from Fairmont Academy to Vivienne Taylor for Harmonious Movement, and I just can't even believe it. How perfect.

I have my mom. I have a dad who wants to be my dad. I have my future with the boy, now man, I've loved my entire life . . . and I have my horse. Harmony is mine. All mine.

Perfect.

ACKNOWLEDGMENTS

I want to acknowledge the entire Amazon team that I work with! They are all great people who support my work. There are too many to list, but the Amazon team in general makes being a writer a truly wonderful thing.

Once again, writing Vivvie's story couldn't happen without the generosity and support of the horse women and girls in my life. I want to acknowledge them, in no particular order, because each one of them has contributed to this story in one way or another: Kaitlin, Terri, Luisa, Lexi, Gina, Bec, Haley, Neely, Tami, Debbie, Jessie, and Gayle. I'm sure there is someone I've forgotten. I hope not! We have an awesome community!

Thanks go to my mom, my husband, and my kids. I have a supportive, loving family and I am grateful for them.

I also want to acknowledge a group of women who are the most supportive group of professional writers around. Not only are they amazing writers, but they are also dear friends. They know exactly who they are.

And, finally—the horses. Thanks go to Mister Monty the wonder pony, Bronte, Will, James, Jamo, Patches, Toby, Krissy, Cruise, Hobbit, Mouse, Little Bit, Uiver, Sawyer, Ben, Peter, Tahoe, Kona, Mia, and Little Grey. They provide me with the inspiration!

ABOUT THE AUTHOR

michele scott lives in California with her family, which includes her husband, three kids, three dogs, a cat, and nine horses. With her days spent in the barn or at the keyboard, she has forged a flourishing career as a mystery writer who is also deeply involved in the world of horses and equestrian riding.